ON EDGE

An Ozzie Novak Thriller

Book 1

By
John W. Mefford

ON EDGE
Copyright © 2017 by John W. Mefford
All rights reserved.

V1.0

Sugar Hill Publishing

ISBN: 978-1709206-00-9

Interior book design by
Bob Houston eBook Formatting

To stay updated on John's latest releases, visit:
JohnWMefford.com

One

The red-stamped letters on the sealed envelope are as big as mountains. A sickening waft of wet ink hangs in the air. And the cacophony of voices sounds like a garbage disposal full of chopped glass.

You, Ozzie Novak, a twenty-eight-year-old husband and half owner of Novak and Novak, LLC—at least in name—think you have life figured out. And then it kicks you in the nuts with a precision that could never be mistaken as an accident. Drowning out the sensory attack, you replay the last few hours to see how it possibly could have been avoided.

A morning almost like every other: an early coffee, always flavored with something like hazelnut or vanilla, and a piece of fruit in your hand. Usually an apple, orange, or pear. Apples are the hardest. Choosing the apple this morning actually has a benefit.

We'll get to that in a minute.

On your way out the door, an air kiss from the wife. She says she can't smudge her makeup. You push the insecurity of her not kissing you—not *really* kissing you for the last two months—to the back of your mind and hang it on her justification. You try not to think about the fact that she's provided five such explanations during this moratorium on anything resembling intimacy. Each, on its own merit, holds weight. But when viewing her broader body of work—yes, you realize you're thinking in terms of acting—the excuses make you wonder if she thinks she is married to a ten-year-old.

As you push open the kitchen door to walk toward your Cadillac sitting just outside of your detached garage, a swirl of wind whips across your face. The lungful of chilled air acts as a drug infusion, sending your mind and spirit into another place, where the pain of a relationship that has so suddenly flipped into the red zone recedes just below skin level. You relish the diversion. As much as you want to stop, close your eyes, maybe even lie down in the lush, green winter rye you had planted to ensure there was green grass even in the winter months, you can't. She might be looking from the house, then wonder if you're losing it. Ultimately, that would lead to a lot of questions. Questions that neither she nor you have the guts to answer.

Instead, you trudge forward, and when the door shuts on your CTS, what little sounds you'd been able to pick up before are now nothing more than a memory. You take a breath and wonder if she or you will ever open up and attempt to repair the damage that divides your relationship. Questions crowd your frontal lobe, but you quickly switch on your favorite sports talk-radio station. It's entertaining, and you find yourself laughing out loud. You realize those medical journals you read at the ER a few weeks ago—when your father thought he was having a heart attack, but it turned out to be a false alarm—are right. Laughter is good for the soul.

You sip the coffee, take in the soothing aroma, and feel your arms tingle from the caffeine permeating your arteries. Fake energy is better than no energy at all. You back out of the driveway, put the car in drive, then feel the buzz of your phone against your chest from the front inside pocket of your suit coat. Before proceeding, you check your phone to see three heart emojis from your wife. You try not to ask why or analyze what she's trying to say. You take it at face value. That lasts about five seconds. In the back of your mind, you realize this "patch of love" will last about four or five hours. And then you'll begin to wonder what tonight will bring. More cold shoulders? Or is there any hope that you, she, or both of you will wake up, grow up, talk through all this crap, and get back to loving the hell out of each other.

A sigh. You turn up the radio and lose yourself in another funny bit between the talk-show hosts. One of them had pranked the evening-drive host by making him believe that his marijuana stash had been found by the Austin police and that he would likely be charged with possession and intent to distribute. You laugh again and try to keep things in perspective.

Nothing is as bad as it seems, right?

The morning show's funny banter, for the few minutes driving through Austin traffic, serves as a thin bandage over the gaping hole in your heart. Twenty-five minutes later, you pass the front of your office building. Instead of glancing up to see your last name listed twice in three-foot letters, you focus on three college-age kids harassing Sam, the old black man who's been shining shoes on the street corner since you were knee-high and tagged along with your dad to work. You quickly park the Cadillac in the underground garage, dump your coffee into the trash on the way out, and then spot those same guys shoving Sam around.

You walk in that direction, tossing the apple in your hand like it's a baseball on fire. A fury builds inside. You're programmed to snap at anyone who preys on those who are the most vulnerable. You can't help yourself. It's mean, and it sickens you. It makes you believe that people are more animal than human.

Up ahead, you spot a cop on a bicycle. You wave, try to get his attention. Too many cars and people, and you lose sight of him. You move around an older couple; then you dodge a guy on crutches and a few others moving too slowly. Then you see Sam.

His fatigue-green sweater is ripped. Blood snakes from the corner of his eye. Each time he tries to bend down and pick up his stuff—brushes, polish, and dollar bills from tip money—he's kneed or shoved against his shoe-shine platform.

Ten yards out, you shout at them to stop. Either they are deafer than you, or they don't care. So, with a running start, you hurl the apple. One of the three guys—some skinny punk with a cigarette dangling from his lips—takes it right on the nose. He screams, falls to the ground like he has just been punched by Ali.

The other two are wearing tight T-shirts. Are they part of some wrestling team? Their foreheads are lumpy, and they're missing a few teeth. They appear to be steroid users. You instantly dub them Lumpy and Stumpy—you suspect their muscles are inversely proportional to their dick size.

Lumpy and Stumpy release Sam, who clings to the side of his shoeshine chair. He sees you, and you nod; then you turn your sights to the steroid robots closing in fast. Your breathing is labored, only because your heart is racing. It's not from fright. Those guys are big, but at six-two, two hundred ten pounds, you know you will inflict damage. If they break your face in the process, so be it. They deserve an ass kicking, or worse.

Lumpy, wearing a blue shirt, lunges with a roundhouse right. Easy pickings. You duck, and as he spins from the missed punch, you thrust a left fist into his kidney. His teeth clap together, and he drops to the ground.

You hear something in the distance, maybe a shrill, but you ignore it. You have to. Stumpy, in a red T-shirt, growls as he reaches for your throat. His hands never touch you. You send a hard side kick directly into his knee. It buckles. You know the feeling of a hyperextended knee.

You rear back, take aim for Stumpy's nose, and just as you begin to throw a punch that will make mincemeat of his cartilage, someone with a whistle jumps in front of you like a referee in an NFL game, breaking up a fight. It's a cop, but his quick arrival scares you. You're used to not hearing distinct noises until they're right on top of you. So you step away and take a breath. The cop calls for backup. The whole story is shared. A few minutes later, Lumpy and Stumpy and the punk with the cigarette are hauled away, while paramedics treat Sam's wounds. They're minor. The cop thanks you, but you can only focus on Sam, whose hands are quivering. You help him pack up his stuff, give him a hundred bucks, and suggest he take off a couple of days. He doesn't say much and toddles away through the parking lot.

You buy an energy drink in the lobby of the office building, crack it open, and drink half of it on the elevator ride up to the fourth-floor offices of Novak and Novak. Three others are in the box with you. You're not fond of small, enclosed places, so you try to calm your thoughts, take your mind off the confrontation, off the spike of adrenaline.

But you can't do it. You replay the series of events on the sidewalk and begin to question if you took it too far. And then you finally hit on a really tough question: were you simply looking for an excuse to get into a fight?

Maybe it goes further back than the defense of Sam. It doesn't take much head-scratching to recall the time of your first real fight. You were in seventh grade, still a scrawny, prepubescent kid whose athletic socks sagged down your ankles. Kids made fun of you for being Jewish, for being too skinny, for not hearing very well, for being…whatever. You didn't pay them much attention, but you also never really stood up for yourself. Not until two bullies picked on a kid with special needs. You don't recall his exact impairment, but Jacob had problems with yelling uncontrollably, and he had this weird twitch. You walked toward the locker-room exit to join the other kids in athletics on the field, but out of the corner of your eye, you saw two kids shoving Jacob over the bench and into the lockers.

You couldn't ignore it. You walked over and helped Jacob to his feet. The two boys got in your face. The leader of the two had such a thick hick accent that he hurled spit at your face as he called you the "p" word—that's what your mom calls it. Then he grabbed you by the T-shirt.

A fuse was lit.

Without thinking it through, you put everything you had into one swing of your fist. The hick took it on the chin and fell back against his buddy's knee, who screamed out in pain. You told them if they ever went after Jacob again, you'd beat the crap out of them. They never said another word to you or Jacob the rest of the year.

A guy behind you in the elevator sneezes, and you inch forward. Then a thought zips to the front of your mind, and it's a bit of a revelation: all those years ago, was the act of defending Jacob not just a defense of him but also a declaration that you would no longer allow yourself to be bullied for who you were?

Instinctively, you reach for your ear and feel the device anchored just behind it.

The elevator rocks to a stop, and you eye the lit-up number four above the doors. People push toward the opening, which shifts your mind into work mode. Lots of tasks to accomplish today. You check your watch—a high-end Tissot that your wife gave you on your honeymoon. It's 8:33 a.m. Dammit, you're three minutes late to start a deposition.

You walk into the main meeting room. Everyone is set up. Brian, a second-year attorney, asks if he can lead the questioning. You're fine with it. The deposition involves a lawsuit related to a bombing at an Austin band venue a couple of months earlier—you and your wife were actually there and survived. The client, one that dear old Dad—Nathaniel Novak—brought in, is hell-bent on suing the club and the City of Austin for not protecting his equipment—he'd supplied all of the stage lighting. You are beyond trying to convince your father that the lawsuit looks petty, considering that three people died, others were severely injured, and the general populace—even those who usually couldn't recite the name of the president because they were lost in their own little bubbles—was shaken to its core.

The deposition goes on for almost an hour. Your mind drifts, initially to the woman in your life. To the time when you thought she might be inside the Belmont, buried under rubble or burned alive in the fire. You can recall that feeling of relief and jubilation when she walked out. You hugged her with everything you had.

A breath catches in your throat as you realize something: isn't the bombing about the time when her emotional connection disappeared?

You sniffle, which draws a look from Brian—he doesn't want anything to interrupt the pristine recording of the deposition. You look off and recall the day you met Nicole Ramsey during your second stint in college.

The first stint? A two-year run at the University of Texas that was summarily halted by the "break-and-shake," a term used by college kids who had nothing better to do than try to humiliate grouchy professors. Too much to address in that hairball, so you move on to that day when you were walking along a path next to the San Francisco Bay, and you looked up to see the most stunning woman. She had brown, lustrous hair framing a face so luminous it appeared to have been dipped in milk. Nicole Ramsey had syrupy eyes. You felt your heart skip a beat. You stopped and talked to her—something that you would usually never do. The connection was instant and electric. You were in bed three hours later, and the white-hot passion didn't stop for three months.

And then she graduated. Said she needed to find herself and her independence. She headed off to Europe. It broke your heart, but somehow you thought you'd see her again. Kindred spirits and all. Fast forward through graduating at Cal-Berkeley, law school at Georgetown—Dad always said you have to experience life inside the Beltway, just to cut your teeth—and then you joined Dad in the firm. Novak and Novak. Your dream job.

Or not.

It's complicated—what isn't these days? So you turn your thoughts back to Nicole. It was about a year ago. Out of the blue, you ran into her at a wine-tasting function where Dad was trying to drum up business. She worked for a bioengineering company in marketing. You didn't say much. She didn't either. But the sexual tension was unmistakable. Again, three hours later, you ended up in bed. After that, you sat on the floor, eating pizza, laughing a lot. You'd found the one. The person who made you whole. You made her whole. She was that once-in-a-lifetime comet. Eight weeks of dating, and then she was talking about marriage. You could see your future all laid out ahead of you.

You asked her to marry you—you could barely utter the words before tears flowed from both of you. *This is what love is all about*, you told yourself. The engagement was a blur. Cake tastings, flower-shop visits, wedding planners, rabbi and pastor discussions—she's a devout Methodist, while you're Jewish in name only, and even that's a stretch.

Again, stay on track. It's about Nicole, not about all this ancillary stuff.

More on the engagement. Caterers, tuxedo fittings, band selection, on and on and on. It wore on you, but you didn't say anything because Nicole was glowing, happy, and showing you how much she loved you every day.

The wedding was spectacular. The honeymoon, though, even better. Two weeks in Italy and the islands of Greece. You settled into a new house, and the relationship continued to grow. Work was…work. But home was what made you get up every day. You started talking about kids. "How is married life?" you're asked almost everywhere you go. Honestly, you say you're lucky to have found "the one." And then she shut down. The flip of a switch. Was it the day after the bombing, or just before? Nevertheless, it rocks you. This could never happen. But it has, and you're not sure what to say. Each passing hour, day, week, the chasm only grows. You're really not equipped with how to deal with it, even though you handle conflict and negotiation every day at the firm.

A nudge on your arm. "How do you think that went?"

You turn and stare at Brian's lips to make sure you understand him. "Nice work," you say. Then people mill about. You walk to your office and tell Stacy, your admin, that you'd like to have a few moments alone.

"But you have a meeting with the leadership council in five minutes," she says as if she's your high-school teacher. She's twice your age, so you tend not to push back.

"Well, okay. Just give me a minute."

Two minutes later, men and women in blue windbreakers and suits enter the office and lead you and everyone they can find to the conference room. They are federal officials.

And here you sit. A man who works for the IRS Criminal Investigation Division holds the envelope. It's a sealed warrant. Meaning, this is no joke. Someone will be arrested and charged with a crime.

Where's Dad, dammit? You glance left and right, but don't find the man who stands four inches shorter than you and has a thinning bed of gray, curly hair. You saw his car in the parking lot in his normal spot, so he has to be here.

Unless he's not. Did he use the restroom, see the raid, and decide to take off?

There are gasps all around, mutterings of questions. You try to understand what's being said, but you know it's impossible. What you do pick up, however, is fear. Fear from people you've known for years, even if it was more as Nathaniel Novak's son than as a practicing attorney at the firm that has been around longer than you have.

You want to get up, pace a little, but two men standing at the side of your chair quash that request.

You watch files being stacked into boxes. Men and women with stern looks writing with Sharpies on the side of the boxes. You've never seen so many Sharpies. Then again, you've never seen anyone raid your office. Maybe a client's office, but not yours.

You stare at the sealed envelope and wonder what's on the inside. What event initiated this raid? With sealed warrants, more than likely a secret grand jury has been meeting for weeks and decided to hand down indictments. And you never caught wind of it? Not with all your contacts in Travis County, the City of Austin, or even, to a lesser degree, inside the state capitol? Someone would have surely tipped you off. Right?

You can't imagine what would initiate such a move. It couldn't have come from any of your clients. Not possible. One of the other six lawyers in the office? Maybe Arie, Nathaniel's old buddy, the only other true partner in the firm. The double mentioning of Novak in the firm name is for posterity reasons only. "Your time will come," Nathaniel always says. You've always wondered what led to Arie becoming the lone second partner, or any partner at all. He's nearly worthless as an attorney.

You glance around the room. No sign of Arie. Hmmm.

But there's also no sign of Nathaniel. Now, you think, *he* has balls. Maybe all this was due to Nathaniel himself. That must be it. He's always treading water where it's the murkiest. All in the name of fees. A legal term for bringing in the cash.

A wave of heat rushes up your neck. You're pissed. You want to pound the desk, find Nathaniel, and wring his neck. But you can't lose control, not in front of all the other employees. They're scared, for many reasons.

And then you hear that whining groan. You can't help but jump out of your chair and look into the foyer. Nathaniel is in handcuffs, falling to his knees as two federal agents jump back, a look of shock on their faces. Nathaniel hits the floor as you run out of the meeting room, drop down next to him. He's sweating profusely, gritting his teeth.

"This is the one, kiddo," he says.

"Dad! You can't die."

Dad has a heart attack. And instead of bailing him out of jail, you rush to the emergency room, followed by two cars full of federal agents.

A second kick to the nuts.

Two

I hate the smell of hospitals. An underlying scent of urine and other bodily liquids lingered in the air, while a sharp, pungent jab of disinfectant tried to smother it out. I call it "the hospital funk." For some folks, the near-constant battle for dominance of your olfactory senses dulls over time…not a very big deal. For me, my sense of smell is always at a heightened sense of alert. It's a natural survival instinct. I'm partially deaf. Actually, "hearing-impaired" is the more accepted term in society these days. But I was born with it, apparently, so it's the only thing I've known.

I picked up a loud clip of heels and turned to see my younger brother, Tobin, walking down the hall, a hand to his ear, nodding at me. He was on a call. My eyes went to his cowboy boots. Made of alligator or something he probably killed while on his African safari adventure last summer. He was quite a character, a little like his father, which, right now, was not exactly a high compliment.

He reached me, but held up a finger. I expected no less, and my sights drifted to two sets of people who had so many lives in their hands. A group of doctors, a cardiologist included, were standing just outside my father's room, discussing his diagnosis. They knew I was waiting to learn of his fate. Another thirty feet beyond them, a gaggle of federal officials also waited to see if their suspect would live or die. For now, they left me alone.

I checked my phone and saw a blank screen. Another dash of disappointment. On my way over in the back of the ambulance, I'd texted Nicole, among others, about the news of Dad's heart attack. I also told her, in as few words as possible, about the raid by the Feds. Maybe she was in a meeting, unable to reach her phone. Or maybe she just didn't care enough to reply.

Tobin touched my elbow to ensure I was looking at him. "Sorry about that, bro. Business never stops."

"Ours did."

One of his considerable eyebrows inched upward. I gave him a brief explanation of the raid and the presence of the Feds down the hallway.

"Fuckin' A," he said.

Typical Tobin response. Some might think he sounded like a skateboard thrasher. At other times, he was all about fighting oppression against… Well, just fill in the blank on the cause of the day. Then, there were his babies—not actual human beings. "Babies" was the term he used to describe his startup companies. Austin was just behind Silicon Valley in the race for the next great idea. Tobin had a lot of great ideas, and thanks to being silver-spooned by our parents, he had lots of babies, although I wasn't sure any of them had yet grown into a toddler.

He asked about Dad just as two women in white coats walked up. They nodded and introduced themselves. The one with a mole the size of a beetle on her forehead did the talking. She was the cardiologist.

"Your father suffered a heart attack."

As if that wasn't already apparent. I withheld a biting response. "Okay," I managed to say. "How bad?"

"He has a partial blockage in two arteries. One is fifty percent blocked; the other is thirty percent."

"That old fart just doesn't know when to lay off the chicken-fried steak and the double shots of vodka for dinner every night," Tobin said with an inappropriate chuckle.

She gripped both ends of the stethoscope that hung around her neck. "Diet is certainly part of the problem. I also understand that he's been seeing a doctor for this condition, but he's been inconsistent in taking his medication, not following the instructions on food, exercise, and stress reduction."

Sounded like Dad. No one else could tell him what to do with his body. Well, maybe one person. I wondered when she would show up.

"Is he going to be okay?" I asked.

She pursed her lips, pausing for a second. "Your father is naturally inclined to have plaque buildup. While this heart attack didn't permanently damage his heart, he's now prone to having another myocardial infarction. And, well…"

She paused, glanced at her colleague. "Your father seems to think he's immune to any further medical issues. We were, uh…rather blunt in explaining the gravity of his condition."

"We know he's stubborn." I reset my feet and loosened my tie.

"Well, we're hoping you can convince him that he needs to follow the protocol he's been given, the full cardiac rehabilitation. If he doesn't, then we can't provide a positive outlook on his longevity."

I noticed movement just over the doctor's shoulder. A Fed was walking in our direction. His double chin made his neck look like a tree trunk.

"Sorry to butt in," he said, finding a small place between the two doctors.

"But you just did," I said.

He eyed me, nodded as if he had some sort of power over me, then went back to the doctor. "When can we take the suspect to our office?"

"You're going to charge a man who's on his deathbed?" Tobin asked with too much dramatic flair. It seemed fake, probably because it was. He was obviously trying to throw up some type of smoke screen for Dad's protection. Not sure why he thought it would be effective.

Double Chin nodded at Tobin, then looked at the doctor. "I'll let the expert give me the answer I need. So?"

"Agent...?" She waited for a name. He didn't provide one.

She looked at me, and I gave her a slight nod.

"So, while Mr. Novak's condition at this moment is not life-threatening, he still will not be released from the hospital for several days, and that will only occur if he follows the protocol I was just explaining to his sons."

"Sonofabitch." Double Chin tugged loose skin around his neck. An image of a walrus came to mind. "We'll keep at least one agent outside of his room at all times."

"Why? He's not a flight risk. And it's not like he can run off."

He looked at me and nodded again. There was a story in there that he wasn't telling me. Or maybe my radar was extra sensitive today. Well, I knew that was the case. He asked to be kept in the loop as Dad's health improved. He started to walk off.

"When are you going to let me look at the charges in the sealed warrant?" I asked, as the two doctors slowly peeled away.

He walked back up, held up a badge that I ignored. He put it away and said, "I'm FBI Special Agent Bowser. Bruce Bowser. You know I can't show you the sealed warrant. Not yet. That's why we need to formally book and charge him. Then we can let the justice process play out."

I could feel my chest swelling, but I let out a slow breath. "I need to know the name of the attorney in charge of the prosecution in the US Attorney's Office."

"In due time. First, we need to formally charge him. We'll do it right here if we have to. But it would be preferable if we went through this at our office. We want to be respectful of his health."

They wanted a live suspect so they could punch a notch in their career belts. I thought about my options. "My father is not a career criminal. Whatever evidence you think you have I'm sure is circumstantial at best. We represent a lot of clients in our firm, and we can't babysit all of them. This won't even make it to trial—that much I can assure you."

He snickered, moved closer, and tapped my chest. *That fucker just tapped my chest.* A quick flashback to seventh grade, dealing with the bully in the locker room. To say I didn't like it was the understatement of the day. But I bit my lip and said nothing. Not yet.

"Ozzie, if I were you, I'd be a little less boastful about what you think of the situation and start worrying about yourself. Get what I'm saying?"

He held my gaze for a moment. I didn't shift my eyes.

"Your firm is essentially shut down. Your father was the lead partner. We know the place can't remain open without a partner in good standing with law enforcement and the bar association. And I would imagine, in a matter of hours, you'll lose most of your clients anyway. Some might even sue you. It could get real messy and very expensive. But that's not the worst of it."

Tobin stepped into our space. "Can it get any worse than that?" Now he sounded like a scared teenager. I wished he would have just kept quiet.

"Oh yeah. For anyone whose livelihood is based upon the man in that room, it could get much worse. Frozen assets. No revenue.

Lots of expenses." He chuckled once. "But you know what, Ozzie?"

I crossed my arms, forcing him to back up a few inches.

"You can protect yourself and your family if you'll help us out. Just need you to corroborate our evidence."

"You want me to turn on my father?"

"You don't want to be indicted as well, do you? Accessory to the crime."

I had no idea what crime he was referencing.

"You want Oz to flip on Dad?" Tobin's voice pitched higher. "You...you're fucking nuts. This is a witch hunt. I'm going to hit social media and soil your career."

Agent Bowser flicked a wrist in Tobin's direction, as if he were nothing more than an annoying gnat.

"Think it over, Ozzie. I'm looking out for you, man." He attempted to pat my chest—I lurched back a step to avoid the bro-contact—and then he turned to walk away. But he wasn't done. He looked over his shoulder.

"Your mother, even your brother here, will thank you in the long run. If you back us up, you'll be the hero. You might be able to save the firm, keep those precious fees rolling in. Like I said, think it over. I'll be in touch."

Bowser went off to join his Fed buddies while Tobin proceeded to bombard me with demonstrative proclamations about what he was going to do to the FBI and how he had friends in high places to make Bowser and these charges disappear. It was all hot air, I knew. Besides, I was hit hardest by a new waft of hospital funk.

Three

Alfonso tore off his greasy apron, hung it on the back door, and tossed the keys to his 1977 Monte Carlo on the counter.

"You home, Alfonso?"

He paused, looked toward the hallway, then shuffled to the refrigerator and opened the door.

"I know you're home."

It was his girlfriend, Lupita. She sounded like his damn mother.

"I need help with the twins." Her voice carried like she had a megaphone implanted in her chest. It literally made his ears ache. "One of them crapped all over my white leather pants," she droned on at a decibel level fit for a rock concert.

"Oh, Lupita. You're wearing me out, girl," he whispered, rubbing his weary eyes. He'd just finished a twelve-hour shift flipping burgers. On his feet the entire time. No breaks. He had grease burns up and down his forearms. His back felt like a twisted pretzel. He was going to plop his ass down on the couch, watch a soccer game, and wait for the Schlitz to help the pain subside.

He leaned over and felt a kink in his lower back. "Fuckin' A, man." Looking inside the fridge, he searched for his cans of beer. Lots of bottles and unwrapped food—a stick of butter, a half-eaten burger from the previous night, molded Jell-O, an old box of pizza. "This is disgusting," he said to himself.

"I hear you out there. Are you going to take care of your little girls?"

Damn, she must have this kitchen wiretapped or something. "This fridge is fucking gross, woman. Aren't you supposed to keep this house clean while I'm off at work?"

Not a beat later, she stood at the edge of the hallway, one fake eyelash flapping like a bird's wing. "Did I just hear you say that it's my duty to clean the house while you're off working, like I'm some kind of servant to the almighty Alfonso?" Her in-your-face attitude was out in full force, as evidenced by both her tone and her twerking torso.

He was so tired, he didn't know how to respond. He shrugged and said, "Well...what the fuck?"

"Real smart, Alfonso." Her eyes narrowed, but he couldn't take his eyes off her fake lashes. He would have laughed at her if he didn't think she'd slap him.

"You sound very educated with your comment. This isn't your old thug world. You can't talk like that and expect anyone to think you've got two brain cells to rub together."

He wiped a hand across his face. He knew she meant well, but damn, he felt like he was about two inches high. His fatigued mind could focus on only one thing right now. "Where's my beer?"

"It's all gone. You had the last one yesterday."

She turned around and disappeared down the hallway, but still yelled out, "You going to take care of your daughters?"

He grabbed his crotch. "You going to suck my—?"

"I can hear you."

Jesus. Really? He snapped his fingers as a smile came to his face. The backup plan. He always had a backup plan. He walked over to the closet that doubled as a pantry. Underneath a pile of newspapers, he found a bucket turned upside down. He flipped it over and found three cans of Budweiser.

"Hell yes," he said. He popped the tab, tipped his head back, and chugged for a good ten seconds. It was warm as piss, but he didn't care. He found his usual spot on the couch and clicked the remote. The soccer game was twenty minutes in, still no score.

"Okay, I guess I'll have to change the diapers…again," Lupita yelled.

He closed his eyes for a moment. Would it ever end? She had no idea the kind of crap he had to deal with every day. No way in hell could she put up with it. She talked all about being equal partners and shit.

Equal partners, my ass.

He slurped another mouthful of Budweiser. Blue ink from the top of his hand caught his eye. Part of the tattoo had been bleached away, but he could still see the outline.

$6 + 7$

It was simple and delivered a deafening message. At least in some circles. Around the house, it might as well be shooting the middle finger to God. But man, in his day, that symbol, along with a host of others hidden under his T-shirt, would bring instant respect. Without saying a word or even looking in their direction, people feared him. They gave him gifts…just so they wouldn't get their teeth knocked in. Yeah, those were the days.

He could hear Lupita in another corner of his mind, listening to his thoughts of the good old days. *"And look what that got you, Alfonso Liriano. Two years of hard time. You were somebody's bitch. Is that the kind of life you want to live, being someone's bitch day after day, wondering when they might decide to gut you like a pig?"*

He noticed an open bag of sour cream and onion potato chips on the coffee table. Had the kids been eating this crap? Damn, they were barely over two years old. He turned his head toward the hallway, ready to grill Lupita about what she was allowing the girls to eat. He paused a moment. What would it buy him? Would she change?

Hell no. She just does her thing, and he ain't allowed to make one fucking comment or even a suggestion. It was like he had no say in his kids' lives…in his own life. No control over anything. Just get up, go work a shit-ass job for twelve hours or more, and then come home to this.

Seemed like he would always be someone's bitch.

He grabbed a couple of chips from the bag and tossed them in his mouth. They were stale, but he didn't spit them out. He ate another handful, chugged more of his beer, and tried to lose himself in the soccer game.

He then heard Lupita speaking in Spanish. She sounded pissed. She had to be talking to her sister. He could make out the gist of what she was talking about. Mainly complaining. Complaining about her lousy house, her crappy car, and her lazy-ass husband.

He went and grabbed his second beer, returned to the couch, and turned up the volume on the game. Still, though, her voice was like a frickin' diamond-tipped needle. It could pierce anything.

He felt a buzz in his sagging jeans. He pulled out his phone and saw the name from his contacts on the screen. He paused and looked back down the hallway, debating whether he should answer the call or let it roll to voicemail. He could hear Lupita cackle, then rattle off a string of cuss words. She had to be talking about him. That was all she and her sister ever did. Sit around, get fat, and complain about the men in their lives.

Fuck it.

He punched open the call. "Yo, Tomas."

"Alfonso, my man. It's been a while."

"Yeah. You know I've got a lot going on."

"That's what I heard, man. A lot of diapers, a lot of laundry, a lot of—" He laughed so hard, he didn't finish his thought.

"Fuck you, Tomas. I got shit going on. It's just, you know… I'm working hard. Trying to provide…to make money. Trying to keep my life on track."

"Life. Hmmm."

Alfonso could feel a rush of adrenaline zipping through his veins. "What are you saying?"

"How's that minimum wage working for you?"

"Wish it was more. But it's steady. A paycheck every two weeks."

"Of course, they gotta take out Social Security, other taxes, and shit so the rich white folks can have their pristine roads in their gated communities. It's all a scam. But I guess you know that, huh?"

Alfonso turned his eyes to the TV screen, but the blur of the action on the field didn't really register.

"You really living much of a life, Alfonso?"

"Dude, I got two little girls I gotta take care of. So, yeah—this life is real."

"I hear you're flipping burgers. You want your daughters to grow up with that picture in their minds? Dear old Dad, the greaser."

Alfonso shot up on the couch. "I ain't no greaser. It's just my first step in the working world. If I put in the time, maybe I can become a real chef and work in one of those fancy five-star restaurants off 2nd Street or something."

"Come on, Alfonso. Get real. No matter how good of a cook you are, you think they're going to hire you to do anything more than clean their toilets? You got more ink on you than a newspaper.

At one point in your life, you were keeping it real, dog. That's right. You commanded respect. You made real cash."

There was silence. Alfonso didn't know what to say, and his thoughts were taking him places he shouldn't go.

But why the hell not? It was a free country. Who said he had to achieve success in just one way? Lupita's way. Fuck that.

He emptied his second can of Budweiser. "So, why did you call, Tomas?"

"I thought you'd never ask."

Five minutes later, Alfonso glanced down the hallway and heard Lupita squawking out a laugh. He grabbed his keys and walked out of the house.

It was time to regain his respect.

Four

I could hear Dad's voice from the nurse's station. Carrying a fresh cup of ice chips, I hoofed it down the hall, took a left, and swung open the door. My brother was pacing on the other side of the bed. He looked like a crack addict who was about to…crack.

"What the hell is going on?" I asked, my eyes shifting to Dad. Pillows propped him up as he sat there and tried to smile at me. His eyes nearly disappeared inside the folds of skin hanging under his eyes.

"We're just having a friendly discussion, Oz. Everything's good. I see you have my ice. Thank you," he said, reaching in my direction.

I handed it to him while looking over at Tobin. I tilted my head as if to say, *"Did you provoke Dad into getting upset?"*

"What?" he said.

Tobin obviously missed my nonverbal signals. I had no choice now. "I heard yelling from down the hall. We both know Dad can't afford to get upset. Not in his condition."

He pursed his lips, then pointed at Dad.

"Spit it out, Tobin."

"What's Tobin's trying to say is that I, uh, convinced him to give me my phone. I just had to check on a couple of things." Dad smiled again and held his phone where I could see it.

I shook my head at the idiocy, the complete lack of regard for doctor's orders. "You heard the cardiologist in here just a few minutes ago. No work. No stress. Not until you go through your cardiac rehabilitation, and after that, only in small amounts."

"This hardly counts as work. I punched a few buttons on a little rectangular device. Your grandfather would say that's the laziest form of work he'd ever seen."

Dad had a tendency to manipulate the situation to his benefit. I wasn't completely certain if that was due to the environment of running a law office or if that was how he'd been since the day he spoke his first word. Nonetheless, it was good to see him have a little spunk, especially with the countless wires crisscrossing his body and the fact that he looked like he'd been given two black eyes.

I dropped the confrontation about him having his phone, although he'd just opened himself up to my questioning. "So, what was so urgent?"

He tilted his head and then shrugged, as if my question were meaningless.

"Dad, please. I wasn't born yesterday."

He splayed his arms and looked to Tobin for some type of political backing. Tobin simply retreated a couple of steps.

"Just a minute ago, you didn't want me to say the word 'work.' Now you want to hold a tense discussion."

He loved putting words in my mouth. Actually, it wasn't exclusive to me. I'd seen him do it with just about every witness, colleague, or family member. Professionally, of course, it made him a damn good lawyer. In his personal relationships, it had the opposite effect. I blew out a breath and tried not to focus on the things I couldn't change. "Did your text or email have anything to do with the federal agents who raided our office?"

He jiggled the cup and let more ice chips fall into his mouth. After we'd endured an agonizing minute or so of watching him chew on ice, he set the cup on his side table. "Now, where were we?"

A delay tactic meant to work on a four-year-old. Had he been taking lessons from Nicole? "The text?" I made sure to keep my tone measured.

"Didn't you know it was Arie's birthday today?"

I looked off, trying to remember if I'd seen any balloons or cards or signs at the office. Nothing came to mind, but I also knew I'd been less than attentive when I'd walked in earlier this morning.

"How old is he?"

He scoffed at me, even flicked a wrist my way. "You think I know the age of every employee we've got? I just know he's getting close to seventy."

He was impossible. I blew out a breath as he picked up his ice again and began crunching away. I saw Tobin looking past me, over my shoulder. I flipped around to see one of the FBI agents casually strolling by the door and adjoining windows. He had his thumbs tucked into his belt loop, as if he were some type of western cowboy ready to round up the villains.

Once he passed, I said to Tobin, "They haven't tried to talk to Dad, have they?"

"Nope. But that Bowser guy keeps passing by every few minutes."

I thought about what could happen over the coming days. Dad's alertness was a blessing, but I knew that might also quicken the time to when the Feds would want to talk to him.

"Son, you look worried."

I glanced up and saw the dad I recalled as a kid. He was demonstrative, larger than life in some respects. But he seemed to have a warm spot for those closest to him.

"Well, our firm is virtually at a standstill. Everyone went home for the day, and I've been pinged by a dozen of them wondering if the office will be open tomorrow."

"So you *are* worried," he said, nodding. Then, just like that, he looked down and started shaking his head. His face had regret written all over it.

"Dad, we can get past this, but I need you to be honest with me."

"When have I not been honest with you?" he asked, pointing a finger.

He sounded offended.

"Transparent. That's a better term," I said.

He tried to pop a knuckle—another habit that wasn't great on the body—as if he were deep in thought, but he didn't say anything.

"Why were you in handcuffs? What were they arresting you for?"

"Honestly, I have no clue."

"So they cuffed you and didn't tell you why you were being arrested? Come on, Dad. This isn't frickin' Russia."

He waggled a finger at me. "I love your sarcasm, son. Don't lose it. It will always be a good way to reduce stress."

And yet again, he didn't answer my damn question. "Agents from the FBI, IRS, FDA, and Homeland Security were in our office. They weren't searching for a couple of joints in someone's desk. They had a sealed warrant. And they won't tell me the nature of the indictment. So, it's probably related to one of your clients, right?"

He shrugged.

"Are you going to force me to log into our cloud service and search through all our historical files? Hell, I have no idea what I'm looking for, but I can at least separate your clients from everyone else's."

"You won't find anything."

There was a knock on the door. "Sorry to interrupt, but I need to review with Mr. Novak his options for dinner this evening." A young woman with dimples waltzed in as I replayed what Dad had just said. *You won't find anything.* How could that be?

Tobin appeared in my space.

"Dad gets all the breaks, huh?" He shifted his head toward Dad and the girl. He was referencing the fact that the girl had to be no more than twenty-one and was rather attractive, in a college-coed kind of way.

"Yep. He just leaves all the shit for us to clean up."

"Hey, man. I know this isn't easy for you. But at least you have nothing to worry about on the health front. I'm the one who has to worry about my heart now."

He was referring to the fact that I was adopted, though that still didn't make any sense—I could have something horrible running through my DNA. I didn't know I was adopted until I was eighteen, when doctors thought Mom was going to lose a kidney. I'd insisted on volunteering one of my kidneys. That was when they finally told me the truth. It rocked me, although once I'd had some time to think it through, the signs were there, in appearances if nothing else. But I didn't harp on it. My family had always shown me a lot of love, and I never felt any different from Tobin. Well, there was one thing—the ownership of Dad's most beloved child, Novak and Novak.

I noticed Tobin's gut hanging over his belt loop. He was a miniature version of Dad. I didn't want to alarm the guy. "You said you got in touch with Mom, right? She was up at some Jewish retreat in the Hill Country?"

"Never actually talked to her, because that group has a weird rule where they turn off all communications during their two days of discussion. I talked to the manager, though. Said he'd relay the message and ensure that she left as soon as possible."

I checked my watch.

"Oh my God. How is my darlin' doing?"

I knew that West Texas twang. I flipped around and saw her. Bianca. The other woman in Dad's life. She put a hand to her face, one that had been stretched and tucked in a way that made her look part alien.

"Nathaniel, my poor baby. You need some Bianca love." Puckering her lips from ten feet away, she sauntered over to Dad's bed while tossing a fur off toward a chair. She missed. All eyes went to her leopard-print outfit—some type of onesie that looked like it was painted on her.

I tapped the face of my watch and traded a quick glance with Tobin. This time, he understood my signal. *Operation Separation*—the term Tobin and I used to keep Mom and Dad's girlfriend from crossing paths—had just hit red-alert status.

"Oh shit," Tobin whispered to me, looking over my shoulder.

I couldn't force myself to turn around.

Five

A man cleared his throat behind me, and I released a deep breath—it wasn't Mom. Yes, Tobin and I were the ultimate enablers for Dad's philandering. I couldn't recall exactly how we had gotten ourselves in this position. Maybe later I'd try to retrace the series of events. For now, though, that painful task wasn't on my top-ten list. Leaving Bianca to dote on Dad in the way only she could, I flipped around and walked to the door to talk to Agent Bruce Bowser.

"What's up?"

"I thought your dad was in such a serious condition that he couldn't take visitors?"

"The cardiologist said as much, and you were right there when she said it. Do you not see the tubes and wires connected to him?"

He nodded. "I see tubes, but I also see a blond bimbo about ready to go down—"

The hospital candy striper interrupted Bowser as she walked past us. "I'll be back with Mr. Novak's first meal in a bit."

"Thank you," I said.

She went on her way, and Bowser moved into my personal space. "You tell your father he better have all the fun he can with Leopard Skin Lilly. Tomorrow, he's going to have to deal with us."

I wanted to shoot back a verbal response that would make Bowser back off. But I knew it would be false bravado.

"You ever going to share with me the specific charges?"

"I guess you'll find out tomorrow, if you plan on representing your father. Oh yeah, depending on the bylaws of the firm, I'm not sure the bar association will allow you to continue practicing law. Looks like you might be on the outside."

This asshat knew things about how the firm was set up that I didn't even know. Dad had always said he'd share it with me in due time, giving me ample opportunity to gain experience and not worry about how to run a law office. Due time had come too late. Well, it certainly had made things more complicated. Dad had to spill everything he knew, or I'd have to hunt down Arie Steinberg, the only minority partner, to understand where we went from here.

I could feel my neck and face turn red. Bowser chuckled and walked off.

I muttered, "What an ass," as I turned around and found Bianca in the bed with Dad, rubbing a hand against his cheek. "Jesus, Tobin," I said, looking for someone, anyone, to be the adult in the room.

"No reason to get your panties in a wad, Ozzie." Bianca smooched Dad on the cheek, leaving her mark of red lipstick. She had always tried to figure out ways to extend her sphere of influence, hoping something would spur Dad to divorce Mom and bring her into a legitimate position. It hadn't happened in fifteen years, so why did she think it would change now?

Dad acted like a shy little boy, not saying much. He just had an "aw, shucks" smile and stared at his phone.

Tobin shrugged, as if to say he had no control over Dad or Bianca. He pulled out his phone and read something on the screen. "Crap."

"What now?"

He walked up next to me. "Mom's on her way up. I'll go try to delay her a bit."

"And I'll try to shove— I mean, I'll urge Bianca to take off."

He took one step toward the door and then leaned back, as we both could hear Bianca talking to Dad like he was a cute puppy dog. I rolled my eyes when Tobin said, "How many times have we pulled this off?"

"Too many. Get going."

A nurse walked in and checked Dad's vitals, which, thankfully, meant Bianca had to roll out of Dad's bed. I pulled out my phone to see if I'd missed anything important. Six text messages from various employees, including Stacy, asking about Dad's condition and if the firm was still in business. But strangely, nothing from Arie. Unless…

I brought my phone to my chin and studied Dad for a moment. Maybe he'd been swapping messages with his old buddy, ensuring the whole operation would sail smoothly while he dealt with these charges. Not that I wanted Dad to worry about anything. He should be focused on eliminating stress and his upcoming rehabilitation. Hopefully, Arie and I could manage the clients and a worried staff.

After the nurse left, Bianca said, "So what are all these federal agents doing around your room, baby?"

Dad looked straight at me. I wasn't going to save him, not with her.

"They want information, that's all. And you know me—I'm a bit of a bulldog when it comes to protecting my clients. So, I drew the line, and now they think they can threaten me with all sorts of warrants. But I'm not intimidated. The good guys will win. We always do."

He gave her this half-wink. That was one of his most epic manipulative moves. I would have been impressed had we been in a court of law. But we weren't, so I wasn't.

She put her hands on top of his, then looked at me and took a hard swallow. "Ozzie, just promise me that you won't let anyone hurt my baby, okay?"

Your baby? I shuffled my feet. "I'll do the best I can."

"Good, because we want Nathaniel here to be around a long time. We still have a lot of memories to make. Am I right, baby?"

She only wanted to make sure that her free ride wouldn't disappear. I was almost certain that Dad picked up every bill she incurred, from her rent on some condo in downtown Austin to her extensive, albeit exotic, wardrobe.

"You're so very right, Bianca," Dad said.

"So you haven't forgotten about that trip to Italy?"

Most people would expect Bianca to be a bit subtle about her arrangement with Dad, especially around one of his sons. Not her. No way. I suspected she viewed us as the outsiders, and, if she wanted, she could snap her fingers and Dad would push us away. I wasn't sure I agreed with that notion, but I never forced it. Probably because we were so young when it had all started. So, it was one of the unspoken truths about our family, which coupled quite nicely with never talking things out. No one did with Dad. But I was now seeing the error of my ways.

You go around thinking that things will always be the same—health, relationships, your job—and then one day you wake up and things change. Instantly. And while you play through scenarios of what you could have done to change the outcome—hindsight is our deadliest weapon to incite guilt—it still feels like a kick to the crotch. It takes your breath away, makes your knees wobbly. You look for something or someone to provide a little bit of sanity and stability. Dad had been that person for me growing up on a number of occasions. In the last few years, though, I'd grown accustomed to dealing with life's pitfalls mostly on my own.

When Nicole and I were married, it seemed like I picked up a copilot. She didn't stifle me or nag me. She was there, supportive but not demanding. It seemed like we were equals in this journey through life.

And then, just like that, we weren't. At least we didn't seem as close. Again, I knew there was at least a small possibility that I was dreaming all of this up. Adding together all her odd brush-offs like it was some type of mathematical equation.

A new thought zipped across my mind, and I quickly felt like an idiot for not even considering it. For her to change this much, maybe she was going through something she hadn't been able to share. Something that had shattered her core to the point where she just couldn't open up to me about it.

I convinced myself not to worry about her not texting me. I'd catch up with her later at the house, pour her a glass of wine—actually, both of us a glass of wine—and give her my undivided attention. Now that I thought about it, I'd been selfish the last couple of months. A couple of difficult clients, new family pressure to have kids. It had been all about me, right? I'd jumped to the sarcastic conclusion of repeatedly being kicked in the nuts. But why go there? Why play the victim? I hated people like that. Not that we didn't all have our moments of self-pity.

Right then and there, I gave myself an edict: stop being so self-absorbed and be thankful for what you do have. Remember the heart emojis from Nicole, not all the perceived blowoffs. Dad was alive. He'd probably be just fine, as long as he focused on his rehab. And the firm? Well, maybe this would be my chance to finally take the reins and lead us out of this storm of controversy.

"Of course not. It's still on my calendar," Dad said about the Italy trip.

I quickly felt sorry for Mom. Yes, she took plenty of trips, but they were with her friends. Never with Dad. He was always too busy. "Next year, when things die down," I'd heard him say countless times.

I felt my phone buzz. I peeked at the screen. A text from Tobin. *Can't stop her. Will be there in less than 1 minute.*

Dammit! I had to act fast. "Bianca, do you still drive that, uh…"

"What about my Mercedes?"

I tried not to choke on my own spit. "It's white, right?"

"What happened to it?"

The color had been a logical guess. White paint, tan interior seemed to match the theme of her platinum hair and leopard-print attire.

She shuffled over next to me, trying to look at my phone. I shoved it in my pocket. "Tobin said he saw a tow truck hooking up a white Mercedes in the parking lot."

"Those two-bit, good-for-nothing…" She bit her lip, then raised her fists to the ceiling. "If they put one scratch on it, I'll have Nathaniel sue them for every penny they've got."

The three of us looked at each other. I wasn't sure who started it, but it was beyond awkward. We all knew that Dad suing anyone was not only a low priority but also difficult to picture, given his uncertain future.

She grabbed her black fur, gave Dad another kiss on the cheek, and said she'd send him a special picture later tonight. I rolled my eyes on that one and ushered her down the hall opposite where Mom and Tobin would likely come up. As I scooted back into the room, I could see Mom and Tobin step out of the elevator. I had maybe thirty seconds. I handed Dad a tissue and motioned for him to clean off his face.

"You know this has to stop."

"What?"

Again with the clueless response.

"You know what. Tobin and I have been covering for you for too many years. Dad, you need to accept responsibility for your own behavior."

He wiped his cheek, then handed me the tissue. "I know, son."

Did I just hear him right? He didn't push back. It was a miracle. So, I took one more leap. "Dad, I'm worried about you and the firm, all the people who depend on us for a paycheck."

He sighed. "Yeah. I'm sorry if I let you down."

That sounded like an admission of guilt. "Just start by telling me the charges."

He looked at me with sad eyes. "Obstruction of justice, extortion, assault and battery—but only a misdemeanor on that one."

I felt the air leave me. "Assault and battery?"

"I said it was a misdemeanor. They said I only threatened someone. You know the law."

Right now, all knowledge and experience was a foreign object. "Did you do it? Did you do everything they said?"

"Two things, Ozzie. First, if you plan on assisting Arie in defending me, then you know to never ask a client if he is guilty. Second, like a lot of the work we do on behalf of our clients, it's gray. We get as close to that thin line as possible. Some might say we cross it; others say we're okay. I guess we'll find out."

He tried to smile, but he never made it there.

I flipped around and could see Mom set her clutch in the crook of her arm and inch her chin a bit higher, as if she were preparing for battle. She was just about to walk into the room.

Back to Dad. "You said I'd never find any records of this client. Is that really true?"

He opened his lips but never got the words out.

"Nathaniel, dear, what did you get yourself into this time?" Mom entered the room, followed by Tobin.

I was forced to retreat from the bed as Mom barely gave me a passing nod. Dad just shrugged.

"Come on, Nathaniel, speak up. You've gone off and had this medical episode, and now I've been pulled out of my quarterly retreat with the ladies. This better be good."

Standing behind her, Tobin and I traded a glance. We weren't surprised at her lack of compassion. To say she wasn't exactly warm and affectionate was an understatement. But she seemed to almost be reveling in her more dominant—i.e., healthy—position.

"Juliet, dear, it's really nothing for you to worry about. I had a little fainting spell."

Tobin apparently couldn't help himself. "Fainting spell?"

Like a good lawyer, Dad chose not to answer the question. "Now that the doctors have completed their tests, they realize it was only a minor thing. I just need to eat a little better, walk a bit more. I'll be back in action in no time."

I just stood there and stared at him. *In action?* He didn't mention the blockages or the increased probability of another heart attack. Nothing. Unbelievable.

"So if this is nothing, then you're okay with me driving back up to my retreat?"

Mom was baiting him, almost daring him to change his story.

"Feel free, Juliet. The boys and I have everything under control."

Mom and Dad had been playing this passive-aggressive game for longer than I could recall. Years ago, I found it tense; now I felt like telling them both to grow up.

Mom turned on a heel and began heading for the door. "Boys, please let me know if your father has a turn for the worse. Until then, I'll—"

She stopped in her tracks. Agent Bowser was walking by again, giving all of us the death stare. Once he disappeared around the corner, she flipped around, her eyes momentarily focused on the ceiling. "I saw three cars in the parking lot that most likely belong to federal agents. Now one of those agents—who knows which department—is stalking your room, Nathaniel. Tell me why, this instant."

My phone buzzed, and, welcoming the respite, I turned my back to what might be a verbal bloodbath. My heart skipped a beat when I saw a text from Nicole. I couldn't open it fast enough.

Ozzie, she started. I felt a click in my breathing. She said my name only when she was introducing me, pissed as hell at me, and recently, giving me the cold shoulder. I read onward.

I'm sorry to hear about your father. I called up the hospital and learned that he was doing okay.

I paused and looked up. She had avoided me to the point of calling the hospital? I blinked twice and forged ahead.

I know the timing of what I'm sharing is not good. But is there ever a good time to break up?

My stomach swirled into an acidic tornado. I swallowed back some bile and forced myself to read the entire note.

I have filed for divorce. I know you've seen it coming, but you chose not to say anything. I assume you wanted the same thing. If not, I'm sorry. I can't read your mind.

I have gone ahead and divided up our money. You are a lawyer, so you can't blame me for getting a head start. There might be some interim rough spots as credit and debit cards are reissued. Until then, I'm sure you'll be okay. To make a clean break, I've also changed the locks on the house. I'll put your stuff in the garage by this weekend and let you know when you can pick it up.

I know you're going through a lot right now. But I can't control my feelings.

Best of luck,

N

On this one, it felt like I'd just been racked by a Venus Williams serve.

I couldn't take any more.

With echoes of Mom and Dad bickering over nothing and thirty years of marriage at the same time, I left the room and headed to my favorite bar. It was time for me to be very self-absorbed.

Six

Alfonso knew this feeling all too well. His pulse peppered the side of his neck. His leg couldn't stop bouncing. He could even hear his own panting. As he stared out of his Monte Carlo, he hardly noticed the light mist coating the windshield or the soft yellow glow of a distant street light. It was as if he were a caged bull, waiting for the gate to open, to unleash all of the pent-up anger he'd kept in check since the day he'd walked out of the state prison in Huntsville.

They say you're never the same once you serve time. No greater truth had ever been stated; that much he knew with certainty. When he went in, he was a wide-eyed nineteen-year-old with a cocky attitude and a chip on his shoulder toward just about everyone. Two days in, he was taught the lesson of his life. A lesson of survival. His mind refused to replay the exact nature of the beating he took—they'd violated him in ways he would never repeat to anyone. It had been his wake-up call. The specific time when he'd flipped from boy to man.

Society outside of those prison walls, though, was so vastly different. It was less about surviving day to day, hour to hour, at least in a physical sense. It was instead the whisper of expectations that, over time, became a weight that crushed his chest. He literally had moments when his airflow was restricted to choppy breaths.

There was the burden of being defined by the job you hold, the responsibility attached to that, and yes, the paycheck you brought home. Every time he thought he'd reached a goal, the line of success had magically shifted. Over time, he came to see it as a moving target, something unachievable.

What about the American dream? Fuck that. It was nothing more than a marketing slogan, pure propaganda, meant to make people feel like this entity known as a country actually gave real opportunity to someone like him. A convicted felon. No one gave a rat's ass about him. No one cared if he rotted away in a sewer. Not really. They cared about his job, his fucking title, his paycheck. Meanwhile, his self-respect had been whittled back so far that he hardly recognized himself.

But now that he felt the familiar fire burning in his belly, he was ready to inflict his will on another human.

The passenger door swung open. He felt a jolt in his chest, and his hand went straight for his waistband.

"Hey, *bato*, it's only me." Tomas slipped into the seat, shut the door. "You're really pumped for this job, aren't you?"

"Yeah, man. Once you got me thinking about what my life's all about, I knew I had to do something about it. So here I am. Ready to take control of my own life."

"Fuck yeah, bro."

Tomas, wearing the familiar blue do-rag over his head, handed Alfonso a sack with a bottle of tequila in it. "Drink, dude. It'll help calm those nerves."

Alfonso unscrewed the cap and took a long swig. He swirled the alcohol in his mouth, let it seep into his gums, and then he swallowed. His eyes closed momentarily as he felt the heat light up his chest.

"You think we're going to get any sleet tonight? They say it's a possibility." Tomas was trying to make small talk.

"I don't know. As long as it doesn't stop our job, I don't give a shit."

Tomas chuckled, smacked him on the arm. "You're hardcore, dude. And you're cracking me up. The real Alfonso has returned from the dead. What's it feel like, dude?"

Alfonso tried to match Tomas's smile. It wasn't possible. Tomas had a grill that he could only dream of, full of platinum. It was dope. He could only hope to one day make enough cash to afford something like that. When Tomas walked into your space, you knew he'd earned his stripes. His grill said it. His tats said it. His clothes said it. And his swagger said it.

"I don't know, man. I don't feel like I've done anything. Just changed my outlook a bit, I guess. But I need to earn back my respect."

"Hell yeah, man. That's what tonight is all about. You do this, and you're back in the game."

For a quick second, Alfonso thought about the implications of being back in the game. What it might mean to Lupita, to his daughters. He glanced up at his visor and saw the photograph of the only two people in the world who could make him cry. His two baby girls had melted his heart when they came into the world. He knew that, when they got older, they'd probably have Pops wrapped around their fingers. He didn't mind. He wanted to spoil them…with love, yes, but more than that. With everything their hearts desired.

Tomas flipped his gold watch around and checked the time, then leaned forward in his seat so he had a better angle to view the top of the building off to their left. They sat on a quiet side street in south Austin, just on the edge of where people had hope and where no hope existed at all. The corner building was four stories, a dark brick. It butted up against another one just like it and blended in with the rest of the area that had been erected long before he was born.

Alfonso strummed his fingers on the steering wheel. That nervous anxiety had returned. "When's this Walter White scientist dude showing his face, Tomas?" He tipped back the bottle of tequila and swallowed another mouthful.

"Walter White. Listen to you talking about *Breaking Bad* and shit." Tomas snickered. "You just got to show a little patience, man." He paused and looked up at the building. "Okay, that's what I was told. Fourth floor, third window in. The light's still on."

"I thought you said this guy would be in his car by nine. It's nine thirty. Someone screwing with you?"

Tomas slowly turned his head toward Alfonso. Red lines splintered across his eyes.

"You should know, dude—no one screws with me."

"Yeah, well…" Alfonso shifted in his seat, turned to look out his window, and saw a dog with its head buried in a trash bag just at the edge of the alley behind the building. "I know you're smart, but maybe someone tipped the guy off. Maybe this whole thing's a setup, just to catch two thugs doing their thing."

"Prison made you paranoid, man." Tomas smacked his arm again. "But I get it. I'd be acting the same way. It's cool. Let's just give it—" He stopped short. "Hold on. The light just went out. Let's get in position."

Alfonso dropped the bottle to the floor of the car. It was about to be showtime.

Seven

The two men quietly exited the car and slipped into the alley, immediately covered by the cloak of darkness. As expected, they saw two cars and a delivery truck. One of the cars and the delivery truck were associated with the bakery. The back door to the bakery was about fifty yards from where they huddled behind a trash bin. Tomas had told Alfonso earlier that the two people working at the bakery played loud music all night long and stayed inside during their overnight shift, making pies, cakes, and donuts for the next day's customers. The rest of the buildings around them were empty, aside from the man who was hopefully making his way down the back stairs to the third vehicle in the alley—a nondescript Buick.

"What's taking him so long?" Alfonso whispered. He spotted a thin dog sniffing the polluted ground.

"Damn, you're antsy. He'll be here when he gets here. Then you can do your thing, man."

Seconds ticked by as Alfonso rested his head against the metal bin. The stench of sour milk and rotten eggs lingered in the air. It made his stomach queasy, yet he still craved more tequila. He blinked twice, and images of his daughters came to mind. Their first birthday party when they both played in their cake. They had to share a cake because he couldn't afford to buy one for each of them. Their presents were nothing more than stuffed animals, a puzzle, and some building blocks picked up at the thrift shop.

He could feel his jaw tighten. He just wasn't able to continue the charade, thinking everything would be okay, when he knew deep down that the cycle of poverty and "no opportunity" would repeat itself. The worst thing he could possibly imagine would be to wake up twenty years from now and see his daughters hook up with losers who were content to be day laborers, or even short-order cooks, demoralized to the point of not being human. He had to take the chance to alter their fate. If he succeeded, then his girls would be on their way to moving into a new house in a nice neighborhood. They wouldn't have to live in fear, and more importantly, they could see examples of people who aspired to make something of their lives.

His perception at a young age had been shaped by two uncles who were busted twice for selling drugs. When they finally got out of prison, one just wandered off and was never heard from again. The other tried robbing his drug dealer and was found dead behind a gas station, his hands tied behind his back. Alfonso had tried to steer away from drugs, but there had been too many other obstacles and temptations to take the traditional path to success.

Just then, he heard a metal bang and the creak of a door opening. Tomas nudged his arm. "Get ready to move," he whispered.

Alfonso moved to his knees and peeked around the corner of the bin, just over Tomas's shoulder. The man was standing just outside the door, at the top of a small flight of steps, under a little cone of light. Clutching his leather briefcase like it was a child, the man swung his head left and right.

"He knows we're coming," Alfonso whispered.

Tomas twisted his head around to look at him. "He only knows he's at risk. I've been assured there are no leaks. No one will know. Don't get cold feet."

"I ain't got cold feet, bitch." He started to lift from his knees, but Tomas pushed him back down.

"Wait until he's walking toward the car with his back to us."

The man cautiously descended two steps, then stopped and looked over his shoulder. Had he spotted them? Just then, the dog from earlier lumbered past them, heading toward the street.

Alfonso let out a breath.

"He's moving again," Tomas said, smacking Alfonso on the leg.

Alfonso removed the gun from his jeans, aiming the barrel toward the dark sky. He watched the man take the last step into the alley.

Tomas nodded his head, and the pair moved out from behind the bin and began moving cautiously down the alley. Their rubber-soled shoes were barely audible. Halfway to the target, Alfonso picked up the sound of a rap beat. It was coming from the bakery. Old-school Tupac? Maybe. It kicked his pulse up another notch.

They closed the distance to the man quickly. He was approaching the back of his car, and they were no more than twenty feet away. Alfonso could hardly contain his exuberance. He would soon be back in the game.

He stepped on a can.

The man whipped around and spotted them.

"Fuck!" yelled Tomas. "Get after him, dammit!"

Alfonso sprang out of his stance so fast that his shoe slipped off the can. His knee dropped to the wet, rocky cement. Regaining his footing, he saw the man darting for the driver's-side door, juggling his keys.

Alfonso moved like the wind. The man put his hand on the door handle, and there was a beep. He opened the door just as Alfonso reached him, the barrel of the gun pressed against his forehead.

"Please don't hurt me." The man's voice quavered. He clutched his bag with one hand and pushed his glasses up on his nose with the other.

Alfonso's heart hammered in his chest. He just stood there for a moment, wondering if some greater force would send a signal for him to let this man live…something that would lead him on a path to redemption.

"You going to do it, Alfonso, or are you going to go back and flip burgers?"

Alfonso didn't answer Tomas. He couldn't. He was so hyped up, he could hardy breathe.

"Alfonso. That's your name?" the man said, now with a bit of hope in his voice. "I'll give you everything I've got, about a hundred dollars in cash, all of my credit cards. Here, you can even take my car." He extended his hand with the key fob in it. "It's all yours. I won't tell a soul. I just want to live."

The gun suddenly felt heavy in Alfonso's hand as a flood of images flashed through his mind, all of which were of his baby girls. Would they one day be proud of their Pops?

He felt tears pool in his eyes.

"Did you hear me? You can have everything—the cash, the credit cards, the car. Just don't kill me. You may not give a damn about your life, but I care about mine," the man said with an air of defiance.

"You hear that, Alfonso?" Tomas said from behind him. "He says you don't care about your life. It's now or never, motherfucker. What do you say?"

Tears burst from his eyes. He squeezed the trigger. The man's head snapped back, and then he slowly crumpled to the ground.

"I choose to get my respect back, bitch!" Alfonso growled.

Tomas laughed as Alfonso grabbed the man's wallet and briefcase. And then the pair disappeared into the dreary night.

Eight

An old song whined from the jukebox in the corner. I think it was a tune by a local Austin act, Monte Montgomery. Hard to tell for certain. Half the lights blinked on and off. The jukebox must have been thirty years old. Of course, my hearing wasn't stellar. In fact, in a public place like Peretti's, with all the ambient noise, it was nearly impossible to hear anything or anyone distinctly. I had to make sure I stared at their mouths, which, for some, can be a bit creepy.

I lifted the tumbler of bourbon whiskey, moved it around until one of the overhead spotlights caught it just right. The booze had taken the edge off my nerves but had also hindered my ability to think very clearly.

It was for the best. Just ask Poppy.

"You gonna sweet-talk that beautiful whiskey or just down it?" She smacked a shot glass onto the wooden bar, leaned a full bottle of whiskey against the side, and poured until it reached the rim. She held up the glass. "You drink the good stuff; I'll stick with the cheap shit. You with me?"

Not exactly in a celebratory mood, I didn't leave her hanging. We clinked glasses—I was a little clumsy and knocked her glass too hard. It began to spill, but she quickly threw back the whiskey and then wiped her face with her arm.

Damn, she was hardcore. Always had been, at least for the last two years that I'd known her. I just smiled.

"What's so frickin' funny?"

"Nothing," I said. She was an original and did what she needed to keep her life moving forward. It wasn't my place to start pointing out her flaws. At this moment, her life was far more stable and, frankly, happier than mine.

I shifted the glass from one hand to the other. No matter what I did, I couldn't help but retrieve a memory from my time with Nicole. Right now, the recollections focused on our California relationship—"phase one," as we'd later called it. A period in our lives when we were so full of spontaneity, sharing our souls with each other, dissecting the meaning of life without taking life too seriously. To sound cliché, we were carefree and madly in love. And yet, we didn't have to say it. We showed it to each other every day.

I recalled one time when we were standing on a pier watching the sun set behind a low bank of fog that was drifting in, seemingly splitting the Golden Gate Bridge in half. The vibrant colors, the rough bay water lapping against the pier, the waft of fish in the air. We just wrapped our arms around each other and took it all in. It must have lasted a half hour. Neither of us said a word. We didn't have to. We were both thinking and feeling the same thing. That was when I learned what intimacy was all about.

"Can I call you Mr. Deep Thought?"

It was Poppy again. Wearing a short T-shirt that allowed people to see her pierced navel, she put a hand on her waist. She was not a small woman, but the proportions were set to perfection. Still, your eyes went either to the colorful tattoos lining her arms and neck—she'd yet to show me other parts of her body—or the red dreadlocks that draped behind her head.

To me, she was Austin. Raw, coarse, yet genuinely honest. Like I said, she was an original.

"My thoughts aren't very deep right now. Very single-threaded."

"Come on, Oz. You need to snap out of it. It's not like you to be this way."

"Can't you just let me drink and wallow in my own self-pity?"

Someone called her name from the other end of the bar. The place wasn't quite half full. Just enough to pay the bills, I'd imagine, and to keep Poppy entertained. She turned her head. "Hold on a second," she yelled at them, then turned back to me, both hands on the edge of the bar.

I tried avoiding her glare. Through the foggy mirror behind the bottles of booze on the opposite wall, I watched a young couple walk by, each with a hand in each other's back pocket. I shifted my sights back to Poppy. I could practically feel the lasers shooting from her eyes.

"What do you want me to say?"

"I want you to *not* do what you just said you were doing…this whole wallowing and pity thing. Isn't that the same thing you told me when we first met?"

Poppy had been my second client. After a preliminary hearing with my first client—a wealthy woman accused of a hit-and-run— I'd lingered in the court a little too long, and the judge ordered me to defend her. Pro bono. Dad was less than thrilled, but he knew I had no choice. She'd been arrested for prostitution and drug possession. She was a mess. Strung out on cocaine, she could hardly connect two words together. She was depressed, anxious, and scared. Her hair looked like she'd stuck her finger in an outlet, and she couldn't stop scratching her arms.

After a listless first meeting with her, I figured I couldn't help someone who didn't want it. But as I lay in bed that night, I thought about why I'd become a lawyer. Yes, I'd dreamed of joining my father at the firm and taking the world by storm—it was an immature if not grossly superficial notion. But before dollar signs had taken control of my motivations, I was inspired to get through law school so I could make a difference in people's lives. And who needed it most? The ones who couldn't afford a high-priced attorney. The ones who thought no one cared whether they lived a vibrant life or slowly dissolved into a shell of a person. That, I realized, was where I could make the biggest difference.

I had gone back the next day to meet with Poppy, focused on helping her, not just her case. I was able to strike a plea bargain on her charges. I floated her some money for clothes, found her a job as a waitress at a diner, and tried to make her feel like she was worth more than being a piece of meat.

It turned her life around. After that, she went through what she called her enlightenment period; she became a tattoo artist for a while, colored her hair, and eventually started managing Peretti's. She was dating some chick she'd met in the tattoo shop, and she was as happy as I'd ever seen her.

Now she was trying to return the favor.

"It's different." That was my comeback? I knew it was lame the moment I said the words.

She nodded, crossed her arms just under her sizable chest. She didn't say anything for a moment, analyzing me, which made me uncomfortable. I finally lifted the glass and sipped my whiskey of choice—Knob Creek.

She huffed out a breath. "Just keep drinking. Drink until you can't stand, and then when you wake up tomorrow, just sit down and write a folksy song about losing the love of your life and how your dog pissed on your clothes."

"I don't have a dog."

"But the lyrics will sound better." She cracked a smile.

I snickered, rolled my eyes, and then thought to check my phone. No reply to a text I'd sent earlier to Arie, asking what the plan was for the office and for defending Dad. Poppy finally moved on to help other customers, allowing me to ponder her get-over-it directive. Easier said than done. I couldn't help but wonder what had caused this instant change in Nicole. After we'd both survived the bombing, if anything, I appreciated her and what we had more than ever. But she had become distant. Or had she been that way before and I didn't notice it? Some event must have triggered her change.

And then I let the dagger theory pierce what little protective shell that was still intact: she could be involved with another man.

I had to repeat the phrase to myself twice to believe I was even thinking it. If someone had uttered that phrase prior to two months ago, I would have not only laughed, I would have bet anything that neither of us would ever cheat on the other. I firmly believed there was a stronger likelihood that the world would finally succumb to some type of apocalyptic event before Nicole and I even had a hint of any trouble in our relationship.

Maybe now was the time to invest in an underground shelter.

I caught myself smiling in the smoky mirror—crazy man. I took another sip of my whiskey.

As for my theory on whether she was cheating or not, did it really matter? She'd apparently been working on this exit for a while. And she'd made a clean break. Maybe, in the long run, I'd appreciate her heartless approach of ripping off the bandage. For now, though, I had to take steps to move forward and focus on something that would get me out of this funk. Helping Dad. Ensuring the firm survived. Figuring out where I was going to sleep for the night.

I pulled out my money clip and tossed down my credit card just as Poppy showed up with a plate full of nachos and a tall glass of ice water. "Eat," she said, pointing at the plate. Then she walked off to ring up my bill. I didn't argue. I'd downed four nachos and most of the water by the time she returned. She flipped the card back on the counter.

"It was rejected."

"What?"

"The card is no good."

And then I remembered that one part of the text from Nicole. *There might be some interim rough spots as credit and debit cards are reissued. Until then, I'm sure you'll be okay.*

I pulled out a different piece of plastic, this one from another bank, and handed it to Poppy.

"You sure you want to be embarrassed again?"

My hands dropped to the bar, defeated.

"Just checking," she said, backing away with both hands in the air.

I ate one more nacho and watched her body language from afar. She attempted to run the card through twice. Each time, she pressed her lips together. Then she headed over to give me the bad news.

"You don't have to say anything," I said, feeling my pockets for cash. And then another memory hit me. "Dammit."

"What's wrong now? Someone steal your dog…you know, the one you're going to write that song about?" She grinned playfully.

Her brand of humor was ill-timed, to say the least. "I gave all of my cash away to Sam, the old guy who shines shoes outside of our office. Nicole shut down all of my cards. I've got nothing, no place to stay. I'll have to sleep in the back of my Cadillac."

"You sure she didn't have the car repossessed?"

"Funny." But I still looked toward the door. I snapped my head back when I found a large black man standing two feet to my right.

He had a hoop nose ring and wore the kind of cap that golfers wear. Except the cap looked as tiny as a yarmulke on his oversized head.

"I saw you take out those three guys this morning. It was badass, Oz." He broke out in a smile.

And that was when I knew I had a friend I could count on.

Nine

An hour later, I stood in front of a painting larger than I was. It was one of the most authentic pictures I'd seen of Santa's sleigh. I was in awe. "You painted this?"

My old high school friend chuckled so hard I thought the floor might start shaking. His jowls certainly were. "Just check the lower right-hand corner."

Under a picture light from the second-floor studio in his downtown flat, I saw his name. Or, rather, his old nickname. "*Tito*. That stuck with you all these years?"

"Yep."

Randal Adams had played defensive tackle on my high-school football team. He had a nasty disposition on the field, but off the field, he was the polar opposite. Always singing a tune or telling a joke, he was the life of our locker room. While quite the performer, the "Tito" nickname had nothing to do with Tito Jackson of the Jackson Five. Instead, it was his penchant for downing burritos at a rate usually associated with food-eating contests.

"Didn't you used to say that you wanted to be a black Jerry Seinfeld?"

He shrugged. "I didn't think it through very well. For one, I'm not Jewish."

I felt my brow furrow.

"That was supposed to be a joke. See? I guess I made the right career choice."

I shuffled to my right and stood under the next cone of light. This painting featured a little boy in a onesie opening a jack-in-the-box in front of a sparkling tree on Christmas morning. The kid's exuberant expression was priceless.

"Wow, Tito. I had no idea."

"I didn't either. Not until I just started painting one day. It just felt natural, like I should have been doing it all my life."

I looked around the room. "I see a lot of Christmas-themed paintings. What other types of things do you paint?"

"Mainly that."

"Seriously?"

"Not sure you knew, but my dad walked out on us when I was still real young. It hit everyone pretty hard. So, when I first started painting, I tried a few other things at first, and they were pretty good. But I knew I had something else I wanted to show the world. So I thought about what made me the happiest growing up. And that was when Ma, my two sisters, my younger brother—my whole family—got together for Christmas. It was special. And so I just try to pass along that same feeling."

"That's really cool."

"Yeah, life is crazy at times. When my dad took off, Ma was worried sick, working two jobs. My two older sisters had to get part-time jobs to help pay the bills. There were no guarantees any of us would amount to anything. And then a few years later, something pulled me into painting. After a while, I became content with my life. I'd found my passion, that thing that makes you think you're helping make the world a little bit better."

He held his fist up high as he spoke. Obviously, he was fully immersed in his newfound path. "Man, once you find your passion, you realize no one can take that away. No one can walk out on you and destroy your life. It's about what's in here." He thumped his chest with his fist. "And how you choose to share it with everyone else."

I nodded, held his gaze another beat. His wisdom seemed to hold extra weight.

I studied two more of his paintings. Both continued the two recurring themes: a Christmas setting with a joyous vibe.

The odd thing about my family was, despite being Jewish, we actually celebrated Christmas. I think we said we were Jewish just because of family roots, which went back to Poland. I hadn't been to the temple in years.

"You do okay as a painter?" I asked.

He barked out a laugh. "Check out the price tag just next to the painting of that little boy. By the way, that's supposed to be me."

I smiled, leaned closer to the wall, and saw the price tag. "Two grand?" I sounded almost too excited for my former teammate. I reached over and gave him a bro hug. "Tito, I'm so glad for you, man. And your timing couldn't have been better for me. I needed something to cheer me up."

"Well, I'm no Santa," he said with another belly-jiggling chuckle, which, of course, made me think of Old Saint Nick. "Seriously, dude, I just wish your world was a little better right now."

"You and me both, Tito."

After finding my car still in the Peretti's parking lot, I told Poppy I was going to leave it there overnight. I was in no condition to drive. I'd given Tito the rundown of this mind-boggling day on the ride over to his place.

He pointed to the couch. "That folds out into a futon."

"No worries. I appreciate you letting me crash for the night. And thanks for picking up the tab at Peretti's. I'll be able to pay you back tomorrow. Just need to get my credit and debit card situation resolved."

"No problem, Oz. It's been a while, but you were always one of the guys who had my back, even after you quit football."

High school. I hadn't traveled down that memory lane in a while. Not sure I wanted to.

"You never told me why you went all ninja on those three dudes today outside your office."

I thought about the prospect of recalling my entire lousy day...again. "I was just helping an old friend, that's all."

"Hey, then I guess you can put me in that category too."

He went off to find some sheets and a spare pillow as I continued my tour of his art. One that really caught my eye was a picture of a kid wearing ragged clothes, had mud or something similar on his face, and was being welcomed into a home with a roaring fire and stockings hanging from the mantle. The family portrayed in the painting was having a blast playing a board game.

"That was never the Novak clan," I said out loud.

Tito appeared from around the corner with a stack of bed linens and a pillow. "You guys weren't into Monopoly or Four Square?"

"We all kind of coexisted," I said, turning my sights back to the painting, making another attempt to recall any moments where we showed that great family bond. I was sure something wonderful had occurred, but right then, maybe because of the day's drama, I was drawing a blank. "I guess I have some decent memories, but we never did things together as a family. Now, don't get me wrong; my parents had the concept of Monopoly down pat. Make money, spend money, and show off your money."

We both laughed at that one. Tito headed off to his room, and I made my palette on the futon. It was surprisingly comfortable, but my eyes wouldn't shut. I was used to reaching out with my left arm and touching my wife's hip. Nicole. Damn, my heart ached.

I turned on my side, and I caught a faint glimpse of another Christmas painting leaning against the brick wall. A couple was celebrating Christmas morning with a toddler, a little girl maybe three years old. All I could think was: *That should be us. Me and Nicole and our first child.*

I flipped to my back and stared at the wood rafters arched across the ceiling. I considered calling Nicole and trying to talk to her. But as much as I wanted to hear her voice, I wasn't sure I could deal with this new person who had been my wife, my lover, and best friend. It sounded all so cliché in my mind, like some type of formulaic romantic comedy.

Where is the comedy in all of this?

Maybe she was lying in our bed at home, staring at the ceiling, realizing that she'd made the biggest mistake of her life. In my head, I replayed the text she sent me, and I felt the air rush from my lungs. While I'd always thought she was warm and compassionate—well, up until about twelve hours ago—Nicole was no wilting flower. Professionally, she appeared to be a bit of an ass-kicker. I'd always found that appealing, believing no one would get the best of Nicole, and I would always be there to support her—and vice versa—if there were ever tough times.

Like right now. Could the times get any tougher?

She, for whatever reason, had jumped from step one to step nine in the break-up process. I knew she was introspective, kept things inside, for the most part. But I'd always believed that she'd shared with me the most important things in her life, her biggest fears or concerns.

But maybe that was where I'd made my mistake. I'd always thought I could read people pretty well, and by that, I mean more than just reading their lips. And Nicole was at the top of that list, which is why we were…uh, *had been* so connected. It appeared my instincts had been thrown off. Love, or lust, or whatever it was had distorted my people-reading radar.

Had I been wrong about Dad too? I knew he had a tendency to push the envelope. He was the Bill Belichick of law. Smart as hell, but he'd been known to skate dangerously close to breaking the rules.

Extortion. Obstruction of justice. Assault and battery. Dad. It was difficult to use those terms and Dad in the same thought. I didn't want to believe it was true, and Dad didn't exactly deny the charges. He downplayed them, yes, but he wasn't pissed like I thought he'd be—like I'd be if I knew the charges were baseless. Hell, the person showing the most emotion was Agent Bowser from the FBI.

There was still so much I didn't know. Who was my dad's secret client? What was he hired to do that would bring about these types of charges?

While I had no experience in this world, I'd studied plenty of cases like this in law school. I learned that an attorney can often be a scapegoat for a client with a lot of money who was used to treating people like puppets. I wanted to give Dad the benefit of the doubt. But, for many reasons, there was a hell of a lot of doubt. It all came down to one thing: did Dad know he was breaking the law?

My phone buzzed, and I reached over to my suit coat and pulled it out.

"Finally," I muttered to myself. It was a text from Arie.

Meet me at the office, 7 tomorrow morning. I'll share everything I know.

I released a deep breath, then put the pillow over my face. It was the best way to force my eyes shut. Maybe I'd wake up and

realize this had all been a bad dream. I clung to that thought as I
drifted off to sleep.

Ten

Arie Steinberg always wore his pants way too high on his waist. For some reason, I'd allowed it to bother me. My annoyance, at the moment, was elevated because of several factors. I was standing in the file room of Novak and Novak, with papers and folders and boxes and Sharpies scattered everywhere. I'd already seen a sign on the front door of the office telling everyone to take a day off—I wasn't sure what that meant. And Arie, the man who had the energy and leadership capability of a person in a coma, had a serious case of halitosis.

He grunted a couple of times at the mess surrounding us, wiped his hand across his face. "Let's go to my office."

I followed him in and sat down in a plastic chair that wasn't meant for comfort. When I looked up, I was nearly blinded by the sun shining through the east-facing windows. "Do you mind lowering the blinds?"

"Sure. Sorry about that." He fidgeted with the pull strings for a good five minutes, but all he did was lift one side and lower the other.

"It's okay. I'll deal with it," I said, cupping my hand over my eyes as a headache began to form. Part of that had likely been brought on by a lack of hydration.

He grunted his frustration with the blinds and sat on the other side of his desk. He opened a manila folder, spread out three sheets of paper, and then stopped. Propping his chin on his anchored hands, he just stared at me. Little did he know, his breath was pumping out air so polluted that the ozone level was probably being impacted in the middle of the winter. I tried shifting in my seat to avoid the invisible fog, but I couldn't escape it. I gulped in some air from the side of my mouth.

"So are you up to the task of leading the firm until my dad gets back?" I asked.

He paused, set his palms on the desk. "Yeah, about that."

"About what? My dad, or you leading the firm?"

He rearranged the pages on the desk, then glared at me. He was studying my body language, wondering how I was going to respond.

"Arie, can you get to it? We need to be at the hospital before the Feds and their lawyers show up and start drilling him."

He sighed. "This office will probably not be open for business—not in the traditional sense."

I leaned forward.

"Not until…"

I waited for him to finish the sentence. He didn't.

"Arie?" He was so stiff, I thought I'd lost him for a second.

"This won't be easy for you, Ozzie."

"What won't be easy?" The pain behind my eyes began to throb.

"As you know, I'm the only other partner in the—"

"Get to it, please."

He puffed out a breath. It nearly dropped me to the floor.

"There is a provision in the bylaws of the firm." He licked his fingers, then lifted a sheet and scanned it with his eyes. "It states that if your father, Nathaniel F. Novak, dies, then all assets of the firm will be sold off and divided amongst the employees."

I let that sink in for a moment. Was that supposed to be some kind gesture by my dad? "Okay, but he's not dead."

"Right, I know. But there's a subclause to that provision that this step must also be taken if your father is incapacitated by illness or is unable to perform the duties as the leader of the firm for a period of more than a week."

I brought my hand down and closed my eyes for a moment. "It's only been twenty-four hours. Not even." I pinched the bridge of my nose and tried to look through the sun to see Arie's response.

He was expressionless, as usual. "Ozzie, he's got two reasons why he won't be back at this firm for a while. First and most importantly, his health. The last thing he needs is to be in the pressure cooker."

The last time I'd heard that term was from my grandmother. "You're right about that," I admitted.

"And second, these charges. They're serious."

"He told me."

"He told you?" His mouth hung open.

"Why do you look so shocked?"

"Well, uh, you know, the sealed warrant and all."

I looked off, wondering if he thought I knew more than I did. My eyes fell upon the lone picture in his office. It was a snapshot of Arie and his wife, purportedly on their honeymoon. It was black and white. Back when life was simpler. Or so I'd been told.

"He told me about the charges, but that's it. I couldn't get anything else out of him. Do you know more than that?"

"You know your father runs a tight ship."

Another phrase from yesteryear. "So you're telling me that you feel like it's your duty to liquidate the assets of the firm?"

"I didn't make the rules. Your father did."

I replayed his recounting of the provision. "If you're going to liquidate the firm, then why don't I just buy it? That will keep it in the family." The moment I threw out the idea, the other half of my mind thought I was nuts. Here I was suggesting that I would buy a business when I couldn't even pay for my bar tab. Surely, I'd work it out with Nicole sometime later today. Yet, I almost felt certain that, by talking to her, I was asking for an invitation to have my heart ripped from my chest. Maybe the most pragmatic approach would be for me to drop by the bank and...

He pressed his lips together. For a moment, it looked like he had no teeth. "Sorry, no can do."

I sat straighter. "Arie, this isn't a will. Even if it was, you know all legal documents are not ironclad. We can figure out a way to keep the office open."

"Perhaps you didn't hear the part about the proceeds being divided among the employees."

"Honestly, I'd bet that they'd rather keep their jobs."

There was a period of silence as he eyed me more. Then he said, "I may be a partner, but I'm also one of the employees, Ozzie. And I'm ready for retirement."

My eyes narrowed as my mind started connecting a few dots. The office was raided, and Dad was caught off guard, or so it seemed. He never flat-out denied the charges and essentially told me there was no record of his client.

So, it sounded as if Dad had acted completely on his own. If so, was there any way Arie knew about this secret work? It was plausible, considering they shared a long friendship. They even played golf once a week, part of the same foursome who had been playing each Saturday for the last twenty-something years. Arie and his wife were members of the same temple, I was fairly certain.

Still though, was there any way that Arie had set up my dad? It was hard to fathom, considering their friendship, and because Dad hadn't suggested the possibility. But maybe my dad had no idea that Arie was somehow behind this. What was *this* anyway? Well, if Arie was the perpetrator, it was essentially a coup. Not a coup to gain power per se, but one to secure his retirement.

Then my mind did a little math. There were eighteen employees, including myself. The firm couldn't be worth that much. Dividing its value by eighteen would whittle the take by that much more. Unless Arie had his heart set on buying a big-screen TV, this so-called retirement money would probably be a pittance. Maybe my coup theory had no legs. But still, why had Arie thrown out the retirement card as a reason he didn't want me to buy the firm?

"I guess it comes down to this." He rearranged the papers again, as if he were playing some type of casino shell game, then stared right at me. "Are you willing to go against your father's wishes just so you can stroke your ego by having your name on the side of the building? This would also mean that you and I would be adversaries. I would be representing the firm, as well as the remaining employees who would be paid, and you would be representing...you."

Arie hadn't spoken ten meaningful words to me since I'd officially joined the firm. I'd assumed his negotiating skills had eroded, or had never existed. It was like he'd somehow tapped into his inner Harvey Specter. Flipping it around to inflict guilt was a classic move. And even though I knew about the tactic, it still had an impact.

"I don't want to create friction, Arie. Especially if we need to work together on Dad's case."

He gave me a grandfatherly nod, as if I'd been a good boy in listening to his advice.

"Okay, then. I guess it's settled."

I stood up, gazed through his door, out into the hallway. I thought about the abrupt changes in my life in the last twenty-four hours. Maybe I'd been blind—on top of partially deaf. Nicole had been preparing for this event for some time. A few days, a week, a month? And Dad had seemed a bit preoccupied lately. Maybe if I'd been more inquisitive, he would have shared this with me before he crossed the line.

I released an exhausted sigh, ran my fingers though my hair. I looked down and saw about a hundred wrinkles in my shirt and pants—yes, I was still wearing yesterday's clothes. I had to get into the house and get my stuff, or maybe buy something later if Nicole wouldn't let me back in. Damn, could things get any worse?

Arie started talking, but because he was behind me, I couldn't pick up anything other than "company bylaws." I flipped around. "I didn't catch that."

"Oh, sorry," he said, tapping his ear, as if I needed a reminder about my deficiency. "I was saying that I forgot to mention one more stipulation in the company bylaws."

I rubbed my face and felt a thick beard. Of course, I hadn't shaved. "So…" I waved my arm, urging him to get to it.

"The division of the company assets is based upon time of service." He paused a second. I didn't bother jumping in with a question, so he continued. "It's set at five years, which eliminates ten of the employees."

I blinked a couple of times, wondering if my mind had correctly processed what he'd said. "You said five years."

"I didn't want this to catch you off guard later, when we're actually dividing up the proceeds."

I'd been with the firm for almost three years, not five. So, not only had my father not made me a partner at a firm with my name on it, but he'd also set it up to basically keep me from receiving my fair share if they had to sell off the assets. I could think of only one reason why he'd done this to me: I wasn't his real son. There could be no other reason.

"I know you must be a little confused right now," Arie said.

A rush of heat invaded my head. "Confused? Not a bit. I'm headed to the fucking hospital. I assume you'll meet me there."

I kicked the top of a box on my way out, hoping I'd never see the inside of Novak and Novak again.

Eleven

Whenever I'd represented a man or woman in a divorce proceeding, I'd always given two pieces of what I considered to be sage advice: don't make key decisions under duress, and learn to be grateful for the small things in life.

Right now, I was two-for-two. For starters, I'd somehow controlled my emotions and not gone off on Arie. The last thing I needed was to create a deeper chasm with the person leading the defense of my father, whose snub of me was still a fresh wound. I wasn't sure how to take it right now. So I pushed it aside. As for finding something to be thankful for, it was simple: the cold wind whipping across my face through the open window of my Cadillac. Tito had been nice enough to drop me off at Peretti's earlier this morning to pick up my car. I was using the time on the drive to the hospital to cool down—literally and figuratively—while also getting some fresh air. After no shower, a night of drinking, and a whole lot of tension, I was....ripe.

I made it to the hospital before Arie and stepped into the gift shop to purchase a package of gum and a stick of deodorant. On the elevator ride up, I made myself presentable, at least as much as I could, and prepared for another round of tension. Then a thought hit me: Neither Dad, nor Tobin, nor even Mom had any knowledge of what Nicole had done. They all thought she was the bomb. So had I, of course.

As much as I wanted to rip into Dad, which, in my mind had to occur well before I shared getting dumped by Nicole, I wasn't going to jeopardize his health.

I exited the elevator and nearly tripped over Agent Bowser.

"You look like, uh…" He covered his nose for a moment.

"No need to go there, thank you." I looked past him. "Surprised you didn't spend the night to make sure my father didn't make a run for the border."

He twirled a keychain around his finger. "We knew he wasn't in any condition to travel, so I told the team to take the night off and meet up here in a few minutes. Besides, I had to drop off my son for early basketball practice."

I didn't move.

"You look surprised."

"You have a kid. Are you married too?" I sounded accusatory. Or was there envy in my voice?

"Two kids. Daughter is eight, son is twelve. And yes, a woman does exist in this world who would marry this ugly dude," he said, pointing at his face.

"I thought it must have been due to your delightful demeanor."

He shook his head. "I realize you may not see it right now because it's your own father, but white-collar crime is a major issue in this country. We're cracking down."

I wasn't about to debate this topic. I started moving around him when he said, "So, do you have kids?"

I stopped, turned, and looked at him.

"I'm just asking because you're married and all." He pointed at my hand. I looked down and saw the ring Nicole had put on my finger a few months earlier.

"No. I don't have any kids."

"Not yet, huh? Still in that honeymoon period?"

"You guessed it. We can't keep our hands off each other."

I turned on the heel of my loafer and headed for the hospital room, hoping to put as much distance as possible between me and Bowser. *What the hell kind of name is "Bowser," anyway?*

I passed the nurses' station and gave a quick wave to one nurse leaning over her computer. Otherwise, the space was vacant. They were probably in a breakroom arguing over who got to eat the last piece of cake.

Man, I was snarky today. I took in a deep breath and tried to find a place that wouldn't piss off everyone with whom I'd interact. It wasn't their fault my life had disintegrated in the last day.

I hung a left at the end of the hallway and stopped as if I'd just reached the edge of a cliff with a thousand-foot drop. All the nurses and doctors had that look of doom. Two nurses were wiping sweat off their brows while talking outside of Dad's room. Inside, I saw two doctors and another nurse. They were moving slowly, shaking their heads. Tobin was cradling his face in his hand. "I can't believe he's gone," he said.

I jogged the last few feet into the room. "Tobin!"

A doctor moved just as I entered the room. My eyes went to the bed. I first saw the ventilator in Dad's mouth. His eyes were shut. He wasn't moving. Not even his chest.

"Dad!" I moved to the bed as emotion filled my eyes.

The cardiologist shifted out of the way. "I'm so sorry, Ozzie. It happened suddenly."

I touched his hand. Cold. I turned back to Tobin and tried to speak, but for a moment there was no air to push from my lungs. "What…what the hell happened?"

He opened his mouth and shook his head. "When I got here, I thought he was sleeping. Then he didn't wake up, and I called for the nurse."

My eyes shot to each person in the room. "How did he die?"

"It appears to be a massive heart attack. As you might recall, we warned that this might happen."

"But you never said it would happen this quickly. You said surgery wasn't needed, only that he had to follow his cardiac rehabilitation."

She looked down and clasped her hands in front of her. "Sometimes I hate this job, because it's so unpredictable. Human bodies, unfortunately, aren't computer programs. Everyone responds differently to the stress and environment they're in. Unfortunately, I think your dad's heart just didn't have anything left. I'm very sorry."

I took another glance at Dad, as if someone might be playing a horrible joke on me. The man who normally never stopped talking was lifeless.

Before I could swallow back more emotion, Tobin grabbed me by the neck. At first it felt odd. He'd never really hugged me before. Well, not since he was about three years old. I reciprocated the hug.

"He's gone, Oz," he said, thumping my back. "I can't believe it. I don't want to believe it."

A moment later, we stepped into the hallway. Bowser walked up, his eyes shifting from me to the window into Dad's room, and then to the doctor. And then Arie came around the corner. He immediately grabbed the wall and shook his head. "It's not supposed to happen like this. Your dad was going to outlive us all."

I felt lightheaded and cold, as if all of my blood had been drained from my body. People were talking to me, offering condolences, but my thoughts were all over the place. I turned and saw more people going into Dad's room.

Nothing seemed right. I knew, even in the moment, that most people in my position probably felt the same. That instant tear at my heart, that sudden loss of emotional balance. And the abrupt ending with Nicole was like putting an accelerant on a smoldering fire. The weight of so many emotions was choking off my oxygen.

But then I mentally pulled back, at least for a few seconds. All the questions from the last twenty-four hours converged into a moment of clarity. Right, wrong, or indifferent, I had to go with my gut.

I yelled, "Everyone out of my father's room. Now!"

Twelve

At my insistence, the hospital staff called the police. Some might say I was in denial or looking to place the blame on someone. Maybe I was, but there was at least a part of me that believed Dad's death to be too much of a coincidence.

"Why are you doing this, bro?" Tobin asked, sipping a coffee as we stood in a spare room two down from Dad's. "I mean, what the hell do you think happened? The doctors said it was a massive heart attack. And we know the reputation of this hospital is stellar."

I looked between the blinds out across the city. I could see the state capitol and the new high-rise condominium buildings behind it. So many cars and people everywhere. College kids, people working government jobs. Nothing stopped, not even for a death. People died every day, but when it was one of your own, it seemed like there should be something different about how the world responded. There wasn't.

"Dad has been involved in some high-profile cases," I said.

"Oz, I know about the charges. I was right here."

Right.

"Do you know anything else?" he asked.

Tobin was trustworthy as far as I knew, but that didn't mean I felt comfortable sharing my deepest thoughts and theories. "No. Dad died before he told me what was really going on. Which is why I don't want to look back and wish we'd allowed the cops to work the crime scene."

Tobin let loose an exasperated breath. "Dude, I just think you're bitter or feeling guilty or something. I mean, this is kind of ridiculous."

I wasn't in the mood to argue. "I'd say you can leave, but I bet the detective will want to ask you some questions."

"Yeah, okay. Whatever."

He'd just *whatever'd* me. I looked in the hallway and saw Agent Bowser talking to Arie—only their profiles, so I couldn't read their lips. But if I hadn't known better, I would have thought they were casually discussing Agent Bowser joining the new opening in Arie's golf foursome.

Two uniformed officers walked by, followed by a person from the crime scene investigation unit. I snapped open the top of my Diet Coke can, took a sip, and started to turn back to the window.

A second later, Tobin was waving his hand in front of my face, then pointing to the door, where I saw a striking redhead standing there. She had a badge on the belt loop of her black khakis.

"Ozzie Novak?"

I nodded and walked toward her.

"Detective Pressler, SA...uh, Austin Police."

The "SA" thing threw me off for a second. I shook her hand and introduced my brother. "You're the one," she said to Tobin, "who found your father this morning. Apparently..." She checked some notes on her phone. She wore not an ounce of makeup, her skin buttery smooth. "Yeah, the nurse had checked his vitals about one hour before you got here."

"I guess so," Tobin said, his voice subdued.

"Sorry to jump right into it." She turned to the door. "Thanks," she told a cop who handed her a coffee. She slurped in a mouthful, closing her eyes for a moment. "Do your magic," she said quietly.

I noticed dark circles under her green eyes. Maybe her night had been like mine. A lot of drinking and not enough sleep.

"I appreciate you coming out this morning. It may not seem like a felony took place, but I have my concerns," I said.

"We need to talk," she said, pointing a finger at me. "I'm first going to talk to your brother. Alone."

"Got it." I gave her a salute and walked toward the door.

Someone shouted my name. I turned around and realized it was Tobin. "What?"

"She was talking to you," he said.

"That's okay," she said, obviously unaware that my hearing was less than stellar. "I know you, both of you, must be upset right now. I was just mentioning that I never went to sleep last night."

Damn, she was the party animal. "Okay."

"I've been working another murder on the south side since just after midnight. Two other detectives called in sick, so I get the extra work. That's okay. I'm the newbie, so I have to earn some respect."

I nodded. "You're a rookie detective?"

"I meant just new to Austin. Before that I worked for the San Antonio Police Department. That's why I said—"

"SA."

"Right. I'll grab you in a moment."

I found a quiet spot in the hallway where I could watch the police do their work in Dad's room and still stay away from the fray. I became restless and found myself pacing in front of a TV in a quasi-reception area, while drinking my Diet Coke. An older guy was sitting there reading a magazine, occasionally looking up at the TV, which was tuned to a repeat of the University of Texas women's basketball game. It was hard to blink in Austin and not see something related to UT or the state government.

I was trying to lose myself in the game when someone tapped me on the shoulder. It was Bowser. "You a big fan of the Lady Longhorns?"

"Eh."

A moment passed, and he seemed like he was growing roots. He crossed his arms and appeared to study the game. I was only hoping he'd give me some space. "My daughter's into basketball big time."

"Oh yeah?" I sounded like I didn't care, because I didn't.

Another few seconds of awkward silence. It was starting to annoy me. Just as I was about to ask for some space, he said, "Are you wondering if this is going away now that…you know?"

"Honestly, I haven't gotten that far. Still just trying to take it all in."

"Oh, I figured that's why you called the cops. You know, just to make sure nothing crazy had gone down."

Did I just hear him correctly? "So you think I'm justified in thinking someone could have killed my father?"

He shrugged. "Not sure I have the authority to release all of the details contained in the sealed warrant."

I pointed at him and came very close to poking the federal agent in the chest, which, of course would have likely led to my arrest. "You seem to be implying that someone might have had justification for killing my dad."

The old guy with the magazine looked our way. Bowser signaled with his head to follow him toward the vending machines. He pulled out a dollar bill and inserted it into the machine; then he punched the C8 button. He pulled a package of pretzels from the bin, opened them, and took a bite.

"Your dad isn't…uh, wasn't the main focus of our investigation." He kept his voice low, and every few seconds, he looked over my shoulder. "But, to show you some good faith, I'll tell you something."

"Go on." I drained the last of my canned drink and tossed it into a recycling container, not once taking my eyes off Bowser.

"We don't know who exactly your dad was working for."

"That's an odd thing to say." I let his words marinate. And then like a crack of thunder, my mind flickered with a new thought. "Wait, did you use these charges against my dad to draw out the person he was working for?"

For the first time since I'd met Bowser, he looked like he was trying to pass a gallstone.

"I'm right, aren't I?" My voice had some steel behind it.

"I told you too much, dammit. But I'll say this…those are legit charges."

"But that doesn't mean you didn't use my dad to get to this unknown person."

"Look, the assistant US attorney is probably going to have my ass for sharing this much. Once they take ownership of a case, they tend to take complete ownership. But no one ordered me to use your dad as bait. That much I know."

"I need to know all the details behind the charges."

"That I can't tell you."

"Can't or won't?"

"Might as well be the same thing."

"You're full of shit. In fact, you probably thought this discussion, by essentially teasing me about my dad's connection to this ghost, would get me to tell you something you don't know, or maybe lead you to this person. In fact, you might think that I'm a part of it, and you just didn't have any evidence on me."

He stopped chewing pretzels for just a second, then he picked back up again. "You're looking at this all wrong. This isn't some big conspiracy to get you to talk. If I thought you had any connection to this character, you think I would have shared what I did? I'd be fired before I could say 'FBI.'"

I flipped around, watched a few officers milling around my dad's room. I turned my head toward Bowser. "I'm surprised the FBI didn't conduct their own investigation of my dad's death."

"I asked Detective Pressler to keep us in the loop. She said she'd comply. Professional courtesy and all."

I watched her finish up with my brother and then give me a nod.

"Let me know when you or someone in the federal government can explain what's really going on. Professional courtesy and all."

I left him standing there and walked over to meet with the detective.

Thirteen

Pressler finished speaking with a male officer from the APD—she covered her mouth for most of the conversation—then joined me in the hospital room, shutting the door behind her.

"Has your team found something?"

"What?" she responded, almost distracted. She let out a yawn, which she tried to contain, and then said, "I'm sorry. Can't seem to find my second wind."

I sighed, or was it more like a huff? It was difficult to hide my annoyance with anyone who wasn't on their A game right now. I spelled it out for her. "I asked if your team found any evidence that my father might have been murdered as opposed to dying of natural causes."

She pressed her lips together. She seemed to sense my irritation. "The team has just about finished up in the room. They've taken prints off everything possible. I've had two officers interview each of the nurses and doctors. I'm going to follow up with the lead cardiologist myself and review the timeline of events with her. We'll also make sure the ME does an autopsy. I'll put a rush on it. So, we're doing all we can do right now."

My eyes were drawn to the window. I saw two men carting away a covered body on a gurney. My father.

"I realize this has to be difficult for you," she said. "I've been around the families of a number of victims, and it didn't matter how they died. It can be very stressful."

She had no idea. My legs had been chopped off at the knees by Nicole, and that was to be considered the most jovial part of the last day. The raid at the office, the sealed warrant for Dad, his first heart attack, the subsequent visits by the two women in his life, a night of no sleep after having no access to my money, learning from Arie that Dad had no intention of giving me even a piece of the firm that had my name on it… then, on the cusp of having to watch him booked on extortion and obstruction charges, he dies. Natural causes or murder? Oh, and how could I forget the tease from the FBI dog, Bowser, saying, ostensibly, that Dad wasn't their real target? I still didn't know what to think of that.

"I'm assuming your wife is on the way and can help you deal with the grief."

I used my thumb to push the wedding ring up a bit. "I guess I'm still married—technically, anyway."

"Oh. I…uh, didn't know."

I huffed out a laugh, but there was no happiness behind it. "No one knows. She dumped me yesterday while I was standing in Dad's room."

Her eyes suddenly seemed puffier as they narrowed into slits so tiny I could barely see her emerald eyes. "She asked you for a divorce in your father's hospital room, as you're going through that crisis?"

"Not really."

"Good. I was thinking—"

"She never bothered to come to the hospital. She did it all through a text."

The detective looked like she'd taken a bite of a nail sandwich. "I don't know what to say. I thought *my* ex was ruthless."

I nodded. "Recent?"

"Just went final in the last month, which is another reason why I moved to Austin."

"What's the first reason?"

"To take care of my mom. It's like being twenty again and having a college roommate." Her tone was laced with sarcasm.

This time, my laughter was legitimate. I brought a hand to my mouth. "I don't mean to be insensitive."

"Laughing helps, even if someone is kind of laughing at your situation."

I received a text and took a moment to read the message. It was from Mom.

Your brother and I have spoken. I don't want to go to the hospital again. I need your help planning the funeral. I hope you won't let me down.

"That was very warm and touching," I said as I showed her the text. "My mom."

The detective pressed her lips together. "Glad you're getting support from somewhere."

"Now I'm the one using sarcasm to cope. My mom has issues."

"I think we have something in common there."

Another quick laugh, which allowed me to relax enough to take in a deep breath. She asked if I wanted to sit, and I actually said yes. She asked me tons of questions, all of which were quite predictable. When I thought she was done, I asked if she was going to share this information with Bowser.

"As a professional courtesy, of course. Why wouldn't I?"

I simply shrugged.

"So there is one more question, and this is really the most important. Why do you think someone would want to kill your father?"

"You are aware that my father was going to be charged with two felonies this morning?"

"I am, but I really don't know the details at all. Care to fill me in?"

"I don't know the details either. But he does." I pointed out the window toward Bowser, who was walking by the window.

"I'll give it another shot," she said, typing a note on her phone.

"A shot at what?"

"Getting the Feds to share. If something has happened with your father, I need to know all the facts, not just the facts they deem appropriate."

I liked this woman's angle. She had a backbone. Handing me her card, she said she'd be in touch as more questions came up.

"Feel free to call if you can think of anything else that might be relevant to this case," she said. "Now, if you call the precinct and someone else picks up the phone, you can't just say, 'Give me the redhead detective.'"

My expression fell to one of puzzlement.

"There are two of us with red hair. Our last names are close as well. Hers is Pressley."

"Seriously? As in Elvis?"

"Crazy, I know. So, just use my first name. It's easier."

I looked at her card. "Brook. I had an old girlfriend named Brook."

"She break your heart too?"

"I broke up with her, right after homecoming."

"Damn, you were cold-blooded." She had a phone call coming in and waved goodbye.

I wondered if I had it in me to go visit with Mom.

Fourteen

Dad had apparently let it be known that he wanted a full-blown Jewish funeral. I found this odd, considering my parents and I had been to temple only on a rare occasion, probably when Dad had his eyes on a potential client.

The last twenty-four hours had been a hellish time, when I was subjected to hearing every complaint possible from my mother's mouth. She criticized almost every decision and act that landed at the feet of my dad over the years. I was actually rather astonished that she never mentioned Bianca. Maybe that one actually hurt too much.

I agreed with her on many of her complaints, but then she started nitpicking the small stuff. And it became too much. I walked away more than once, but somehow stayed at the house, helped her plan the funeral, listened mostly.

While the Jewish faith called to hold the funeral as soon as possible, those twenty-four hours had felt like twenty-four days. And it didn't help that I still didn't have my legs underneath me. My wife was still absent, my job had apparently disappeared, and none of my questions about Dad's death or the indictment had been answered. Thankfully, I had access to a shower. Some old but clean clothes were still in my closet at my parents' home.

Standing near the fireplace, I plucked a glass of punch off a tray being carried by a caterer—Mom went all out on the reception since the funeral was simplistic, a typical Jewish ritual. No flowers, a plain wooden casket. I was still wearing my yarmulke—again, trying to appease Mom—but it felt like a beetle burrowing into my thick mane of curly blond hair.

I felt a nudge on my shoulder. I turned to see my admin…uh, my former admin, Stacy, chugging her drink. "Is your drink spiked with vodka?" she asked me.

"No, is yours?"

"I was just hoping, that's all. Funerals are the worst. Nathaniel, I mean…" Her voice cracked, and she wiped a finger near her eye. I gave her a one-arm hug and swallowed back some emotion. I'd shed a few tears at the funeral home, after I read a passage. It felt like Dad was hovering just above me, listening and nodding, and not talking. Later, when I thought about it, I wondered if those tears weren't just tears of sorrow. Well, not just for the loss of Dad, but for everything else that had piled up at the same time. And still, so many unanswered questions.

"Your dad was a lot of things, Ozzie, but he was still loyal. I've been with the firm for almost fourteen years, and I'm so touched that he wanted to take care of me if something happened."

She'd apparently talked to Arie. At that moment, I spotted him speaking with two other men; they were quietly laughing. Probably telling an old story about Dad. I supposed that was how old people coped with loss, since they were surrounded by it so much. Regardless, I needed to bend Arie's ear once the reception ended.

I went back to Stacy's comment about loyalty and Dad. I felt a surge of food moving up my chest. "Yep. Dad knew how to take care of everyone." She had no idea that I hadn't been included in the distribution of funds from selling off the company. I had no reason to make her feel guilty.

"So, are you going to take some time off, maybe go on vacation with Nicole, and then possibly start your own firm? Even though I'll have a nice little nest egg coming my way, I'd be open to coming out of retirement to help you."

The Nicole question. Surprisingly, I'd been asked that question only a couple of times. Mom had asked while I was over there listening to her bitchfest. I'd told her Nicole had the flu. Today, a couple of folks from the office had asked, and I gave them the same response.

"She has the flu." As soon as I said the words, I realized they sounded forced.

"Nicole has the flu?"

"Uh, yeah." I drank my punch, wishing more than ever it was spiked with vodka. I spotted Mom receiving hugs from friends and extended family. She looked genuinely touched by their show of respect. She could put on a hell of a game face.

"Is she going to be okay?" Stacy said.

"Mom's a strong woman. Nothing brings her down. She'll be back to doing her thing within the next week, I'm sure."

"I meant Nicole."

"Oh, her." I felt my chest tighten, and I tried to inhale.

"Oz, is everything between you and Nicole—"

Tobin appeared out of nowhere, and I grabbed him. "Where have you been?"

"Around. Hey, Stacy," he said.

She nodded as both our eyes went to his hand that slipped inside his suit coat. I was almost certain I'd seen a flask.

"Is that the hard stuff?" Stacy was excited. "Can you give me a little nip?"

"You can't smell it on my breath, can you?" he asked.

His eyes were bloodshot. He took a mint from a small canister and tossed it in his mouth; then he covertly poured the contents from his flask into Stacy's drink. She chugged it down.

"Did Mom say anything about me not being around much?" he asked me.

"Not really. But I noticed."

"Uh, sorry. You know, business never stops."

One business had stopped. I kept my snide comments to myself. I noticed Tobin wiping at his nose a couple of times. Dad's death must have really rocked him. He was, after all, the only blood child. "Are you okay, Tobin?"

"I'm fine, just working hard and dealing with all of this...I don't know, somber bullshit. It's just so depressing."

"That's what happens when your father dies."

"I get that, bro. Geez, do you think I have my head stuck up my ass? Whatever." He walked off, pissed.

"That didn't go over too well," Stacy said.

"I guess we all have our ways of dealing with tragedy." *Or not dealing with it.*

Stacy clung to me like Velcro for the next few minutes. We got food, tried changing the topic to something other than Dad and death. She seemed to have also picked up on not inquiring further about Nicole. We were discussing the weather when all heads in the room turned. It was Bianca, dressed in a black mini-dress that hugged her body like it was made from cellophane.

"What the hell is she doing here, bro?" Tobin had just rushed up to me.

I shook my head, put my food and drink down. "I'll go take care of it; let her know that this isn't the time to make a claim on the Novak fortune."

I made it about five steps before I was intercepted by my mother. She interlocked my arm in hers and pulled me into the dining room where there were only three or four other folks. "Have you tried this dish that the Clancys brought over?"

I just looked at her. "I'm sorry, Mom."

Her grip on my arm became tighter. "Now isn't the time to make a scene."

"But Mom, you haven't talked about—"

"I don't want to hear her name in this house. Is that clear?"

"Okay." She was protecting herself. I couldn't blame her.

"Just to make you feel better, Oz, I'm going to be fine."

"Yeah, I thought you would. It's just that everyone has their own way of grieving and all."

"Your father was a lot of things…"

"Yeah, I know. You told me that yesterday."

"Sorry if I unloaded on you. I guess that was one of my stages of grief, like you just mentioned."

"I get it."

Mom continued walking me through the house, as if she were leading me on a tour.

"I can go ask her to leave, you know. I have no problem doing it."

"She can have her few minutes. I just don't want to create a scene."

"I can be subtle."

She patted my arm, then stopped and looked me in the eye. "You are a worrier, Ozzie. That's one of the reasons I love you."

I felt a tear bubble in my eye.

"Your father…he planned ahead. I have a nice insurance policy to cash in."

I'd always thought they spent every penny he earned. I also felt certain Bianca spent whatever pennies were thrown her way.

"I'm glad you don't have to worry about money. But realize, it can run out, so try not to go too crazy."

"It's worth five million. And we own the house outright. So I think I'm set."

Five million. Was that why she was able to deal with Bianca showing up? From the sound of it, she might even let Bianca know about the insurance policy. Her own way of showboating my dad's lover.

She finally moved on to say goodbye to some guests, and I tried to avoid Bianca on my way back to Stacy. I rounded the corner into the living room and nearly ran over Arie. Before I could apologize, he waved to a friend behind me, popped me on the arm, and kept walking. He must have known that I was restless and looking for answers.

I made a diversion and headed to the bathroom. I splashed water on my face, then stared in the mirror. I wondered what had spooked Arie. He'd made it quite clear about how the dissolution of the firm would be handled, so that topic was essentially a nonstarter. My questions involved Dad's death. While I waited to hear back from Detective Pressler, I needed to know more about what had led to the charges, specifically, the evidence the Feds had—or thought they had. And what were they really after? In cases like these, the Feds usually cared less about the lawyer and more about the person the lawyer worked for. But as Dad had told me, there was no official record of this client. He, or she, was a ghost.

I flashed back to Bowser talking to me at the hospital. Not in the waiting area when he thought he was throwing me a bone—implying that someone might have had justification to harm Dad—but earlier when I ran into him coming off the elevator, before he started jabbering about his son and daughter and basketball practice. He mentioned that he took the guard off duty the previous night because he knew Dad couldn't travel.

A surge of bile moved into the back of my throat. Was there any way that Bowser had been asked, or told, to remove the guard? Maybe by the person or group that wanted my dad to be silenced?

The internal replay of my theory made it sound all that more ludicrous. Bowser was an FBI agent. He wasn't the top cop in a one-light hick town in West Texas. Yes, there were corrupt FBI agents, no different than any other government entity. But what few federal agents I'd run across in my time at the courthouse meant serious business.

But why, then, did I still have a bad taste in my mouth? Dad died during the time when a guard wasn't watching his room. Bowser, in so many words, hinted that other forces might have wanted him silenced. In my limited experience as an attorney, I had never offered up the "C" word as a reasonable defense.

The "C" word in the lawyer community was "coincidence." And, frankly, it was considered to be a laughable, if not indictable, act on behalf of a client. Sure, coincidences happened, but convincing a judge or jury of that was practically impossible. And did I mention laughable?

I couldn't just sit back and wait for a gust of wind to enlighten me with answers to every question.

A bang on the door. "Oz?"

It was Tobin. "Yeah. Just give me a minute."

"Bianca is downstairs mouthing off about reading the will. Can you come help?"

I looked in the mirror: *you can't leave here until you figure out something actionable to do, something that will bring you closer to the truth.*

"Fucking A, Oz. I can't deal with her right now. All the guests are looking at her; even Mom can't hide from it. She's causing a big stink."

94

Something he said just sparked a thought. "I'll be right down. Give me a minute."

I made sure he was away from the door, then I made a call to the one person I thought could actually help.

Fifteen

Even in my limited capacity to differentiate sounds, I could hear the whining of electric wrenches. Beyond that, the symphony of clatter in the closed-in garage—the temperatures had dipped down into the upper thirties as darkness fell on Austin—made my head feel like it was being smashed by two marching cymbals. I turned down my hearing aid, hoping to thwart a massive headache.

Finally able to think a second as I waited to enter the back corner office, I blew out a breath and typed in a text to Nicole, or at least my final draft. After stopping and starting the text about a dozen times between me sitting in my Cadillac and walking inside the garage, I told myself to keep it short and unemotional.

Please let me know when I can drop by and pick up my things. Thx

I waited a second, my thumb hovering over the screen. I wanted to say so much more. But my thoughts debated over whether to ask questions—countless whys and hows—or to go with a more direct approach, telling her I was pissed that she'd cut off my ability to support myself. But then I thought about the desired outcome. That was what I'd often asked myself during a case. If I said or asked one thing, then what would I expect the outcome to be? If it wasn't the right answer, then I needed to move on and think of a different approach.

So glad that my law degree had helped me learn how to negotiate with the woman who, up to about sixty hours earlier, had been the center of my world.

The door to the office opened, and a woman in a pencil skirt ran out with a tissue to her face. She bumped into my shoulder and then smacked me in the arm. "Sorry?" I said, while at the same time turning up my hearing aid. I sounded as if I were asking a question, even though she'd run into me. She burst into tears and then quickly exited Gartner Automotive.

"Hey, Oz." Ray Gartner, whose brother Steve owned the automotive repair business, picked something out of his teeth and then held out his hand. "I want to say how sorry I am to hear about your dad. He was a good man."

Ray was a private investigator often used by Novak and Novak to handle sensitive investigations. While I'd interacted with him only a couple of times and this was my first visit to his official office—his unofficial office had been Peretti's—he was discreet and damn good at his job.

"Thanks, Ray."

Something dropped to the garage floor—a loud boom—and I looked over to see a mechanic kicking a tire. Apparently, he was frustrated.

Ray shrugged, and I followed him into his office. His gait appeared as if he'd been strapped to a horse for the last ten years. Almost instantly, I was hit with a rancid odor that made me think I knew why the woman had been in tears. I pinched my nose. "Is she okay?" I threw a thumb over my shoulder.

The edge of his lip twitched, which made his thick, bushy mustache move like it was a live animal. "Jilted wife. She just saw the pictures of her husband banging his secretary. Didn't go over well. Never does. But sometimes it takes the reality of the pictures for them to believe. Know what I mean?"

I could feel a knot take root in my gut. "Uh, yeah."

"You want a little of my chew?"

I glanced around the room, and besides the stacks and stacks of newspapers, manila folders, magazines, and a whole bunch of other crap, I found at least six leftover cups that Ray had used to dispose of his chewing tobacco. I was just glad I didn't have an instant gag reflex.

"I'm good, thanks."

"You've never been to my office, have you?" He was all country. If it was allowed, I wouldn't have been surprised to see his horse tied to a pole out front.

"Don't think I've had the honor," I said, looking for a place to sit.

He chuckled as he first found a chair, then placed two enormous stacks of crap onto two lesser stacks by his desk. In order not to disturb the precious stacks, he climbed over his desk. His cowboy boots banged against the hollow metal. I found my spot as he leaned back in his chair and took hold of his spit cup, at least the one he was using right now. I could see the wad of chew tucked inside his lower lip.

"You said on the phone that we had to talk in person. I'm all ears. Hit me."

I wasn't sure how to jump into the subject. "It's about my dad." I looked over at one of the stacks. The frayed edges of the newspapers were brown.

"Good old Nate."

Dad hated being called that name, but maybe he let Ray get away with it. He paused. While some might take a breath, Ray used the spare moment to spit into his cup.

"They don't make 'em like that anymore. God rest his soul." He crossed himself as if he were Catholic, but his outline looked more like a cursive Z. I wasn't even sure he was Catholic. I remembered Dad had told me that Ray had been married five or six times, and once even had to cross the border into Oklahoma since he wanted to get married so quickly after a divorce. I'd soon join that club. Maybe he and I could make a run at double-digit marriages.

"You think you got a malpractice lawsuit lined up against the hospital? I got contacts all within the medical world. Lots of nurses. If you need some inside scoop, I can probably get that done from just about any hospital in Travis County."

My brow crinkled, doubtful.

"You don't believe me? I can do it; just point me in the right direction."

"Oh, I believe you. No worries there." He had flecks of gray in his mustache and a head of wavy hair, but his leathery skin gave his age away. Dad had said Ray was nearing sixty-five.

I thought about his leap to malpractice against the hospital. I'd actually never considered that as a possible reason for Dad's death. Still, though, Detective Pressler seemed capable of leading that investigation for now, even though Ray appeared mighty eager to be knocking boots with one of his many nurse friends.

"So I need to be frank with you, Ray."

He spit into his cup and nodded. "I thought you already were."

"I was…I am." I took in a breath and rebooted my approach. "Our office was raided two days ago."

"Say what?"

"Federal agents from the FDA, IRS, Department of Homeland Security, and FBI."

"That's a frickin' acronym orgy ready to happen."

He was right. Absolutely right. "Yeah, it got our attention, all eighteen of us working at the firm. But they only wanted one of us."

He nodded, and I paused, wondering if he'd pick up on who that one was. He just spit into his cup and stared at me. I sighed and went on with it. "They arrested Dad. They tore the place apart, taking files, computers, everything they could carry. Gutted the office."

"Damn, that must have been tough to sit through."

"I thought it was the worst, until Dad dropped to the floor as they were walking him out."

"That's when he suffered the heart attack?"

"The first heart attack, yes."

"He had more than one?"

I walked him through the sequence of events: how Dad had gone from having one heart attack, hearing the feedback from the cardiologist that he did not need surgery but would instead require a change in lifestyle, and then having a second heart attack, the one that killed him, moments before I arrived the next day.

"Sounds like malpractice to me, but I don't know much." He leaned forward, rested his elbows on the desk.

"Maybe, but my thoughts didn't go there."

I waited another moment, wondering if he'd start connecting the dots. He just spit into his cup again. He was either not as bright as Dad had described or he had a reason for allowing me to lead him down the path. Just before I was about to speak up, he said, "You think someone knocked off your dad." He said it as more of a statement than a question.

"It's very possible. I only know the high-level charges. It was a sealed warrant, and as of yet, they haven't released the details behind it."

"Even though he's dead?" He spit into his cup. "I don't mean to come across as insensitive, but Jiminy Cricket, what the hell's the holdup?"

"That's how the Feds work, I suppose." I tapped my thumb on the edge of the chair. Detective Pressler had come across as reliable, even if she was overworked. But I wasn't sure I could count on her to find out who my dad's mystery client was. There was a part of me that thought this client could have killed Dad—personally or through some proxy—and figured out a very crafty way to cover it up.

But I also knew that Brook didn't work for me. I couldn't command the direction she should take, or blow off, in her investigation. She may or may not find Dad's client relevant to the investigation. Or, after looking at the evidence, or what she had reasonable access to, she might conclude that he died from natural causes. Maybe I was grasping for something or someone to blame for my dad's death. Right now, with my emotions swirling, it was difficult to fully believe in my instincts. Basically, the reasons were numerous for why I needed someone I could trust to find the person who'd hired my dad.

I looked at Ray. "Maybe the Feds have their reasons, but the more I thought about it, the more I couldn't trust the justice system to figure out what, if anything, happened."

"Happened to what?"

"To my dad." I moved to the edge of my seat. "The lead FBI agent, a guy named Bruce Bowser, hinted after the fact that someone might have a reason to keep Dad quiet."

"No shit? He admitted it?"

"He didn't use those exact words, and when I tried to pin him down, he backed off a bit. By that time, I'd already called the Austin police and asked for an investigation into Dad's death."

More head nodding, and then a repeat of the spit-cup routine. His eyes left mine and scanned a stack of magazines next to him. Was he searching for something specific, or was this how he went into deep thought?

Finally, he put a hand on his desk and said, "Who?"

"Who…what?"

"Who was trying to keep Nate quiet?"

"That's the thing. Bowser told me that, while the charges against Dad were legitimate, they were really trying to get to the person my dad was working for."

"His client."

I nodded.

"So, did they just use your dad to draw out this other guy?"

"They better fucking not have." I could feel a flutter in my chest. I released a deep breath and dialed back my intensity.

We discussed the specific charges that I knew of, and Ray did some more scanning of the artifacts in his office. Maybe that was why he hoarded everything—his way of thinking through a problem.

"Man, I could sit here and ask you questions from now until next Christmas, but I doubt you'd have many answers," Ray said with a snicker. "So, besides just keeping me in the loop, which I appreciate, what do you want me to do?"

I'd hoped he would have seen the obvious next step. Apparently not. "I need you to find the person who was my dad's client."

He didn't immediately agree, which sent a wave of heat into my face.

"Wait. They raided your office? Somewhere in those files is the name of Nate's client, of course."

I tried to laugh, but I never got close. "The Feds might think they'll find something, but if what Dad told me was true, they won't find any evidence of the client in our files, hard copy or electronic. During the brief time Dad and I talked about it—really, it was more me trying to pull information out of him—he said one relevant thing. The Feds wouldn't find the name because it wasn't in the records."

Just then, one of the mechanics put his face against the window to my right and started sliding down the glass. Was he playing a game? Ray got out of his seat and shut the blinds. "Stupid chuck-wagon kids don't know when to act professional."

By the time he sat back down, I felt a buzz in my pocket. I pulled out my phone and saw a text from Nicole. Ray might have been talking, but I wasn't listening. My eyes went to the screen.

Feel free to drop by tomorrow at noon to pick up your things. Thx.

That was it? No wondering how I was doing after my father had died, or how the funeral had gone? No remorse, or better yet, maybe some enlightenment into how she had turned into a piranha? I slid the phone back into my pocket and saw Ray with his mouth hanging open.

"Sorry, did you say something?"

"I said I'll take the case, but only under one condition."

"What's that?"

"That it's on the house. Pro...whatever you lawyers call it."

"Pro bono." Given my lack of access to my funds, I was certainly glad to hear he didn't want a sizable retainer fee up front. I would definitely take *free*. "That's nice of you, Ray."

"Your dad brought me plenty of business. He was a good man who tried to do the right thing." He looked over my shoulder into the garage for a moment. "Before I get started, any reason to believe that the text you just got might help me out?"

"Nope," I said, hands on my knees. Then I felt the urge to just let it all out there. "It was my wife."

"Right, the old ball and chain. Glad I don't have to answer to anyone."

"I don't either anymore. She's basically kicked me out of the house. She was just telling me when she'd *allow* me to drop by and pick up my stuff."

He shook his head and went back to the cup. "Damn womenfolk. Can't trust any of them."

I smiled.

"Tell you what, I can put a tail on her and see if, you know, she's got anything going on the side."

The knot in my stomach just expanded. I really didn't want to go there. "It's okay. I'm fine."

"You sure now? Sometimes if things get contentious, nothing will sway a jury more than a few vivid images of said slut kissing her new boy toy goodbye."

He was making it more difficult not to think of Nicole being with another man. "I've used that same strategy for my clients. It's not like that. But I'll keep your offer in mind."

Ray said he'd jump on the case immediately and would share information as soon as it became available. I walked out of the building. I found my car sitting in the parking lot, with key scratches up and down both sides. A perfect end to the day.

Sixteen

A blustery wind whipped across my face as I stood in front of my open garage and stared at everything that was supposed to have meaning in my life. A low, gray sky was spitting out a light mist, but I didn't bother wiping my face. I was too busy assessing how my life with Nicole could so easily be boxed up.

I shuffled closer but still moved at a tentative pace. It was as though all of my stuff was made of kryptonite. Touching the boxes might instantly drain me of what energy I had left—as if I'd been kicked in the nuts. If I were to pore through my belongings, it would mean that I'd fully accepted the edict of Nicole.

Get over it, Ozzie. You wanted your shit—now you've got it.

I pulled open one box and found my law books. The one next to it contained a bunch of CDs and DVDs, many of which had entertained me and Nicole many times over. There were CDs from the Foo Fighters, the Red Hot Chili Peppers, Green Day, and even one from Bon Jovi. Among the DVDs was *I Am Legend*, a few of the Harry Potter movies, one of the Jason Bourne movies, and *P.S. I Love You*. I picked up that one and recalled how Nicole would tear up.

Looking back, I wondered what was behind those tears. I began to question if she was sharing the intimate moment with me. I remember her once putting her hand on mine as she thumbed a tear in the corner of her eye. She didn't say anything because she didn't have to. It seemed rather obvious—she didn't want me to die like Gerry, the character played by Gerard Butler, and leave a huge hole in her heart. I thought it had brought us closer.

But maybe her mind had been on something else. Someone else. Not a lover, but maybe an uncle or close friend. Nicole's behavior the last three days had gone straight to the top of my most-shocking list, but I knew one thing for sure about her—she was a one-man woman.

Yet, I knew she'd been unhappy. That was rather clear.

Maybe all along she'd seen flaws in our relationship, one that I had considered to be almost magical. It was strange to feel so close to someone and then end up questioning if that bond ever really existed. As I perused my personal effects while kneeling in the chilly garage, I felt a lack of assuredness in just about every aspect of my life. Emotions clamored for supremacy in my mind, making it difficult to get my bearings and figure out where to go next.

I completed my cursory check of the boxes and suitcases and began loading up my car. I had to put my golf clubs in the front seat—maybe I could throw a hat on top and pretend the clubs were a person, giving me an excuse to use the HOV lane.

Wow, that was a lame thought. I was about to punch the start-engine button when I tried to remember if any of those boxes contained the one picture that held any meaning for me. It was a shot of Dad and me just after one of my swim meets when I'd won my first medal. Not many guys can say they quit football to take up swimming, but it was just a way for me to stay in shape and keep my competitive juices flowing. I'd always loved the water. Mom called me a trout when I was a kid and we'd go to the beach, like a pseudo-normal family.

As I slipped out of the car to inspect the garage, my phone rang. I answered the call.

"Hey, bro." I decided to speak in Tobin's language.

"Bro? Okay, listen, dude, you gotta get to Arie's place. And I mean *now*."

The reading of Dad's will. I looked at my watch. "I still have thirty minutes. I'll be there on time, even if I have to speed a little."

"Do you not hear the stress in my voice?"

Loud and clear. "What's wrong, Tobin?"

"Fucking Bianca, that's what's wrong."

I continued moving around the garage looking for even a small box or container that might have more of my stuff. I was coming up empty. "What about her?" I knew I sounded almost disinterested. To a degree I was, at least in the drama.

"She's in the other room."

I stopped moving. "She's at Arie's? Why?"

"Good fucking question, bro. Arie and his wife are off getting drinks and food together, so they're not saying a word."

"Sounds like she was invited to the reading of his will."

"Dammit, I thought you'd say that. Now, how can I encourage her to leave?"

"You can't. Well, you can encourage her to leave, but you can't force her, not unless she's creating a scene."

"I'm not sure if she's going to create the scene or Mom is going to create the scene."

"Crap."

"Now you're getting it. Dude, I just got here, and I'm already sweating like a whore in church."

How original, but I understood his concern. "I'll be there as soon as possible."

"Where are you anyway?"

Here came the questions. It was a miracle no one had realized that Nicole had disappeared from my life, and their lives too, for that matter.

"I'm running an errand. Gotta go. I'll be there soon; don't worry." I hung up before he could continue peppering me with more questions.

I'd leave as soon as I got my picture. I stood in front of the door to the house, staring specifically at the doorknob. Was it locked? Did she really change the locks? I moved a hand toward the knob but didn't touch it. I felt like I was violating some sacred rule by even thinking about entering…my own home.

Okay, the lawyer in me said I wasn't allowed to act naïve. Nicole had established the ground rules, and even if they were ridiculous—most anyone would agree with that—I hadn't pushed back or tried to find middle ground. The office raid, the felony charges, and Dad's hospitalization and subsequent death had stolen my attention, so I had a good reason not to address this part of my life. But I knew that didn't absolve me from adhering to the basic principle of this imposed separation.

I walked back to the car and opened the door. I thought about where I was going…to the reading of Dad's will. This would, in fact, probably be the final event that surrounded his death. I still had a lot of things to work through in relation to how he treated me, especially in our professional lives, but right now, I needed a positive memory from at least one part of my life. Something that might actually bring me a smile, maybe offer some encouragement that my entire life hadn't been fake.

I shut the car door and looked at the house. I only wanted my picture. She could have everything else, at least for now. Last I remember, it was in the office that we shared. It was on my late grandfather's antique desk. I walked over to the door leading into the house and tried twisting the knob.

It didn't budge. Not unexpected. I tried my key, and it didn't fit.

So, she had done what she said she would. The locks had been changed.

I snapped my fingers the moment the thought hit me. I walked around to the far side of the house and found the window to the office. The lock hadn't been able to latch since we moved in. The foundation was likely the culprit. Actually, it was the always-shifting soil and rock beneath the house that was the root cause. A Texas issue. I would just open the window, grab my picture, and be out before feeling an ounce of guilt.

I put my hands on the window but stopped short of pulling it up. We had an alarm system, but she had never used it. Not once. Had she changed that habit? Anxiety rippled through my body, my heart pounding my chest. The strain of everything was getting to me. The last thing I wanted or needed was the alarm going off, cops showing up, me trying to explain what I was doing. I could just hear the ridicule from Nicole, or the new Nicole. All I wanted was my picture. Was that so bad?

Fuck it.

I pulled up and held my breath. All was quiet. I exhaled, glanced around like a thief in the night—except, of course, it was broad daylight. I curled my body over the windowsill and shut the window behind me so no one walking or driving by our house would suspect anything. I turned around and scanned the office, took in the familiar oak smell. It was mostly in order. There were gaps in the bookcase where Nicole had pulled my books out and boxed them up. An old-fashioned grandfather clock ticked from the top of my antique desk. Just to the right of the clock was the picture. I walked over, picked it up. Dad's smile couldn't get much bigger than that. I had this goofy teenager grin. My dimples looked like divots in my cheeks. He was reaching up, an arm around my shoulder. I was probably close to six feet tall, just a couple of inches shy of my current height—and I still towered over him. He was the one holding up the medal that dangled from my neck. Damn, he was proud of me.

I was glad I'd taken the risk. This picture meant something to me.

My eyes grazed over Nicole's desk setup, a simple wooden structure with an ergonomic chair. Colorful presentation slides, as usual, cluttered almost every inch of space, even covering most of our home laptop, which was closed. She worked in marketing— go figure. I felt the pull of wanting to somehow take half of the laptop with me. Of course, that was a ludicrous notion.

I shook my head and released a quiet, almost mocking laugh. How many times had I advised clients to protect themselves, not to let blind stubbornness direct their actions, to allow the process to play out?

Protect yourself? I must have sounded like a pompous, insensitive ass to my clients.

As I flipped around, my eyes spotted a small card on Nicole's desk. The logo in the upper left-hand corner appeared to be flowers, something red and yellow.

I stopped breathing for a second.

Don't be tempted, Oz. Once you go down this path, you'll question everything.

"I already am questioning everything, dammit." The sound of my voice startled me. I actually paused, somewhat expecting to hear Nicole ask me to speak up from the other room.

There was a note written on the card, but it faced her chair on the opposite side of the desk. My eyes studied the handwriting. She wrote like a schoolteacher. This handwriting had more flair to it, bigger loops. Like a kid about to dig into the proverbial cookie jar, I looked around to make sure no one was watching me. I knew it was nothing short of a paranoid move.

I picked up the note and read it.

My Dear Nicole,

The gleam of your beautiful smile is only eclipsed by the blaze of your red-hot passion. Every time you look at these flowers, think of my body against yours.

C

I don't recall ever actually *hearing* the thump of my heart, but right now it felt like it was connected to an amplifier beating in my head like a bass drum. I slid the card into my pocket and turned to the window.

Almost immediately, I stopped. I couldn't take the card with me. She would know I'd been inside the house—that I knew about her and this *C* person.

Nicole would never cheat on me, regardless of what kind of craziness we were going through. That had been my staunch position. It was what my old geometry teacher called a postulate—something absolute, unchanging. But I had been wrong about Nicole. So very wrong.

My thoughts were scrambled and irrational. I pushed out a slow breath. At the moment, I wasn't sure if I wanted to learn more about Nicole and this *C* person. I'd seen enough to make me want to throw up. She and I were over.

My advice from earlier zipped through my mental haze: *protect yourself.*

I carefully set the card back where I'd found it, then scooted out the window and made my way back to my car, where I couldn't help but notice the key scratches on the side panel.

This day, like the previous two, was off to a roaring start.

Seventeen

The outdoor façade to the Belmont had a new, brighter finish to it. Other than that, the iconic indoor-outdoor music venue in Austin looked just about the same as when I was here two months ago, when a bomb ripped through the complex, killing three and wounding twenty.

Similar to that night, white lights were strung across the outdoor space, glowing against the nighttime sky. With the club/restaurant on one side and the ivy-covered brick wall of an adjoining building on the other side, there was no wind. The place was only half full. No live acts were on stage; it was only recorded music tonight—currently an old tune from INXS. The place had reopened only in the last couple of weeks or so.

The waiter and the person I was meeting arrived tableside at the same time.

"I guess this is for you?" the waiter asked Brook, who wore a pair of fashionable boots over her denim leggings. She looked like anyone other than a cop, except for one thing. Really, it was two things. Two stress lines seemed to be permanently sculpted into her forehead.

She thanked the waiter and sat down. "I appreciate you ordering my drink in advance, even if I am sticking with a virgin mojito." She had texted me twice earlier, once while I was still at the reading of my father's will—that couldn't have been any more dramatic—to say she wanted to meet and discuss her progress on the investigation, and then again about fifteen minutes ago, apologizing for being late.

I held up my drink, and we clinked glasses. I'd gone with my second-favorite drink: Knob Creek and Coke on ice, as opposed to Knob Creek neat.

"Tough day at the office?" she asked, digging through her purse. I thought I saw "Kate Spade" on the side of her bright-orange and hot-pink bag. She appeared to want to define herself, or at least her look, as the anti-cop, more like someone we'd run into at the country club. *We*. I needed to stop thinking of myself as part of a team with Nicole. I was on my own in many ways right now.

I crunched on a piece of ice. "If I had an office, maybe. I've got a desk. But, ohhh, the stories I could tell," I said with what felt like a tired smile.

She pulled out her phone, checked something on the screen, then gave me her full attention. "I'm sure you've had a lot of fallout from your father's death."

With the background music in the air, my hearing was particularly limited, so I had to watch her lips as she spoke. "Not the least being the silent feud between my mom and my dad's girlfriend."

Her eyes got wide. "You have to deal with one of those triangles on top of everything else?"

"My brother and I have been dealing with it for about fourteen years, helping keep the peace, trying to make sure the wrong people don't run into each other at whatever event."

"Seriously? They put you in that position?"

"Most of that falls on my dad's shoulders. Then again, as we crossed that threshold into adulthood, my brother and I…well, we could have stopped. We were enablers."

She sipped her drink and glanced at her phone again. "I hope I didn't pull you away from anything important."

"Hell no. I just got done attending the reading of my dad's will. And, man, that event might be one for the ages."

She raised an eyebrow.

"Yes, it was that memorable."

"Lots of drama?"

"Let's see… First, my dad's girlfriend shows up. My brother begins to freak out. I wasn't there yet."

"She came uninvited?"

"No, she was invited. I'll get to that chapter in a second. Then, my mom shows up."

"Good Lord, I'm starting to sweat, and it's fifty-something degrees. Did she lose it?"

I sipped before speaking. "Not exactly, but she had her own way of getting even…well, until the will was read."

She moved her phone to the side and clasped her hands on the table. "I'm all ears."

"I'm glad my misery is so entertaining," I said with a sarcastic chuckle.

She shrugged and took a drink. "We all need distractions; at least I do. I recently stopped smoking. So don't stop now."

"Mom walked in with a friend. I'd never met her before. Her name was Hilda."

"And?"

"They were arm in arm, kind of how you might have seen me and Nicole a couple of months ago."

"Are you saying that Mom and Hilda are…?"

I held up a hand. "Stop. I don't want to envision it."

"Is that too out there for you?"

"Hardly. I've got friends of all kinds. But when it comes to your mom, you don't want to think about that stuff. Would you want to think about your mom and anyone doing—"

"I get it." She closed her eyes for a moment.

"Mom's act didn't last long. When Arie read the will, I thought she was going to jump across the table and grab him by the throat."

"What made her so pissed?"

I huffed out a breath as I relived the anxiety of that moment. "She was almost bragging at the funeral reception that she was going to receive five million on an insurance policy. Turns out that was only half right."

That eyebrow of hers lifted again.

"Yep. Dad gave half to Mom and the other half to Bianca, who actually pumped her fist like she'd just won the Super Bowl."

"Ho-ly shit."

I raised my glass and took another gulp. The waiter came by, and we ordered seconds.

"How have you been dealing with this?" she asked.

"It's been exhausting, and up until today, it almost felt normal. Well, normal for our family."

She snickered and held up her drink. We clinked glasses again as she said, "Here's to the new normal."

"I love it. That'll be my new mantra. 'The new normal.'"

Eighteen

A couple walked in from the street entrance, and for just a moment, I thought the woman affixed to the side of a man was Nicole. Her dark-brown hair was up in a bun on top of her head, wispy ringlets draping down either side of her face. She had the same high cheekbones and walked with a confident grace that drew your attention. I could actually feel my pulse quicken as I wondered if the man looked anything like the *C* person who had sent my wife flowers and written her that love note.

"Do you know that person?"

Brook had seen me gawking. "Oh, no." I scooted my chair forward for no particular reason. I had this urge to get up and walk around, or just leave. I felt lost. Maybe I'd go walk the streets and try to figure out what I should do next. "So, you called this fun meeting."

"Right. I appreciate you meeting me outside of the precinct office. It's kind of stuffy in there. For me, anyway."

"Sounds like there's a story there."

"Eh. It's just breaking into rituals and cliques of a new department, especially the detective pool. Everyone is very judgmental, and there are a lot of old-timers."

"They're not used to having a woman around?"

"Oh, they want women around…to get them coffee, file reports, do menial research work. You know, anything to make sure we understand that the glass ceiling remains."

"That sucks." My mind went to how Nicole would handle a situation like that. Well, the old Nicole. She would have broken the glass ceiling, but in the process won over about ninety percent of the good-ol'-boy clan. For the remaining ten percent, she'd probably ignore their requests until they treated her as an equal.

"Yeah, it's basically taking every ounce of self-control to avoid a shoot-out—and I mean that figuratively, of course…well, sorta—with a couple of the alphas. But right now, I'm knee deep in these two investigations, so I have no time. Which is probably a good thing."

"I'll drink to that."

She laughed. "Cheers." We sipped our drinks to seal the toast.

She turned the discussion to my dad's case and started by saying that she'd gotten a warrant for his cell-phone records.

"Are you saying you think he was murdered?"

"No, I'm not saying that. In fact, the cardiologist was very convincing in explaining how your father's heart was weakened and how he could have suffered a second heart attack that killed him."

"You said *could*."

"She didn't use that term. I did. I have to leave the possibility open that something more sinister could have happened."

"So you went for his phone records. Why?"

"Well, for starters, we need to identify who he was interacting with, especially recently. Beyond that, in looking at the logs from the hospital, we see where there are gaps when no one was in the room with your father. Between the nurse on duty, the hospital cleaning crew, the person responsible for taking food orders, and family and friends, there are still periods of time when he was alone."

I nodded. "Since he wasn't in intensive care, there's no sign-up process for visitation, so it's difficult to track who dropped by or didn't."

"You got it."

She gave me the hospital's regular visitation hours: 8:00 a.m. to 11:00 p.m. "But," she added, "the staff admitted that those hours aren't strictly enforced, not unless Nathaniel was on the pediatric or neonatal floors. Some patients have friends or family who spend the night in the room with them. Some visitors might stay later; some show up earlier. After questioning a lot of the staff, it appears that unless there is some type of emergency health situation or a visitor is creating a disturbance, they don't usually question a person walking the halls."

I scratched my face, felt the thick stubble. The razor I'd borrowed from Tito hadn't done a very good job. My sights drifted upward to see a squirrel scampering along the wire of white lights to the next building.

"Three-quarters of the world seem to have a camera in place to capture video. Have you looked into the hospital surveillance?"

"I just got that warrant approved. Hospital security is working with one of the APD video techs. I've been told they don't have the whole place covered. But you never know; it might turn up something."

Her phone buzzed, and she asked me to hold on for a second as she read something. During the spare moment, I was able to spot two outdoor cameras. I was almost certain they'd been installed since the explosion.

She let her phone drop a little too hard on the table, but I had to ask her a quick question before addressing her phone message.

"Do you have any inside scoop on authorities finding the people who bombed this place?"

She swished a lock of hair out of her face, then waved at the waiter. "I'll take another one of these, but make it leaded." She pointed a finger at me. "Don't judge."

I smiled, held up both hands like she had a gun on me. "I'm not saying anything. It's what, nine o'clock at night? You're technically off the clock."

While we waited on the drink, she informed me that she had no real inside information on the bombing suspects. "Basically, I know what you know. They're calling it 'domestic terrorism.'" She used quote marks with her fingers on the last two words.

"What's up with the quote marks?"

"Well, labeling it something like that only scares the public more, which if it's truly terrorism in the classic sense, isn't that their intent? To scare the public?"

She had a damn good point. "I like the way you think."

"Not sure my male colleagues would agree with that notion, but I appreciate it." She took in a breath, her eyes drifting away for a second. "For those of us who were here that night when the explosion occurred, it was horrific. Like something you'd see in a country on the other side of the world."

I stared at her lips, wondering if what I'd seen her say matched what I'd heard. "You said *us*. You were here?"

We then discovered we'd both shared this tragic moment in Austin's history and that we had a connection—Zahera Subzali. I'd known Zahera since college; we had a brief little thing while I was still attending UT. One of those college nights that went a little too far. But we'd remained friends throughout the years. Nicole and I were invited to The Belmont for the same reason Brook had been in attendance, to watch her friend, Cristina Tafoya, perform with a local Austin band, the Batistas.

The waiter arrived with Brook's drink, and she immediately took a pull from the straw. "For this case, we at the APD are out of the loop. I just know the ATF and the FBI, and even the Department of Homeland Security, are involved. I realize the public is clamoring for information. The Feds are being really hush-hush on this one, which means they're either really close to finding these nutjobs or not close at all."

My hands felt a vibration running through the table. We both reached for our phones. I saw a text from Ray.

Just checking in. I've been working a couple of old sources at fed agencies. Other than that, can u get me access to your dad's personal email?

I couldn't recall seeing an email from Dad that didn't go through the Novak and Novak domain. Maybe he had one. I could ask Mom...or not. She had checked out on Dad and the firm business, on or off the books, long ago. She might be the last person who'd have any interest in getting involved in this investigation—unless it would lead to her prying the other half of Dad's life insurance money out of Bianca's fingers.

Maybe Arie was someone I could ask. I typed in a text to Ray letting him know that I'd do some digging of my own and get back to him.

He responded with: *Have started talking to ur colleagues at firm and other old-timers ur dad knew.*

I didn't want to set off alarms and make people think they might be the target of some investigation. Word could start to spread, and if the wrong ears heard it, then any hope of staying quiet on the search for Dad's mystery client might be forever ruined. I thumbed a quick reply. *Be discreet.*

He came back with: *Discreet is my middle name.*

I looked up to see the wrinkles on Brook's forehead even more pronounced. I almost didn't want to ask.

Nineteen

"**E**verything okay?" I asked.

She sighed. "If I start bitching, I might never stop. Real quickly, I want to tell you about the people your dad called or received calls from in the last week."

"Good. What do you have?"

She scrolled her finger down her phone screen. "Okay, so we have Bianca Chastain." Her eyes glanced up at me.

"That figures."

She continued. "You, of course. And then there's your brother Tobin, Arie, a handful of calls into the actual Novak and Novak office, your mother, a Cadillac dealership, and then one last one." She swiveled the phone back and forth, as she studied me.

"Am I supposed to guess?"

"It's a burner phone. No longer active."

"Who called whom?"

"Good question. There were twelve total calls. He received seven and made five."

"Who made the first call?"

"Damn, you're a bulldog. I can see why you're a high-paid attorney."

"Right now, I'm a no-paid attorney."

She showed her teeth, then answered my question. "First call was made by the owner of the burner phone almost three months ago."

I didn't understand how this could be the same dad I'd known almost my entire life. He was a bit of a showboat, bombastic at times, and he'd taken on some questionable clients and pushed a few judges. But I'd never seen him act with absolute disregard for the integrity of the firm or, as might be proven, his own safety.

Why get involved in something that required communicating via a burner phone? The more I learned, the more it was obvious that Dad was involved in something shady. For what, though? He must have at some point sensed he was in danger. He admitted that we'd find no trail of this client at the firm, so he knew it was illegal. But what could have been his motivation to do business with this person or group of people? I couldn't begin to wrap my head around it. Right now, nothing in my life made sense.

"Anything else to share?"

"Not yet. I'll let you know if we find anything usable on the surveillance tape at the hospital. Unless we find you walking into your dad's room in the middle of the night." She raised an eyebrow.

"Believe me, when the Feds raided our office and I knew he was the reason, I was ready to do some bodily damage."

"The Feds," she said with an eye roll. "I tried to get more info out of them."

"Dead end for you too? They won't share the details of Dad's case with me. It's frickin' crazy."

She gulped another mouthful of her mojito. "They're a pain in my ass on two investigations."

I turned my head.

"First, your dad's case. They want me to share any evidence I find, but they won't tell me squat…who he was involved with, what exactly he'd done."

"Supposedly, they don't know who he was working for."

"Right. Well, I bet they have a strong idea or two. They start throwing around this love-of-country crap just to guilt me into being their personal cop. But I can't do my job if they withhold information. Or, it will just take me a hell of a lot longer."

The more I hung around Brook, the more I appreciated her candor and feistiness. "So if you suddenly disappear, I need to question the FBI?"

She playfully rolled her eyes again. "Something like that."

"You mentioned two investigations."

"Did I tell you about the murder of the doctor in the alley on the south side?"

"I didn't know he was a doctor."

"Keep it to yourself, but his name was Dr. Harry Clem."

I didn't move for a second. "Clem. Does it start with a 'C'?"

"Yeah. Why?"

I casually took a drink, although my veins buzzed. "It's a pretty common name. I think I might have gone to school with a kid named Clem." I hadn't, of course, but I couldn't think of another reason to sound so interested in his name. I was in this strange place…feeling guilty for crawling through a window, then finding the love note, while at the same time feeling so utterly betrayed by Nicole. It was like she had an evil twin or something.

"Yeah, well…" She paused, stared at her phone.

"You don't have to share anything with me about the case. I understand protocol and all."

"It's not that," she said, shifting her eyes to me. "You've got experience working criminal cases. It might help me to bounce a few things off you…if you're game."

"My experience is limited." I didn't want to get into the fact that we used Ray for any deep investigative work. With him leading the non-governmental charge to figure out who Dad's client was, I'd just rather keep his name off anyone's radar for now.

"I understand if you're busy or just preoccupied with your dad's situation."

"It's not that. In fact, I don't really have a true job right now. The firm will be dissolved. Not my decision, of course. But Arie has his marching orders, and he seems rather intent on following through with Dad's intentions."

She took another pull from her drink, then lifted her phone. "So, I just got back the ballistics report on the bullet that killed Dr. Clem."

I sat a little straighter in my chair. For some reason, her investigation into the death of this doctor whom I knew nothing about intrigued me. It seemed absurd to think I was interested just because his last name started with a "C." Did I actually believe he was the person who sent the note to Nicole? For starters, how many people sign their name with one letter, using the first letter of their last name? Beyond that, how many people in Austin had first or last names starting with the letter "C," or even a nickname? The number was impossible to fathom.

But that still didn't squelch my desire to know; if for no other reason, I could mark this person with a *C* in his name off the list.

My mind then hopped to another level of shit to worry about. If for whatever crazy reason this doctor was the person Nicole was involved with, he was now dead. Did she know he was dead? Could she be in danger just because of her association with him?

"Do you find this kind of stuff boring?"

"Oh no, sorry. I was just thinking. What did the ballistics show?"

"Hold on a second." She waggled her phone another second, then called over the waiter and asked for the check. "I'm picking up the bill. Then I'd like to take you to the crime scene, if you're game."

"Nothing else better to do. Count me in."

For the first time in days, it was nice to be of use to someone. Even if I was the one with the ulterior motive.

Twenty

Twitching my nose, I watched Brook count her steps as she made her way out of an older office building and down an alley.

She flipped around, pointed the flashlight from her phone up to her face, and said. "Forty-one. That's how many steps it took me to get from the bottom of the staircase to where the body was found, right here. And it took me about twenty seconds or so."

"No offense, but that's kind of a creepy look for you," I said, walking in the middle of the path she had taken and glancing back at the office building.

She snorted out a quick laugh. "So, what are you thinking?"

I put my hand against my ear. "Is my hearing aid going haywire, or do you hear some type of thumping bass in the air?"

She pointed a thumb over her shoulder. "The bakery at the end of the alley. The two guys who work overnight crank their music."

I nodded, walked to the top of the steps, and looked up and down the alley.

"What?" she asked from her spot forty-one steps away.

"How do you know the doctor was in the building?"

"You answer a question with a question. O-kay. Well, I've confirmed he has a small lab."

Now my eyes stayed on her. "A lab. For what?"

"We're not exactly sure at this point. We have some strong guesses, but we've asked the FBI for assistance. All they did was refer me to Special Agent Bowser. He asked me a few questions and told me to keep him in the loop on everything I uncovered."

Bowser. The same guy assigned to my dad's case. Was it a coincidence? Anything was possible, but aside from weather events or completely unrelated elements, there were reasons—whether logical or emotional—for just about everything. I recalled the lessons learned about using coincidence as a defense strategy. It didn't fly with judges or juries.

"You said you weren't 'exactly' sure about the type of research the lab was doing. So what are your theories?" I glanced up at the back wall of the building. Not a single light was on through the windows that I could see.

"Well, we have a few chemistry nerds in the forensics group, and they think the lab was set up to research a new type of drug."

"As in Dr. White, *Breaking Bad*, and—"

"Crystal meth," she said, nodding. "Although they didn't see any specific evidence of crystal meth, per se. But they did see an interesting combination of elements that led them to believe drug development was a goal."

I scratched my chin and let her feedback simmer in the corner of my mind. "Earlier, you counted forty-one steps in about twenty seconds."

"Right. I might be off by a second or two, but that's what I'm thinking."

"And on the drive over here, you mentioned he was killed with a single gunshot wound to his face."

"Yep."

"Where you're standing?"

She looked down for a second, and I noticed white paint around her. She said, "The doctor's car, a Buick, was next to him, facing the bakery. The front door was open."

I scanned the alley. It was littered with trash. I also spotted five or six small crates scattered from the end of the alley to the green trash bin near the opening of the alley. A few bags of trash were huddled against it. Apparently, the trash collector had not made a recent visit. The toxic mixture invaded my senses.

"Here's the strange thing, Ozzie. The office space used for his lab wasn't in his name. It was in his former wife's maiden name."

Former wife. My thoughts snapped back to the *C* in his last name. "You mean his ex?"

"I used the wrong term. He was a widower. His wife died seven years ago from some type of fever she picked up while hiking in the Amazon region of Brazil."

I nodded. "Was there signage on the door?" I asked, pointing at the building.

"It's on the fourth floor. And no signage at all."

A few seconds passed where all I could hear and feel was the thumping bass from the club-like music emanating from the bakery. "That's annoying."

"It's frickin' nonstop until they leave. But somehow they get their work done—typically bake a hundred or so pies and cakes."

"We might have to raid that place here in a bit." She laughed, but I didn't.

Then I asked, "Are you thinking that he didn't want to draw attention to this little lab operation?"

"Actually, there's more than the lab operation that doesn't seem right. A couple of officers and I visited his residence in Round Rock. Not much there, honestly. And when we spoke with his neighbors, they hadn't seen the good doctor in weeks."

"But let me guess." I held up a hand. "When they had seen him, they said he was a normal guy who kept to himself."

"Did you feed them their lines?" she joked. "Seriously, we both know that, these days, the whole neighbor thing doesn't mean a lot. People keep to themselves and tend to only notice people if they—"

"Turn up the music to an obnoxious level?" We both laughed at that one.

"So," I said, getting us back on track, "Dr. Clem parked his car in the alley, not along the street or in the parking garage a block down. He exited this door behind me." I flipped around and pulled the door open. "Okay, assuming the door remained unlocked after it closed behind him, he would have run back inside if he had seen his assailant anywhere from halfway to his car or less."

"We believe it was unlocked. At least it was when the first officers arrived on the scene."

"Which tells me he didn't see anyone, not until he was at least halfway to his car." I scampered down the steps and walked toward the trash bin. Brook started to follow me, but I asked her to grab one of the crates and place it in the spot where the body was found. She did and then joined me near the trash bin. I huddled behind it.

"From my vantage point, I can peek around the edge of the bin to see the back door and stairs and probably not be seen. There is no light over here at all."

She got right behind me and looked toward the back of the building. "Right. I'm with you."

I shuffled a couple of steps into the middle of the alley. "So, the doctor checks the alley out, sees it's all clear, and heads to his car. The perp, I'm guessing, is wearing soft-soled shoes and sneaks up on him. Maybe the doctor sees him at the last minute with his car door open, and pop, he gets hit with a bullet."

Brook walked a few steps toward the crate, her boots crunching on some broken glass; then she turned back to me, waving a hand in her face.

"*Now* you smell it?" I asked.

"No one would want to hang out back here for long."

"Just long enough."

She tapped her finger against her chin. "So part of me thinks it's a professional job. Whoever did this has killed before."

Before I could comply with her theory, she raised a finger and said, "But."

"There's more?"

"He had no wallet on him when he was found."

"Killer could have taken it," I said. "Or, maybe after he was shot and the killer had already left the scene, someone found the body and stole the wallet."

"Hadn't thought of that one."

"But if the killer took the wallet, then that would make me think it wasn't a professional hit."

She pointed toward the building. "The drugs. I keep going back to that lab, wondering if this was some type of drug-related hit. Maybe it was done by a professional, maybe it wasn't, but the wallet is missing, and Dr. Clem was concocting something in that lab."

We paced the alley for a couple of minutes, both of us lost in our own thoughts.

I stopped and held up a hand. "Back at the Belmont, you mentioned the ballistics report."

"I almost forgot. The bullet was 9mm, and they believe the handgun was a Ruger."

"Not sure if that helps or hurts the professional-hit theory."

"Well, for what it's worth, the Ruger 9mm is a semiautomatic. And it's one of the guns most often used by gang members."

Austin, not unlike any major city, had its share of gang problems. I'd represented one former gang member a few years earlier, once again as a pro-bono case. The kid seemed like he had legitimately changed and didn't want to go to prison, unlike some of the thugs who almost taunted the judge until they were sentenced. While I was able to get his sentence reduced, he still had to serve two years in prison. And from what I'd seen and heard, even a few days in the Texas prison system would change you forever.

We debated going into the bakery and asking for any leftover pie or cake but, in the end, decided against it. She pulled up on the side street near the Belmont, where my Cadillac was parked in the garage, and thanked me for taking the time to walk through the crime scene with her.

"No problem. I hope Bowser and the FBI will stop treating you like the enemy and start sharing information with you."

She gave me a fist bump. It seemed appropriate.

I pushed the door open, then turned back and said, "On both investigations."

She said she'd reach out to me with any updates. I found my car on the second level all by itself. As I approached the four-door sedan, I sensed something was off. I stopped a few feet behind it. The car leaned to the back right.

"Sonofabitch." I lowered my body and saw that the back tire was flat. I ran my fingers across the tread and found a hole.

Just what I wanted to do: change a tire. Nicole, of course, would have told me to call AAA or some service to change my tire. But right now my funds were limited, thanks to Nicole. As I pulled off my jacket to throw it inside, I spotted something white under my windshield wiper. I removed the piece of paper and read a handwritten note:

Your dad died for a reason. You will, too, if you don't stop snooping.

For a moment I forgot to breathe. I glanced around, saw no one. Then I changed the tire and headed straight to Tito's place.

Twenty-One

As Alfonso surged away from the light at 6th and Guadalupe, he took a bite of his burger, then washed it back with a long chug of Schlitz until the can was empty. He crushed it, tossed it over his shoulder, into the back seat of his Monte Carlo.

"Watch out, Fonso; we don't want to get too close," Tomas said from the passenger seat, drinking his own bottle of Colt 45. "This surveillance shit is about chilling, staying back, and watching."

Wiping his arm across his face, Alfonso glanced at his running buddy, then took his foot off the gas pedal, falling three cars behind the navy-blue Cadillac. "How's that?" He didn't like asking for validation. It made him seem stupid, weak even. But he'd never done anything this subtle.

"That's cool, dude. You're picking it up real nice. Before long, Five-O will be sending you to Hawaii to go undercover. Can you imagine that, being an undercover cop or FBI agent in Hawaii? Those bitches twerking their hips in those skimpy bikinis, drinking those fruity drinks on the beach. Damn!" Tomas held out his hand, and Alfonso smacked it. "Don't know how you got me there, but sometimes I think about crazy shit like that. It's a free country. Who's to say we can't just haul ass to Hawaii and join up with our brothers out there?"

Even with his blood rocketing through his veins like nobody's business, his mind in a hyped-up daze, images of his two little girls—and yes, Lupita too—flashed before his eyes. A trickle of doubt reentered his mind, and it still gave him a sinking feeling. He was questioning the decision he'd made, if the path he'd chosen would truly pay off, not just in terms of the cash he would bring in. Would his family accept him for who he really was, his roots?

Alfonso pulled his tight grip off the steering wheel and shifted his sights to the jerseys he and Tomas were wearing—Kurt Warner's 13 jersey when he'd played for the Rams.

"Give me another beer, man." He couldn't let this buzz dissipate.

"Sure 'nough." Tomas reached behind the front seat into the Styrofoam cooler and pulled out an ice-cold Schlitz.

Alfonso grabbed it, popped the top, and drained about a third of it, then let out a belch that rattled the windows.

Tomas cracked up. "Fonso is the man!" he yelled, laughing. Then he faced forward and pointed. "Hold up, dog. He's taking a right at the light. Don't lose him."

"I got it, bitch." Alfonso executed the turn onto Nueces before the light turned red, still a couple of cars behind the Cadillac. "I'm a pro at this, Tomas. Make sure you tell Boss Man that."

"Absolutely. Boss Man said we got to pick our spot carefully—you know, like a panther tracking its prey," he said, scratching his fingernails on the dash and cackling.

"You don't sound like no panther. You sound like a fucking hyena."

"Just drive, douche bag. We can't afford to screw this up. Know what I'm sayin'?"

"I'm all business," he said, chugging more of his beer. "Which is why I need to stay calm, keep my focus, man."

Traffic moved along at the same basic pace. The blue Cadillac took another right on 11th, running east, just south of the state capitol. A red light had stopped about ten cars, including the one they were following, at the intersection with I-35. Alfonso stared at the red brake lights of the old Nissan just in front of his Monte Carlo. For a moment, his thoughts went back to the night he'd made the decision to change the course of his life forever: when he took the life of that man in the alley. He had no idea what the man had done to deserve to die, but Alfonso wasn't the judge or jury, merely the executioner. He was damn good at carrying out orders. Danger to him was nothing more than a challenge of his willpower over the elements of evil, the suffocating oppression that was always trying to knock him down, to lessen his role in this world.

The prison, his life since then…all of it had stripped Alfonso of almost everything that made him a man. He knew Lupita wasn't going to accept this new path, not at first. Hell, she might even come after him with a knife. She had an epic temper. But in the long run, she would eventually come around. She'd have to. It was all about the money. If he could pull off this job, gain the confidence of Boss Man, then he might be put on… What did Tomas call it? Retainer. That was it. Consistent pay, even if a small percentage went to the crew. Enough to change their lives. He could move the family into a neighborhood where they wouldn't worry about the girls running outside to play. And if anyone even thought about endangering his girls, he'd make them pay.

He knew how the game went. He'd seen it with his own eyes. It didn't make a damn bit of difference if the players were thumbing each other's nuts while wearing two-K suits in some fancy boardroom, toasting their latest acquisition. Everyone played the same ass-kissing, ego-stroking game. He and Tomas…they were keeping it real. No fancy suits. No bullshit games. And if or when something hit the fan, their crew would have their backs.

"You lost in your Schlitz world?" Tomas said, smacking Alfonso's arm.

Alfonso jabbed the gas pedal. The eight-cylinder engine launched the Monte Carlo forward, squealing the tires.

"Dude, we can't be drawing attention to ourselves," Tomas hissed. "Where's your head at?"

"Hey, man. I got this. No need to hit the alarm. I'm cool as a cucumber."

"That ain't what your momma told me," he said, laughing uncontrollably, grabbing his crotch.

Tomas and his momma jokes. Normally, Alfonso would hit back, one-up that prick. But he had to rise above, keep his focus on the blue Caddy. "He should be turning left up ahead, right?"

Tomas nodded. "As long he doesn't make some unexpected booty call or gets sentimental and wants to head back out to the burbs or shit. He's in the artsy-fartsy part of the city. You ready with your piece?"

Alfonso reached under his seat and gripped the Ruger. He lifted it from the floorboard and placed it on the seat next to him. The weight of the weapon gave him a blood rush.

Just then, lights flashed in his rearview.

"Fucking cops, dude." Tomas sunk in his seat, then peeked over the front seat to look out the back window. "We're fucked, man. The booze, your fucking gun. Dammit!"

Alfonso tried to swallow, but his throat had clamped shut. His mind hit the panic alarm; it was all he could do not to pee in his pants. He was doomed. In mere seconds, he'd be on his way back to prison.

Back to being someone else's bitch.

Twenty-Two

The Cadillac was just three years old—a gift from Dad when I joined the firm. At the time, I believed it was just the beginning of greater things. I'd be crowned partner of Novak and Novak, the in-waiting top dog. The Cadillac, as it turned out, was a gift for putting in the work—grinding it out through one of the toughest law schools in the country and then passing the bar exam. The message of what type of privileges, or lack thereof, would be bequeathed to me because of my surname was never completely delivered, at least not in a timely, definable action.

Perception and desire, I'd learned, can often have no resemblance to reality. Dad probably needed to teach me some lessons in humility—given my expectations that had never been doused during my years of schooling—although I think I would have responded just as well to a sit-down discussion over a couple of Heinekens. But given how I couldn't undo the past, including Dad's untimely death, I'd never know how I would have responded to a frank discussion about his expectations of me and the firm he'd built from client number one.

As I slowly accelerated on 11th, heading under the I-35 bridge, I spotted a police car with its lights flashing in my rearview.

"Crap!" I lowered the volume of my car stereo—I'd been trying to chill out to some old Texas folk music by Robert Earl Keen.

Just my luck. The police car had probably been tucked away in one of those dark parking lots just off the highway and had seen the tiny spare tire on the back of my Cadillac. It was actually the backup to the backup of the real tire. I'd rolled over nails in the neighborhood twice in the last few weeks. New construction was a part of everyday life in Austin and its sprawling suburbs.

Before I had a chance to put on my blinker, the police car pulled to the side of the road behind a brown car, a lowrider of some kind.

My shoulders relaxed. I wasn't really sure why I'd freaked out. I would have shown the officer my license and proof of registration and...

My mind wandered then. The cop might have asked me where I was heading, and then I'd have to explain how I'd taken up temporary residence at Tito's place in East Austin. No big deal there, although that would have led down the path of sharing the nauseating information about my separation from Nicole. That was just painful, not illegal.

Unless, somehow, Nicole had found out about me sneaking into our home and reading that note from her shit-stick lover, *Mr. C.* Or was it *Dr. C*? Whatever. Was it possible that she'd had cameras installed? I didn't see any cameras outside or inside the home, but I knew a camera could be on the spine of a book or the frame of a picture. She could have seen everything I'd done. And she would be pissed, possibly vindictive.

She could have called in a favor with a friend or colleague at the APD—she was in marketing, and it seemed like she had contacts all over the private and government sectors—made up some crazy story about her lunatic husband who was harassing and threatening her, shown them the video footage of me breaking into our home, all to convince them that I'd stolen the Cadillac.

In other words, why not pour gas on me and light a flame, then step back and watch me burn to death? It would be hilarious to the evil twin sister of Nicole to see me homeless, moneyless, *and* carless.

My line of thinking was becoming more radical by the day, but in this new life, this *new normal*, as Brook and I had called it, I had no real foundation. And it was about as much fun as a daily proctology exam.

The fluorescent image in the road reached my brain just in time for me to jab my foot on the brake. My tires squeaked as the car stopped on a dime. It was a construction worker, holding out an arm as a lumbering bulldozer made its way across the street.

"Sorry," I said while holding up a hand. Of course, he couldn't hear me. In fact, his facial expression told me he was pissed. I got it. In his job, if someone wasn't paying attention for just a split second, he could very well end up as roadkill.

As the bulldozer creeped along at the pace of a snail, I picked up the note and read it again.

Your dad died for a reason. You will, too, if you don't stop snooping.

Now in a more relaxed mindset, I wondered why I hadn't called Brook, let her team come and process the scene. My eyes looked up and saw the construction worker still standing guard, his jaw set, his hand defiantly pointing in my direction. I connected with his disposition. I didn't like anyone trying to threaten me or even intimidate me. It made me want to fight back. By changing my own tire and leaving, it was my way of saying, "Screw you and your veiled threats."

Just replaying the whole ordeal in my mind caused my heart rate to skyrocket, my body to tense up. I wanted to take action.

Now. But as pissed as I was about the note, there was no definable enemy. To a degree, the person who wrote the note was like my own personal domestic terrorist. They were trying to scare me.

With the bulldozer nearing the edge of the road, I picked up my phone and considered calling Bowser to demand that the FBI release more information about Dad's investigation.

But you know what that will get you, Oz. Squat, that's what.

I took a breath. I would let Brook know, but what would that get me? I'd probably erased any fingerprints on the note. Or maybe there were no prints to be found. This person wasn't stupid. My thoughts circled back to when I'd started this day: I had to find out whom my dad was working for and why. While Brook might be on the fence about whether or not he was murdered, I was convinced he had been. If I found the person he was working for, then I would probably find the person who wrote the note.

Ray. He was my best hope. Unlike Brook, he wasn't shackled to following the letter of the law. Then I recalled that he wanted access to Dad's personal email—*if* Dad had a personal email account. I punched a button on my steering wheel and said Arie's name. A few seconds later, his line rang. He picked up on the second ring. He sounded like he'd either been asleep or was on his fourth after-dinner drink. The discussion lasted no longer than sixty seconds. He claimed he had no idea if Dad had a personal email account. Then he summarily dismissed me, saying he was working night and day to sell off the company assets, including the Novak and Novak client list.

With my agitation level nearing the red zone, I wanted to push back—strongly—to convince him this wasn't really what Dad would want. I knew Dad better than anyone, and I knew he would prefer the firm to live on, with me helping to run the show.

Thankfully, I somehow stopped myself from saying a word. It would be useless and would only increase my anxiety that much more. Arie, like any strong attorney, had the document in hand that gave him all the power he needed to execute the plan of dismantling the company. I'd been excommunicated—not by Arie, I had to remind myself, but by my dad.

The construction worker moved off the road and waved traffic on through. As I passed by him, I took another opportunity to wave at him in apology or appreciation, whatever, but his sights were on the cars behind me.

As I increased my speed, out of nowhere an idea came to mind about Dad's personal email. Stacy, my admin—well, former admin—knew everything about everyone. If she didn't know it, it didn't exist. With an extra burst of positive energy, I called out her name and heard the phone ring.

I was certain I was about to hit pay dirt.

Twenty-Three

Alfonso wondered if he was having a heart attack. His chest throbbed, he was sweating profusely, and his mind was scrambled, as if he'd smoked two massive joints.

"Chill, dude. Don't move a muscle." Tomas sat as straight as a mannequin in the passenger seat, his eyes looking straight ahead.

Looking into his side mirror, Alfonso saw the officer approaching the window, one hand on his gun. He kept his hands on the steering wheel, hoping, praying that the officer wouldn't smell the booze on his breath. If that happened, the cop would ask him to step out of the car; he'd find the empty beer cans and then the gun. Alfonso would be toast.

Two knocks on the glass to his left. Alfonso cranked the window down.

"Hi, Officer. I wasn't speeding, was I?"

With his hand still on his sidearm, the officer twitched his oversized nose. He had gray in his sideburns and a pair of deep lines on either side of his mouth. This was no rookie cop.

"License and proof of insurance, son."

"Yes sir. I'm going to reach into my back pocket." He knew it was best to tell the cop what you're doing. Don't give them any excuses. "Yo, Tomas. Get out the insurance card from the glove compartment, will ya?"

"Sure thing, Alfonso."

The second Tomas's hand touched the glove compartment, the cop yelled out, "Stop right now!"

Both froze.

The cop bent over to where he was eye level with Alfonso, but spoke to Tomas. "Put your frickin' hands on the dash."

"Sir, I was just—"

"Don't back-talk me, boy." The officer glared at Tomas. "How do I know you don't have a weapon in there?"

Tomas opened his mouth.

"That's called a rhetorical question, boy. I guess you don't know the difference." His nose twitched again, and then his deep-set eyes scanned the car, stopping on the floorboard for an extra-long pause.

Alfonso had his hand at his back pocket, but he dared not move. "Sir."

"Hold on." The officer lifted up and used his free hand to speak into the radio mic attached to his shoulder. He was calling for backup.

"Crap," Tomas whispered. "We're fucked, Fonso. We're totally fucked."

He was right. If more cops showed up, they'd be taken out of the car, given breathalyzer tests, which they would likely fail. Then, the cops would find the gun. They'd probably have a way of connecting the gun back to the shooting of that man in the alley.

He closed his eyes as horrific memories from his time in prison pinged his mind. Ironically, it wasn't the handful of beatings he'd suffered that stayed with him. It was the never-ending reminders that he was enclosed in a cage full of vultures, and it all centered around one central theme—fear. The nightly catcalls, the toxic smell of body odor, the threatening glares, and so much more. If there was a way to punch a hole in his psyche, that place could do it. His self-worth exploited incessantly, to the point where he thought he might want to end his life rather than endure another hour in prison.

He couldn't go back. Not now, not ever. He'd lose every bit of freedom. He'd never see his girls grow up. His life would cease to exist.

A tear bubbled in the corner of his eye. He looked up at the officer as his mind sent a signal to his arm.

Pick up the gun and shoot the cop. If you don't, your life will end.

His heart felt like it might explode, as if a force from within was slamming an iron wedge into his chest wall.

It's now or never, Alfonso. Grab the gun, take control of your own life. Don't leave it to chance.

He leaned forward, his eyes glued to the cop. Slowly, he inched his right arm lower.

A loud squawk followed by a screaming voice came over the cop's radio. He snapped back against the seat and listened. Something about an officer being down. The cop quickly replied, then put his hand on the door. "I got no time for you two screwups. I gotta run. Stay out of trouble, hear me?"

He ran off before they could respond.

Alfonso held his breath until the police car screeched off with its sirens blaring away.

"Ho-ly shit, dude." Tomas smacked his arm. "Damn, that was dope. We live to fight another day."

Alfonso emptied his lungs, wiped his face.

"Did you hear me? We got out of it!"

Drained as if he'd just run a marathon in the middle of an Austin summer, Alfonso turned his gaze to Tomas.

"What you looking at me like that for?" Tomas sneered.

Alfonso's mind had so many thoughts and emotions flinging around, but he didn't say a word. He wasn't sure what he thought.

"Just because of one hick-ass cop, you're not going to get religious on me or anything, are you?"

"No."

Tomas studied Alfonso for an extra second. "Don't play me, man. I saw your hand dropping down to pick up the gun. You were going to shoot that motherfucker. He deserved it, for treating us like we're second-class citizens. We pay our taxes just like everyone else," he said, holding up a hand like one of those loud-mouth politicians.

"Dude, don't play me. I ain't stupid. When's the last time you even paid taxes? You make money from selling drugs and doing jobs for people like Boss Man."

Tomas frowned, and he appeared ready for a fight. But just as quickly, his lips turned up at the corners. "Look at us, fighting like a couple of bitches. We should be thankful. Hell, I'm thankful. How about you?"

"Yeah, I'm thankful."

"So, dude, that's a sign. A sign that we're untouchable. A sign that we're meant to do this job and many others just like it."

Alfonso rocked his head up and down.

"Why should everyone else in this world get paid except us? We deserve to get paid. That's it. Bottom line. And in the process, we're going to make these fuckers respect us."

Alfonso could feel that fire burning in his belly. The one born from being disrespected by so many people, and the pathetic paycheck he'd been earning from flipping burgers.

"Do we still have time, you think?" Alfonso asked, turning on the engine.

"We could. We know his destination. Let's go check it out and see if we can make something of this night after all. Given our luck, we might hit that jackpot."

Alfonso steered away from the curb and zipped down 11th Street.

Twenty-Four

As I eased the Cadillac into the parking lot at Tito's complex, I slowed to a crawl. The ten-foot-wide pothole was as deep as Lady Bird Lake, or so it seemed, knowing I had a little donut for a rear tire. I braced myself for the impact.

Whaboom!

I grunted at the crunch of the Cadillac's undercarriage into the jagged concrete.

"You okay, Ozzie?"

Stacy was back on the line after stepping away to investigate my query.

"I'm good, although I can't say the same about my car."

"Don't tell me you got in a wreck. Are we going to have to call you a lawyer?" She giggled in a way that made her sound like a little old lady.

"Ha ha," I said without enthusiasm. I made my way into the parking space on the end, just next to Tito's green VW bus. He'd called it a 1965 classic. I'd retorted with my own description: a classic piece of garbage.

"Were you able to find any evidence of a personal email account for my dad?"

"I didn't want to say anything at first, but…" She stopped short. I thought I picked up a giggle, but I couldn't rely on my hearing.

"Were you saying something?"

"Sorry. Will you promise not to tell Arie?"

"Arie. Why him?"

"You promise?"

I crossed my chest. "I just crossed my chest."

"I snuck out my laptop. Am I a bad person?"

"No worries, Stacy. I'm not the FBI, IRS, FDA, or Homeland Security. Did I miss anyone?"

"Crap. You think they're looking for my laptop?"

"How many secrets are you keeping on it?"

There was a pause, and I thought the call had been dropped. "Stacy?"

"I'm here, Ozzie. I'm thinking that somewhere on my laptop I have my grandmother's famous Fried Pineapple Explosion recipe."

"Are you serious?"

"She actually won a blue ribbon at the state fair in Dallas back in 1960-something."

"Your secret is safe with me. How about Dad's email?" I loved hearing Stacy's stories, but after my night, before my head hit my pillow, even a borrowed pillow, I needed to feel like I'd made some progress.

"Just as I expected, I found an email I had forwarded to his personal account."

That got my attention. "When did this occur?"

"It's dated about eighteen months ago. I remember what happened. He called me from the golf course, said he couldn't get to his work email from his phone. He asked me to check on something. So I just forwarded the email to his personal account."

"Do you have it there? What was it about?"

A quick moment of silence. "Is this going to get me involved in this FBI investigation, Oz? I don't want any trouble."

I watched two women come out of the building, arm in arm. It was dark, difficult to get a good look, but they seemed happy and carefree, as if life were just a breeze. That was me a couple of months ago, but it felt like another lifetime. I sighed.

"You have nothing to worry about, Stacy. I'm just trying to figure out who my dad was working for. And I'll be damned if anything or anyone is going to stop me from finding out." The moment the words left my mouth, I knew I'd taken it too far. "That sounded harsh. I'm sorry. It's not directed at you. It's just been one of those days."

A car drove by on the side street, its engine rumbling. It looked like one of those old Corvette Stingrays. It was as if I were living in the world of vintage cars.

Stacy responded. "If it's anything like the funeral reception, I can't imagine. So, the content of the email is pretty innocuous. It has to do with his client, a city councilman who was charged with DUI, and the client was paranoid about any word of this leaking to the press, so he insisted on routing his emails to your father's private account. I don't even think the guy is in office anymore."

"Do you know if Dad's account is still active?"

"I don't see why not."

I asked her to text me the email address. "Wait, do you know the password?"

"Pfft. Do cows shit in barns? Come on, Oz. I don't forget things like that."

Wow, I'd forgotten how lucky I'd been to have such a talented person as my admin. "You're the greatest, Stacy."

As I pushed the car door open, I saw another car driving down the tree-lined side street, one of those lowrider cars, going about five miles per hour. Two guys were in the front. It didn't turn into the parking lot.

Instead, it stopped right there in the street. With one foot still on the floorboard, and a gust of chilly wind making my eyes water, I stopped moving. Something was off. The driver's-side window of the lowrider was rolled down, even with temperatures in the thirties. Were they going to ask me a question? But the driver didn't lean out the window.

I picked up a strong waft of wood burning in a fireplace. Not many people still had wood-burning fireplaces. Back in San Francisco, when Nicole and I had frozen our asses off just from walking five blocks toward the wharf, we'd scoot into a coffee shop, grab two warm mugs of coffee, and huddle near the public fireplace. We jokingly dreamed of someday having our own fireplace, one that used real wood, where we could snuggle by the roaring fire and hug and kiss each other without worrying about offending other people.

At this very moment, someone was probably doing the same thing that we'd talked about all those years ago. I had this strong urge to have her close to me, her body against mine in front of our wood-burning fireplace.

I blinked and saw a glint of metal. I didn't think; I just dove back into my car. In midair, I heard a series of muffled pops, and as I landed—the gear shift slamming into my ribs—glass exploded just above my head. A second of silence. Were they coming after me? I wouldn't be able to hear if someone was walking toward me. Should I lift my head? I was a sitting duck, no way to protect myself.

Just then, a woman's scream pierced the still air. The kind of scream that chilled your bones. I pushed up, spotted the woman near my car—one of the two women from earlier—and followed her gaze to the driver standing next to his open door, pointing his pistol at a man huddled on the ground. Where did that guy come from? He held up an arm, trying to protect himself. They were both cloaked in darkness. Words were exchanged, but I couldn't hear what was said. The thug was going to kill the man.

I kicked open the door, jumped out of the car, and yelled at the top of my lungs. The shooter swung around and fired his gun without even looking. I lunged for a row of trees lining the back of the narrow parking lot. I felt the breeze of a bullet whiz by my forehead, clip a tree trunk, and spray tiny chunks of bark into my eyes.

I took a breath and realized the shooting had stopped. But that sense of relief lasted only a second. I lifted my eyes and saw the shooter turn back to the man, who was now crawling away. I also noticed a shopping cart turned on its side. I leaped out of my stance and screamed, "No!" It must have scared the shooter, who lurched just as his gun fired.

The man on the ground cried out, grabbing at his leg. I ran at the shooter, screaming, waving my arms, determined to stop this madness. He turned, aimed his gun right at my chest. I screamed louder, dodged left and right, but kept running toward him. I hoped I was freaking him out, scaring him. He shuffled closer to his door and jerked the pistol at me, but nothing happened. I saw a guy's head pop up on the other side of the car. He was yelling at his buddy to go. The shooter glanced at the other guy, but then turned back and tried to shoot me again. The gun didn't fire—he must have run out of bullets.

Out of nowhere, I saw a blunt object a second before it connected with my head. I literally saw stars, then my knees slammed to the concrete. My vision was blurred, but I still saw the car race away, fishtailing around the corner.

A moment later, the woman ran up to the man who'd been shot. She put her hands to her face and cried. My efforts had been for naught. An innocent man had died.

Twenty-Five

The ambulance driver flipped on his siren, carefully negotiated the massive pothole, and drove off to the hospital. I was leaning against a police cruiser, holding an ice pack to my head as I watched the screaming woman from earlier sob uncontrollably in the arms of her friend.

The woman's name was Janet Patterson, I'd learned. She was twenty-four, a recent graduate of the UT School of Arts. Her first art show was scheduled for the next night. The two women had a blanket around them, huddled between two officers. Fog pumped into the nighttime air like a sea of smokestacks. The temperature must have dropped another ten degrees in the last hour.

"She's really upset, but at least she has a friend, Ozzie." Brook gingerly touched my elbow as my eyes shifted to the shopping cart still lying on its side at the mouth of the parking lot, empty tin cans scattered around it. Officers and CSI techs were milling about, scanning the ground for evidence. They had already bagged the object that had smacked my head—a full sixteen-ounce beer.

I wasn't sure when Janet would be able to fully recover mentally from this trauma. I hoped she would get help. But nearly all of my concern was for Sam, the man who was shot in the leg…the same man who'd shined shoes outside of the Novak and Novak office building for more years than I could recall. Due to loss of blood, Sam had gone into what one of the paramedics called hypovolemic shock. He'd opened his eyes briefly when I had dragged myself over to him earlier. He muttered words that no one heard, but I could read his lips: "I was just looking for some spare cans so I could make a few dollars on the side, Oz. Damn, I guess luck isn't on my side." Then his eyes flickered and shut.

"I hope like hell that Sam is going to make it."

Brook nodded, let out a tired breath. "These drive-by shootings are so senseless. The perps are usually young, cocky, and just trying to prove something. They don't give a shit about human lives."

"I don't think it was a random drive-by shooting."

She'd just turned to watch her colleagues near the shopping cart and scattered empty cans. She stopped moving for a second, then slowly turned to me. "What are you saying, Ozzie?"

I told her to hold on a minute. I walked over to my car, asked one of the CSI techs if I could look for a personal item, and, given the okay, I pulled the item out. When I turned, Brook was standing right there. I almost plowed into her.

"What is this?" she asked as I held the note in front of her face. She mouthed the content of the note and said, "I'll ask you again: what is this?"

I explained that I'd found the note attached to my car in the parking garage earlier when she dropped me off. "That, along with a little present." I pointed at my back tire.

"They put a donut on your car?"

I didn't laugh. My face was so cut up from the shards of glass that it hurt to stretch the skin. "They slashed my tire, Brook. It kind of goes with the theme. First they threaten me, and then, apparently, they try to kill me."

She raked her fingers through her hair, then put her hands at her waist. "Jesus H. Christ. This was no random shooting."

"I already said that."

"This changes everything." She glanced at the note, then up at me. "Why didn't you call me when you found this? We could have tried to get prints off the paper."

I was expecting that question, but I didn't have a good answer. "I don't know. I was just pissed and wanted to fix my car and leave. It was irrational. And now…I wish I had called you. Then maybe Sam wouldn't have been shot." I blew out a breath, dropped my hands to my side.

She took the ice pack from my hand and put it against my head. "Believe me, you need the ice."

"I got this injury from a can of Schlitz."

"How did that happen?"

"I think the guy in the passenger seat chucked it at me. Some luck I have, huh?" I winced as I grabbed hold of the ice pack. "Schlitz. I didn't think people still drank that piss water." I was trying to change the topic, anything to keep my mind off the fact that my action, or rather, inaction, had likely led to an innocent person being shot and possibly killed. I went to my second tactic and bit into the side of my cheek, keeping my emotions at bay.

"Listen, Oz, in my line of work, you second-guess yourself all the time. But it's useless. We can't predict human behavior. Certainly not the kind where people just start shooting a gun at random people. Frickin' nutjobs."

"You're right. They came after me, but Sam just happened to be in the wrong place at the wrong time."

Police had checked his ID earlier and learned that Sam lived just a couple of blocks away. They called his home and found out he was living with his sister's family. They were going to head out to meet the ambulance at the hospital.

Brook spoke to some other officers, then led me over to the sidewalk so her colleagues could continue doing their work.

She held up the note and read it out loud: "*Your dad died for a reason. You will too, if you don't stop snooping.* What do you think they're talking about here?"

I tried to pull my thoughts off the replay of the shooting, of seeing Sam on the ground. "I…I'm not really sure." I wanted to rub my face, but as soon as I touched it, I was zapped with a sharp sting from one of the cuts.

She looked off for a second, then back at me. "This note is implying that your dad was indeed murdered. As you know, we've yet to see evidence of that fact. Maybe we missed something. Maybe the video from the hospital will identify the perp. But how many people admit to murder? Not many, in my experience, that's for damn sure. This note is essentially doing just that."

The intensity in her voice was palpable. She was feeling the heat that would likely come as the note was shared with others in the APD.

"Doesn't sound like you're too convinced that you'll find anything in the hospital surveillance video that points us to the killer."

"I think it could go one of two ways. Either it comes up blank, which means we have no idea if they're just taking the opportunity to take credit for the murder, when in reality he simply died. Or the murderer was absolutely brazen, the kind of guy who would stare at the camera, flip it off, and then go put some drug in your dad's IV or something like that."

I huffed out a breath, which sent a stabbing pain straight to the bump on my head.

"So, Oz, for starters, don't tell a person about this note. Got it?"

She was good at giving orders. "Yes ma'am." I sounded like I was mocking her, but I wasn't. I was just tired and beaten down by everything.

"Okay, back to the note and what this means and who might be behind this…" She set her feet shoulder-width apart and stared at me. Maybe she thought there was something I hadn't told her. If that was the case, she'd be right. It was Ray. I'd brought him in to try to figure out who Dad's client was. But Ray was one of the best at his line of work, from what Dad had told me. It was hard to imagine that he would have been compromised, especially so quickly. He was still waiting on me to get him Dad's email-account information. He did say that he would talk to some of my coworkers and even some of Dad's old buddies. Was one of them connected to the person behind this? Possibly. I had to talk to Ray, to share the note—yes, the exact opposite of what Brook had just asked of me. I had to find out whom he'd spoken to and if he believed any of them might be connected to Dad's mystery client, his death, or this shooting. The list of tragedies was growing by the hour.

"What are you thinking, Oz? Come on, don't hold anything back."

I knew I had to, at least for now. "I'm guessing that someone found out that I brought you, the APD, in to investigate Dad's death."

"And that's it? You haven't done any other snooping?"

I shrugged. "What can I do? Dad told me he didn't keep any record of this client."

"You know this changes everything. I need to start questioning people at the firm, your mother, Bianca, everyone, to find out what they know about your dad's work. This investigation just got bigger. I'm going to need a lot more help."

She ran her fingers through her hair, brought up her phone, and started typing out a message. I wasn't sure if she was asking her superiors for more support or what. The next thing I knew, someone hugged me from the side, nearly knocking me over. My ribs felt a prick. "Your name is Ozzie, right?" It was Janet Patterson, tears in her eyes.

I tried grunting out a response, but she spoke first. "You saved that man's life. Sam's. If you hadn't tried to distract that shooter, Sam would have died. Thank you, thank you, thank you." She squeezed so hard it hurt my ribs…again, but I didn't say anything.

I patted her on the back of her head. "I just hope Sam makes it."

She cried more. Her friend came over and joined us as a VW bus drove up. Tito hopped out with two trays full of coffees.

"Just in time, my friend," I said.

Tito handed out the coffees to APD's finest and then finished up where we were standing.

"You're the greatest, Tito," Brook said. "The guys all appreciate it too, even if they didn't say anything," She sipped her coffee.

"It's the least I can do, Detective." He turned his sights and scanned the scene, shaking his head. "Man, I've lived here for over five years, and I've never had a shooting or anything violent take place here before."

"I've only been your roommate for two nights," I said, tongue-in-cheek. While I tried to be funny, the comment just sat there. As Janet and her friend drifted over to the grass, Brook, Tito, and I traded glances.

"Listen, Tito, it might be wise if I find a cheap motel until I can find more permanent digs."

"What? That's nuts, Oz."

"Tito, they were after me. They left me a note earlier." I could feel Brook's eyes on me, and I addressed her for just a moment. "I'm living at his place. He needs to understand the kind of danger he's in."

"Pfft," he said.

I turned back to him. "This isn't a joke, Tito." I took the note from Brook and let him read it. His facial expression didn't change. I said, "They used real bullets. Sam was shot and may lose his life."

He handed the note back to Brook and said to me, "Did you invite them over for a late-night dessert?"

"Do what?" I wondered if he'd added some whiskey to his coffee.

"You didn't ask them to shoot you, right? You didn't put a hit on anyone in their gang, right?"

Gang. A thought zipped into my mind, and I turned to Brook. "There is one thing that I just remembered. This could help us figure out who shot Sam, who could be behind the threats against me, maybe who murdered Dad."

Twenty-Six

Before this moment, the most recent woman who had taken me by the hand and led me anywhere had been my wife, Nicole. And that was when she'd taken me into the bedroom and rocked my world. Well, I'd also done my best to uphold my end of the bargain. She'd even told me as much.

While I now questioned the authenticity of every loving moment we'd shared, what I was currently experiencing was nothing like that. And Brook was nothing like Nicole, version one or two.

"You too," Brook snapped at Tito, indicating for him to follow us. We made our way inside Tito's building and headed up to his loft. The moment Tito turned on the lights, Brook had a difficult time focusing on the matter at hand.

"You did all of this?" She swung her finger left and right.

"I painted every one of them, yes." He smiled, brought his thick fingers behind his back in an "aw, shucks" kind of way.

I was more inclined to focus on being dragged away from the gathering downstairs. "Brook, what's going on? The word 'gang' comes up, and you start to freak."

"I didn't freak." She set a hand on her hip.

I wasn't going to challenge her. "Okay. You became tense, concerned."

She sipped her coffee, found a small corner of a table, and set it down. "It wasn't as much the word 'gang' that got my attention as it was who you were describing."

My recollection of the shooter had included him wearing a shirt that was white with blue and gold trim. It reminded me, I said, of a Rams football jersey. "We don't work for the APD. Can you give us some insight?"

"Lately, Austin, like a lot of cities, has had a rash of crimes associated with a notorious gang called MS-13." She moved her head from me to Tito and then back.

"And?"

"MS-13 is like a small army. There could be as many as ten thousand members across the nation. They're ruthless and attract real maggots to their cause."

"You think the guy who shot at me is a member of that gang?"

"I'd bet my badge on it."

She went on to explain that Kurt Warner's 13 football jersey was often used by gang members as a sign of solidarity, given the name of the gang. "They'll also use other numbers that add up to thirteen. Sometimes it will be shown through tattoos. Or maybe two guys who are tight…one will wear a jersey with the number one, and the other guy will wear a jersey with the number three, or maybe a six and a seven. Most people don't notice unless they are aware of the gang symbols."

Tito walked across the loft, turned on a couple of other lights, picked up something from his bar, and walked back over to us. I focused on Brook. "So, why were you so concerned when I brought it up?"

"The MS-13 gang has a lot of the characteristics of a terrorist group. Domestic, international…it makes no difference. They prey on the young, the uneducated, those who feel like they have no way out. And for law enforcement, what makes it extremely difficult is that they have sympathizers in a lot of places. You think you're getting close, you think you have an eyewitness, and then the next thing you know, that witness forgets what he saw or heard, or even worse, he simply disappears." She stopped, her eyes probing mine. I think she wanted to tell me more, but I was guessing she wasn't authorized.

"These sympathizers are, say, on the fringe of the gang, maybe family members and friends?"

"Yes." She lifted her chin slightly. "And more."

I paused, wondering if she would say what I was thinking. She didn't.

"Law enforcement," I said.

She nodded again, appearing hesitant to admit it verbally, as if someone might be recording our conversation. That would be ludicrous. "Including *your* police department?"

A slow nod as she sighed. "No definitive proof, but I've heard that the brass is concerned."

She paused a second as Tito edged closer, holding a frame against his chest. He motioned for her to continue.

The sound of Brook's voice pulled my eyes back to her.

"They're not sure how to deal with it. If they open an internal investigation, something this salacious would likely be leaked— the press apparently has contacts on the inside as well. So, from what my captain told me, if even the possibility of such a thing gets out, then public trust in the department will be ruined. After that, it could result in chaos on the street."

"And then the gangs would win again," I said.

She flicked her fingers against my arm. "Now you know why I wanted to talk to you privately." She took out her phone, started thumbing a note, adding, "I know you're staring."

"Looking intently," I joked.

"This is how I remember stuff. I send myself a text message."

I was about to ask her how progress could be made in finding the shooters when I realized Tito hadn't said much. He was still standing there with a frame against his chest. His vacant expression told me he wasn't amused with our banter. In fact, I wondered if he'd heard us at all.

"You okay?"

His eyes snapped back to attention. "Uh, yeah."

"What do you have there?" Brook asked, dipping her head toward the frame he gripped tightly.

He swallowed hard, reset his feet. I recalled that he wore something close to a size-seventeen shoe in high school.

"My, uh…" he garbled, his voice full of emotion. He cleared his throat.

I said, "Tito, you don't have to—"

"Yeah, I do," he said, his moist eyes shifting to me. "I need to, Oz."

We gave him a moment to gather himself. This enormous, kindhearted man needed every second. Finally, without saying a word, he flipped the frame around. It was Tito back in the day, a huge smile on his face, his arm wrapped around a younger kid.

"Your brother," I said, noticing the similar body types.

"Jamal was only fifteen." He enunciated every syllable as if these would be the most important words he would ever utter.

My heart sank, but I kept my eyes on him. This wasn't about me.

"Tito, I had no idea," Brook said. "How did it happen?"

He swallowed hard. "When I moved out of the house, he started running with the wrong crowd. Dad was long gone; Mom was working two jobs. No one was around to keep him out of trouble."

He wiped tears from his face, rocking back and forth on his feet. "He got in trouble a couple of times, suspended from school, kicked off the football team. I tried talking to him, but I wasn't sure I was getting through that thick skull of his." Tito poked a beefy finger into the side of his head, and it wasn't a gentle poke. More tears from the big man.

"You can't put it on yourself, my friend."

He shook off my comment, took a couple of heavy breaths. He had to get it out, it seemed. "I thought he was doomed. I actually braced myself for the worst. But then, a friend of his died of an overdose. And that was Jamal's wake-up call."

Tito broke off his faraway stare and focused on me and Brook. It was as though he hoped that, by reliving this horrific story, somehow it would end differently. I felt a lump in my throat.

"Jamal told me in our last phone conversation that he was done with the thug life. He said he was going to beg his way back into school and tell his so-called brothers that he was done with it. Three nights later," he said with a shaky voice, "he was shot. Word is the gang or group of thugs, or whatever you want to call them, told him he'd never be able to leave. He apparently told them to go to hell, and they just..." He gasped. I put my arm on his shoulder, but he held up his picture. "They just shot him like he was a possession, something they owned."

Brook and I both said how sorry we were, but I knew it had to feel so hollow to Tito. Nothing would bring back his brother. After a few seconds, Brook couldn't help herself. "Did they catch the scum who did this?"

He pressed his lips hard against his front teeth. "Nope. Detectives thought they had someone who could name the shooter, but then the witness just disappeared. No one would say where he went. The fear of reprisal from fellow gang members stomped down the whole investigation. It was like something straight out of Kabul or Aleppo."

He asked for a moment to gather himself and went to the bathroom. A minute later, with his tears dried up, he returned. He was no longer holding the frame. "I didn't mean to get so emotional, but I guess the pain is still just below the surface. So, I know the dangers of gang violence and the ripple effect it can have on a community. We can't bury our heads in the sand and think everything is fine." He swung his sights to his paintings, finally focusing on Brook. "My painting of all things Christmas has allowed me to find some happiness in a world where some people want the exact opposite. It's all about hate. I refuse to give in to that hate. But at the same time, we need you, the cops, to find these gutless thugs and put them behind bars."

"I'll do everything I can, Tito," Brook said, intensity in her tone.

Twenty-Seven

We made our way back downstairs. I saw the two ladies from earlier speaking to someone near the yellow police tape. Brook split off to speak to one of the crime-scene investigators as I took in the condition of my car from a different angle. It had several bullet holes, and one window had been blown out by a bullet meant for me. "I might need to find a rental car," I said to no one.

"You can borrow the Tube," Tito said.

I followed his gaze over to his green VW bus. Not exactly my style. But the development of my so-called "style" was before my life had cratered before my very eyes. Now, I was lucky to have a friend who wanted to help. Besides, I still had no access to my money, so renting anything might be difficult. "I appreciate the offer, Tito." I popped him on his back.

Brook walked right past me, making a beeline for the two ladies over at the police tape. I could see them talking to a guy with glasses and a notepad. He was short and wore the odd combination of a sweater vest and a shiny pair of running shoes, like a cross between academia and a triathlete. Curious as to what had grabbed Brook's attention, I found myself being pulled in that direction. I was about halfway when I saw her extend an arm toward the man.

"Did you hear me, asshat? I said *no comment.*" She put her hand on his chest.

I shuffled closer, hoping to save her from being baited into doing something she'd later regret.

"Asshat. That's original," the man said.

Janet Patterson swung around the moment I got to the tape, whispering to me, "I hope we didn't do anything wrong. We were just answering his questions."

Crap. This guy had to be with the press. I put my hand on Brook's arm. She shook it off and held a finger up near the chin of this guy. He shoved it away.

"Just because you wear a badge doesn't give you the authority to treat me like I'm pond scum," the man said, bowing out his chest.

"Hold on, you two," I said, moving between them. I looked up, wondering if anyone would jump in to assist me. No one in a uniform seemed to notice or care.

"Pond scum," Brook said, talking around me. "The name fits you perfectly."

"You can call me every name in the book, Detective Pressler, but that won't change a damn thing as to what I write about." He put his hand to his chin, looking up to the sky in a mocking way. "Maybe we could add a nice sidebar story to this gang shooting. The headline will say something like, 'Detective Loses Temper, Assaults Innocent Citizen.'"

Brook began to cuss so fast I thought she might have been an auctioneer in a previous life.

"Guys, can we just agree to disagree and part ways before someone loses their cool?" I suggested.

That instantly silenced Brook. She took a breath, then looked my way. A few seconds passed, and I wondered if she might deck me for butting in. Then her lips turned upward, and she giggled. "Damn, Oz, your timing is something else."

"Glad I could help ease the tension. I think."

I was introduced to Tracy Rowlett, crime reporter for the *Austin American-Statesman*. His name sounded familiar. He dialed back the intensity, and they both chilled out as they actually traded a couple of stories about previous crime scenes. Usually, I might find that type of conversation interesting, but not after being shot at and seeing Sam sent off to the hospital with his life in jeopardy. Plus, I had too much on my mind, wondering what event or person had triggered this retaliation against me. Of course, the note and subsequent shooting basically confirmed it—my dad had been murdered. I knew the key to finding the person who killed him started with finding his mystery client. From there, I could hopefully learn what Dad was actually doing on behalf of this client, and what compelled his client—or someone working on his behalf—to kill my dad.

Saying those words, even in my own mind, brought about an array of emotions. Sadness, anger, and a feeling of emptiness. He wasn't my biological dad, but in his own way, he'd been there for me, taught me the ways of life.

A lump formed in my throat. I shifted my eyes to Brook. Now that she was in the loop, I should be able to back off and let the law-enforcement machine take over. She had resources and access to information that I didn't, starting with the video from the hospital. That would hopefully yield the key piece of evidence regarding who had murdered my dad. His heart hadn't been well. That much was rather obvious. I then thought about the what-ifs. What if he had gone through rehab, changed his habits, maybe even moved to part-time or left the firm altogether to reduce his stress? He could have lived a long time just playing golf every other day. Sure, maybe someday I would have taken over the firm, but with him now gone, the thought of that seemed beyond selfish.

With Brook and Rowlett still playing nice, I turned to quietly walk back inside. I needed to sleep. Or try to sleep.

"Mr. Novak, one more thing…"

I flipped back around and didn't hide my eye roll. "Yeah?"

"Can you confirm for me if this was an MS-13 drive-by?"

"Mr. Novak is…was my father. I'm Ozzie. But I can't answer that question. That's her territory." I looked at Brook.

"You don't have to answer that," she said quickly before realizing I'd essentially passed the baton to her. She then turned back to Tracy. "And I have no comment. So, that's your official statement, Tracy. Give us some time, and we'll provide an update on the investigation. We're not miracle workers."

I nodded and made my second attempt at walking away. But the crime dog clamped a hand on my forearm. He happened to hit a cut.

"Ouch," I said, removing his hand as I gnashed my teeth.

"Maybe you have another story to tell me, Mr. Novak. Did you possibly screw these gang members on a drug buy?"

Brook leaned closer to me. "It appears the cease-fire is officially over."

"Hey, I'm just doing my job," Rowlett said. "You guys look at me like I'm the bad guy. I'm the voice of the people. If it weren't for people like me, then the public would be given a line of PR bullshit."

He had a point, but now wasn't the time to jump on his bandwagon. "Your drug angle is wrong, Mr. Rowlett. Let's just leave it at that and let the cops do their job, okay?" My voice sounded like I'd smoked half a pack of cigarettes. I was tired as hell.

"Then what are you doing in this part of the city?" the reporter asked, flipping a page in his notebook before pointing his pen hand at me. "We've seen an uptick in drug-related crime all over the city. It's like there's some type of squeeze going on."

"I'm staying with my friend. As for analyzing the latest crime stats, I'm not the right person to ask."

I flipped around and walked off, even as he continued quizzing me about my friend and if he had any connections to gangs or might be part of a drug-dealing network. I resisted the urge to run back and jab his pen into the side of his neck or, better yet, to let Tito come over and pile-drive his head into the ground, like he used to do to quarterbacks in high school. Instead, I kept walking as my eyes were drawn to my shot-up car.

That was exactly how I felt inside. Full of bullet holes and smashed glass.

Twenty-Eight

I spent most of the night volleying between things I should do. Or not do. Figure out if or how I should continue pressing to find my dad's killer. If I should call Nicole and talk to her for the first time in days. The mental exercise, which I thought would put me to sleep, had the opposite effect. It was as though someone had shot me up with an IV bag full of caffeine. My pulse skyrocketed, and sleep was nothing more than a pipe dream.

"You want me to rustle up some eggs for you, Oz, before I head out?" It was morning, and Tito was moving with the quickness of a deer. He was in constant motion as I sat on the edge of the couch and rubbed my eyes, wondering if I could conjure up some semblance of energy.

"Uh, no thanks. I'll grab something when I head out."

He stopped for a moment. I looked up and saw that he had two paintings in his arms. "Yeah, about using the Tube today... I have a new art show tonight, and I've got a lot of errands to run to get ready for it. You want to ride shotgun? Along the way, I could maybe squeeze in a couple of stops for you. I'm sure you've got a lot on your plate."

I emptied my lungs. I felt like an idiot for temporarily forgetting my car had been impounded by the cops. Who knew when I'd get it back? On top of that, I wasn't sure if my credit cards would work. Still, I said, "I'm good, Tito. Thanks for the offer and all. I'll grab a cab or something. You've done enough already."

"Well, if you change your mind, give me a call. And I know you have a lot of shit going on, but if you have time tonight, I hope you'll drop by the grand opening of my new exhibit. I'll text you the address."

"Do that. I'll make it a point to show up."

"By the way, hot coffee is in the kitchen. Help yourself."

He gave me a wink and headed out the door. I dragged my aching bag of bones to the bathroom and stood under a hot shower for a good twenty minutes, hoping to gain some clarity on what the hell I could, or should, do.

It worked. When I came out and loaded up on some coffee, I had enough energy to feel like I'd get something accomplished, hopefully on both fronts—with my dad and with my soon-to-be ex-wife. Sitting around the loft and staring at a TV would only bring about another night of worry and restless sleep.

Step one was to talk to Ray. I felt fairly certain his initial probing had alerted Dad's killer, or someone close to the killer, that I was questioning his death. His digging had apparently broken the seal on the scum bottle. Did I think that Dad's mystery client was someone in the ranks of MS-13? Not likely. But perhaps someone had a connection to that group, aware that members of the gang had been known to carry out brutal acts without a second thought. Plus, thanks to Stacy, I now had Dad's personal email-account information to pass along.

I put in a text to Ray and waited a couple of minutes. No response. Then I dialed his cell-phone number. Of course, it rolled to voicemail. I didn't want to get into the sensitive details of why I called, so I left a short message and asked him to call me.

Before I went down the path with Nicole, I called to get an update on Sam. He was stable and would likely be okay. *Something in the world is still right*, I thought.

I thumbed through my contacts and found the one for Nicole. I had real questions for her about having access to my money…well, our money, so that I could find my own place to live, get my car fixed, and eat on occasion. But my mind went straight to the note I'd found on her desk.

The gleam of your beautiful smile is only eclipsed by the blaze of your red-hot passion. Every time you look at these flowers, think of my body against yours.

C

A poisoned dose of reality quickly drained twenty percent off the top of my adrenaline. Every bit of news in that part of my life was being absorbed as a body blow, as opposed to just another noteworthy data point. Sure, it was understandable, but it sure as hell wasn't sustainable. I had to find the middle ground of being human, yet buffer myself from being impaled every time I learned more information or thought about the past.

I loved to swim. In a pool, in Lady Bird Lake, at Barton Springs Pool—the temperature was never higher than sixty-eight—and even in the ocean. Sure, I'd been a lifeguard and competed some through our country club and school swim teams, but it wasn't the competition that drove me. It was finding that perfect balance of thinking through things in my life—whether it be about one of my clients or something more personal—without those thoughts disrupting my breathing. As a swimmer, breaking your breathing cadence was akin to losing a wheel in the Daytona 500. If it happened, you couldn't recover. You were toast. I needed to find that sweet spot right now, outside of the water. My swimming mindset.

Move forward, I told myself. I reached my thumb for the little green circle, but just before I dialed Nicole, my phone buzzed. It was a text from Ray. I switched over and read it.

Sorry about missing ur call. I'm stuck in a meeting with a client. One of those husband-cheating investigations. The wife's a mess. Why don't u drop by this afternoon? We can talk about what I've learned.

It seemed like he had some progress to share. Of course, he had no idea that I'd been shot at and my life threatened. Lots for us to discuss. I locked down our meeting time as early as I could make it.

I'll drop by at 1.

No sooner had I finished my text than he sent off a quick reply.

Better make it 3. I have a new client coming in around 1. New clients are the most unpredictable with my time. Later.

I confirmed the midafternoon time slot with Ray, then walked into the kitchen to clean out my empty mug and the coffeepot. In other words, I was finding something to occupy my time before I called Nicole.

Dammit, Oz, get over it, or her. She's just a woman.

"Right. The most beautiful, caring soul you've ever met," I said out loud.

The sound of my voice nearly made me laugh. As I dried off the coffee pot, I punched up her number before I could talk myself out of it.

"Yes." She sounded in a rush, exasperated.

"It's me, Ozzie."

"I know your number. It's still a contact in my phone. How can I help you?"

You're swimming in the frigid waters at Barton Springs, in the middle of a fifty-lap workout. Maintain the form of your stroke and in no way allow her to—and I say this with the intention of using a pun—don't allow her to take your breath away.

"It's nice to talk to you, Nicole." I paused, if for no other reason than to let her know she had a choice about being rude. She said nothing in response, which told me that she knew she was, as my mom would sometimes say, "being an itch with a capital B."

"So, thank you for allowing me to pick up my stuff."

A nice compliment to try to throw her off her bitch perch.

"Uh, sure." She was abrupt, but at least it wasn't combative.

Point for me, or at least my sanity.

I tried to continue the win streak. "During this time while we're separated and working through the process of finalizing our divorce, I'd like to figure out a way where I can have access to some money for living expenses."

Can't get any more non-confrontational than that, I thought.

"Well…" She sighed, which, in our past life, told me she was stressed about something at work. But at this moment, what could be causing her stress, other than unwrapping her fingers from some cash so that I wouldn't have to continue mooching off of Tito?

"I don't think you should have a problem right now," she said.

"I'm not sure I'm following you."

"The credit cards. At least one of them should be turned on now and working like a charm." She sounded like a second-grade teacher on the first day of school. Everything was happy and perky.

"That's a good sign," I said, trying to maintain a positive vibe. "Can you tell me which one so I don't have to worry about a card bouncing on me when I'm buying pots and pans at Target?"

"You act like you're above buying things at Target. Not all of us come from such a wealthy family."

Left uppercut just connected into my already bruised ribs. I blew out a breath, concentrating on not taking the full brunt of the blow. But I was still taken aback. Was that her big beef with me, that my family had money? That was not exactly new news. She had been raised in a blue-collar family, from what little I knew. Her father had died of lung cancer from working the coal mines in West Virginia, and her mom had worked odd jobs just to keep the lights on. She had died prematurely as well, apparently after drinking enough vodka to cause her kidneys to fail.

Nicole had told me early on that she didn't want money to drive our every decision, nor did she have any desire to live a life that was all about our status. She wanted us to be defined by how we treated others, not by materialistic gain. It was one of the things I loved most about her.

I tried not to address the personal dig. "If you don't know which credit card, I'll just use the process of elimination, I guess."

"Okay."

That was an odd answer. But then again, I'd been doing backflips to make sure I kept my cool and didn't let her strikes pierce a vital organ.

There was an awkward silence. "Okay," I said just to hear someone say something. "How do you want to handle the bills at the house?"

"I'll figure it out and let you know."

She'll let me know. My pulse couldn't help but tick faster on that comment. I tried to alter the statement. "Okay, how about you take a first stab at it, and then I'll provide feedback." I didn't go to law school for nothing.

"Well—"

I had to break in. "And while we're at it, I need to create my own bank accounts, so don't be surprised if I take out half the money and create my own account."

"Uh…" That one utterance sounded as if I'd left her homeless. She said, "You can just use the money from your paychecks for now. We'll settle everything else through the lawyers."

"I guess you haven't heard."

"Heard what, Ozzie? You're giving me a headache."

Keep that swimmer's mindset. "The firm is being sold off in chunks."

"Perfect. You can use the proceeds from the sale. You see, I'm not such a bitch after all. But try to be frugal with it, please. Just remember that half the money you're spending is mine."

"Wish it were that easy. I think you recall that I'm not a partner in the firm."

"Oh yeah, that's right."

Now she was playing naïve? I suddenly felt like I was talking to a used-car salesman. Actually, that sounded disparaging to anyone who earned an honest living selling used cars.

My phone buzzed. It was a text from Stacy.

Do you need a pick-me-up? How about we meet for lunch?

Damn, she had good timing. "Hey, Nicole, I have to go. Just wanted you to know about the withdrawal I'm going to make from our joint account."

Before she could say another word, I told her she could call or text when she had something to share, and then I ended the call.

I'd survived. Barely. But a win was a win, even if it was a narrow victory. I typed in a text to Stacy and told her to pick the spot and I'd meet her there.

Twenty-Nine

Thankfully, Franklin's barbeque was less than a mile from Tito's loft, just east of I-35 on 11th Street. A blustery wind blew leaves into mini twisters along my path, but the walk was just what my lungs needed. A block away from the joint, I picked up the sweet aroma of barbecue. My mouth was already watering by the time I walked in and spotted Stacy sitting in an old wooden booth.

She jumped to her feet and was about to give me a hug when a grimace crossed her face. "What happened?"

"I cut myself shaving?" I shrugged, trying to make light of my minor injuries from the previous night.

Knowing my sense of humor, she simply tilted her head and flicked her fingers. "Spill it, Ozzie."

I first encouraged her to take a seat, and we ordered our meals and soft drinks. "I would ask you to keep this to yourself, but it might be in today's paper or even on the news. Someone shot at me last night."

She gasped, accidentally knocking her fork and knife off the table. "For the love of God, are you okay?" She scanned my body, as if I might be hiding another injury.

"I wasn't hit. I have superhero powers. You're actually having lunch with Bruce Wayne," I said with a wink.

She didn't laugh. In fact, she appeared to thumb a tear out of the corner of her eye.

"I didn't mean to make you upset, Stacy."

"It's just that we already lost your father. We can't lose you too."

I put my hand on top of hers. "I guess someone upstairs thinks I have something to offer, so I'll be around a little longer."

"Who are these people that tried to kill you? And what is really going on?"

Our waiter, with a dirty apron and skin that mimicked the barbecue on our plates, delivered our food. I pulled a piece of meat off the rib. It melted in my mouth before I had a chance to chew. The door to the restaurant dinged open, and I caught a little tick in my breath until I saw it was a couple of college kids walking in. I was jumpy, and I had every right to be. I'd been the target of a hit. Thankfully, Sam's condition had improved. But the reality was that the two thugs who'd tried to kill me had failed. Would they try a second time? Or would they and this person who'd hired them—that was my running theory—crawl into a hole now that the APD was involved? All of this made me wonder if I was putting Stacy in danger simply by having lunch with her.

"What's wrong, Ozzie? Something's on your mind. I can see it in your eyes."

I finished chewing my mouthful of ribs, then washed it back with a gulp of Diet Coke. I scanned the well-known, laid-back joint. It was bustling with people, but no one seemed to be looking our way. "Before the shooting, I found a note left on my car last night telling me to back off from snooping into Dad's death. *Or else.*"

Her mouth opened, and then, slowly, she brought a hand up to cover it.

"Oh yeah, for good measure, they also slashed my tire. I wasn't happy. In fact, I was quite pissed. I changed my tire and headed over to Tito's place."

"Tito? Tito Jackson? And I thought I knew everything about you."

A knot formed in my gut, which didn't settle well with my barbeque. If I told her the complete truth, then I'd have to open up about why I was at Tito's place. I'd yet to go public with my new Facebook status—separated from Nicole but not looking. I had to start sharing that part of my life, especially with those closest to me. I gave her the thirty-second elevator version.

"I don't know what to say. It's just so unexpected, Oz. You and Nicole…I just thought you'd…"

"I did too. I did too." I sighed unexpectedly, but then went back to my drink, trying to move my mind off of Nicole. "But the good news is I changed a tire. First time since high school. I think I might be asked to join a pit crew."

A smile formed at the edge of her lips. "I know you're like your father. Not exactly mechanically inclined and all."

I tried to match her smile, but I didn't get there.

"You're not joking about this note. Someone threatened you?"

I nodded. A tear ran down the side of her cheek. She picked up her napkin and wiped it away.

Our waiter, who was walking by with a tray of food for a nearby table, slowed down and glanced at Stacy, then at me. It appeared he thought I was making her upset.

"We're good. Thank you," I said, trying to calm his unease.

He squinted one eye and kept walking. Not sure my words did much for him.

I turned back to Stacy. "I think it's rather clear that the people who wrote the note followed me to Tito's, where they knew they wouldn't have a ton of witnesses, and… Crap. I almost forgot to tell you about Sam."

"You're talking about Sam, the guy who's been shining shoes outside our building since before George W. lived in Austin? What on earth could he have to do with any of this?"

I explained how I'd seen him get shot, how he'd been at the wrong place at the wrong time.

She momentarily pressed her eyes shut and gripped the side of the table. "Our world just seems like it's crumbling, Ozzie."

She'd said what I'd been feeling—this had occurred countless times over the years we'd worked together—but never wanted to admit. I gave her the latest update on his condition. "So, it's looking like he's going to be okay."

"I need to send him some flowers." She fished through her purse and pulled out a small pad with a vase of purple and yellow flowers on the cover. It matched her outfit. She found a pen and made a note. "I'll add in a couple of balloons as well," she said.

"That's nice of you, Stacy. But you're not working for the firm any longer. It's not really your job."

She stopped moving her pen and looked up at me, her face as serious as I'd ever seen it. "This is who I am, Ozzie. I can't control who I am or what I've experienced in my years at the firm. Not everything in my time at Novak and Novak has been perfect. Far from it, as a matter of fact." She pulled in a breath and appeared to try to calm herself. "But kindness and compassion doesn't end just because the company is being sold. It's the right thing to do for Sam."

While part of her delivery seemed a bit intense, to hear her speak of the importance of kindness and compassion was heartwarming, especially when all I saw around me was either some type of vitriol or outright violence. "You're a real sweetheart, Stacy."

She grinned, batting her fake eyelashes a few times. She finished writing her note, then went back to her plate of pork. I made some headway on my ribs. The waiter dropped by and gave us refills on our drinks. "Everything okay?" he asked, his eyes on Stacy.

"Just fine, thank you."

"Let me know if you need anything." He was addressing her, not both of us. With my face cut up and a sizable bruise on my forehead, I was sure I gave off a vibe of someone most people avoided. Whatever. It wasn't as if I were trying to gain a new client.

Yeah, what about that next gig? I'd need to talk to some of my lawyer buddies up at the courthouse to see if they had any openings at their firms. Hell, most of the folks I knew had asked about joining Novak and Novak in the last year. Apparently, many outsiders thought we had the best of both worlds—a smallish firm, but one with financial stability.

Still, something about taking that next step in my career seemed...I don't know, maybe forced? I'd always known I would be a lawyer, because my father was one, and I was endlessly intrigued by all of his stories. Looking back, I felt certain he'd done his fair share of embellishment. Yes, I had convinced myself that helping people, those who really needed someone to stand up for them, was my motivation. How many people, though, had I actually helped?

"Did you lose your appetite?" Stacy asked, jarring me back to the here and now.

I picked up a rib. "I can't let great food go to waste," I said, then proceeded to take a bite.

"So, that email address I gave you... Did you give that to the police? I'm assuming with the threatening note and the shooting, they're going to look into everything?"

I wiped my mouth with my napkin. "I'm sure it will come in handy." I paused a second. "Have you had a visit from—"

"Ray Gartner. The PI we use...well, used to use at the firm. I know him pretty well. He stopped by my place yesterday."

"Good. I'm glad he's making headway."

She looked down for a moment. "You haven't shared everything with the police, have you?"

"More or less, yes."

She gave me the signal that my answer wasn't sufficient.

"Well, I'm the one who demanded that they go to the hospital to investigate my dad's death. Their initial investigation hasn't shown any evidence of a homicide. But now that I've been threatened and shot at because I was snooping into my dad's death, they realize there might be something to my suspicions."

Her face seemed to harden. "And that's it?"

"It isn't that I don't trust the cops. One detective in particular I trust. She's a bit of a bulldog, and that's what I want to see. I also have Ray working the case, since the police have obvious limitations based upon something called the law."

We both chuckled.

"Well, okay. Just let me know what you learn on either front. I care; you know that."

"I do, Stacy. Thank you for caring so much."

We finished our lunch and turned to more mundane topics. The typical questions around "How's your family?" as if we hadn't seen each other in six months. In reality it had been closer to four days. But I learned that when you work with someone every day, you tend not to ask about the routine things, since your collective energy is focused on legal briefs, depositions, and making sure clients pay their legal fees. I found out that Stacy's mom was ill, something about having her gallbladder removed, and she was a little beaten down with taking care of her.

"My mom wasn't a good mother growing up. She was curt, spiteful, and generally no fun to be around. So, I'm having a difficult time being the type of caregiver I know I should be."

I was surprised Stacy could be anything but kind. "Well, give yourself a break. And if anyone knows about parental flaws, it's me. None of our parents are perfect. My mom has issues. My dad certainly had issues. I guess you have to focus on the best parts, since before you know it, they aren't around."

She nodded. "So true." Her eyes wandered away before settling on her half-empty glass that she was twisting. She seemed somewhat conflicted, which was understandable. I decided not to probe further. The waiter arrived with our check. She wanted to pick up the bill, but I insisted.

"This will be the big test to see if Nicole was pulling my leg. The only question is which credit card will work."

I closed my eyes and pulled from a deck of six. "The green one," I said, setting it on a tray and watching the waiter walk off with it.

A moment later, he returned. His scowl told me everything. I pulled out my wallet as he set the tray back on the table. I saw two pieces of paper and a pen. "Come back soon." And then he walked off.

"It worked!" You would have thought I'd just won the lottery. I signed the receipt and walked with Stacy to the door. We agreed to make this a weekly thing. Once outside, she walked to her car, and I waved goodbye from the sidewalk. She then realized I was on foot.

"You're not walking in this weather. Where can I take you?"

I didn't push back against her generosity. I hopped in and gave her directions to Gartner Automotive.

Thirty

I arrived thirty minutes early, but when you have no ride and very little money—none in cash—you have to take what you can get. I thanked Stacy for the ride, and she again asked me to stay in touch with any new details. I hoped Ray would have positive news and continue my lucky streak—yes, I considered my credit card being accepted as a victory.

The main garage door was rolled shut, and I saw only one car in the side lot, a banged-up Ford pickup, whose red color looked like it had been bleached by the wicked Texas sun. I tried the pedestrian door, and it opened. Inside, the lights were on, but there was no buzz of activity. A couple of cars were up on lifts. I bent over to look for human legs but saw none. All the mechanics were gone.

"Is anyone here?" My voice echoed. No one answered. To a degree, it felt like I'd walked right into someone else's home. I flashed on an image of me standing in the office at my former home, reading the love note from "C." The parallels were not lost on me, although I realized my name was actually on the deed of the house that Nicole lived in and where I was no longer welcome. I still had a lot of curiosity about the infamous "C." Well, curiosity that was wrapped around a bundle of seething anger, jealousy, and general disgust.

Perhaps the person behind *C* was only called *C* kind of like *Q* of James Bond fame. I chuckled internally, thankful that I was slowly learning to find humor in life's little jabs.

I made my way around the array of tools and spare tires until I saw Ray's office, and then I stopped. The light was on, but the shades were shut. Was that his red truck outside?

I moved to my left and saw that the door was open, the piles of magazines and newspapers stacked nearly to the ceiling. Not confident I could hear anyone sneak up behind me, I swiveled my head back and forth and padded closer to the office. No one was in the shop. Just before I reached the door, I saw a boot, then a jeaned leg, and then drops of crimson on the concrete floor. I ran inside his office.

"Ray!" I dropped down next to him. He tried to raise an arm. His hand quivered. Was he trying to say something? I leaned over his back but couldn't pick up what he said.

I gently turned him over. "Oh my God," I said. His face was barely recognizable. He had purple bruises on top of other bruises. One eye was completely shut, the other about halfway open. The pupil I could see was dilated, but he seemed catatonic.

"Ray, can you hear me?"

He grunted something, but I couldn't make it out. *Damn my hearing!*

I asked him to repeat what he said. His lips moved, but they were so swollen it was impossible to figure out what he was trying to say.

I quickly looked around the office for a rag or towel, finding none. Ray's face was covered in blood—seeping out of his mouth, his one eye, his nose—with splatters across his beige western shirt. My hands, too, were coated with his blood. I leaned back down to get a closer look at his injuries.

"Holy shit." I swallowed back my barbeque as I examined an ear that appeared to have a chunk taken out.

"Ray, where's a towel around here?"

He lifted his arm toward the window that looked out to the garage. I ran into the garage, stumbled over a hose as I feverishly scanned the place for anything to use to stop the blood. My eyes went to the corner, where there was a foot-high stack of what looked to be recently laundered hand towels. I grabbed the entire pile, found a sink, soaked half of them in water, and ran back into the office. Ray was actually sitting up against the wall.

"You showed up early." He grimaced as he spoke and then touched his jaw.

I put a towel to his ear, and he squealed. "Let me do it."

"Ray, a piece of your ear is missing. What the hell happened?" Drops of sweat trickled off my sideburns.

"Did you see it running out of here? If so, go catch it for me."

At least he still had his sarcasm, so I knew he wasn't too bad off. He took another towel and dabbed his eye, then his nose. "I guess I look pretty fucked up, huh?"

"Let's just say you're not a candidate for the sexiest man alive."

"Have you seen my six-pack?" He patted his paunch, but quickly regretted it.

"Ray, who did this?"

He tried to scoot up some more and grunted. Near his desk, my eyes found a blood-stained tire iron. "Is that what the person used?"

"Does it have teeth?" He tried to chuckle, but he quickly stopped.

I pulled out my phone and punched in nine-one-one.

"Put it away," he said, swatting at my hand. He missed by a good six inches.

"I'm calling the cops. You can give them a description; maybe they can pull a fingerprint. If we're lucky, they can find this fucker before morning."

"You're not calling the cops." Again, he reached for my phone, but he got nothing but air.

I surveyed his pulverized face, the blood that was covering the floor and his clothes. "This is nuts. I need to call the cops." I stood, my thumb on the green button.

"You can't."

"Ray, what are you saying? We need to find whoever did this and have him arrested."

He arched his neck to look up at me. "You do that..." He coughed and then flinched from the pain. "You do that and I'm a dead man."

I slipped my phone into my pocket. He had my attention. First things first: his condition. "I suppose you don't want to go to an ER?"

"Nope."

"How about a first-aid kit?"

"I think Steve's got one mounted on a wall over by the first bay."

I ran into the garage and found the metal box, covered in dust so thick it might have been there since the Beatles had come to America. Back in the office, I opened the box, found bacitracin and a foot-long roll of gauze bandage. He decided to take the lead, starting on his ear. He used up three towels to wipe it clean, applied the antibacterial ointment, and then tried to wrap his ear. I jumped in to help.

"Sorry about the mess," he said.

I began wrapping his ear. "You know who did this to you, don't you?"

"Eh. I'd rather not get into it."

I taped off the bandage. It might hold for a couple of hours, if he was lucky.

"Do you have any ice?"

"Steve has a machine in his office, but I think it's broken."

"Where is everybody?"

"It's a bank holiday. President's Day or something. My brother looks for any reason to take off and go hunting or fishing. And he's known some of these guys for a while, so he lets them take the day off as well."

I wondered if the man who'd assaulted Ray knew that he'd be alone.

He smacked his lips.

"Water. Let me find a cup or something and get you some water from the sink in the garage."

"Hold up. Just hand me the small thermos on the shelf behind my desk."

I found it and handed it to him. He twisted the cap off and took two gulps. "That's some good shit," he said, staring at the thermos.

I pushed some crap to the side and leaned my butt against the side of his desk. "Ray, does this beating have anything to do with you digging into who my dad was working for?"

His one eye looked straight ahead. I waited a moment and then waved a hand in front of his face. "I thought I was the deaf one."

"What?" he barked.

"Are you going to answer me?"

He shook his head.

"You're refusing to answer me?" I was stunned by his stonewalling. "Ray, it's me. I'm not a cop. You can tell me anything."

"Can't."

I stood up. "What the fuck, Ray?"

"Won't."

My head felt like it might explode. "Ray, I'm paying you. You have to tell me."

He glanced up at me. "Don't you remember, I'm doing this pro…?"

"Bono. Oh, right. I forgot."

He scooted his feet underneath him.

"What are you doing?"

"Help me up."

I tried questioning his judgment, but he wouldn't stop, so I did the best I could to help him to his feet as fresh blood made an appearance on his face. Then I got a whiff of his breath. He collapsed into his chair.

"Your thermos has booze in it, not water."

"Really, Sherlock? Damn, your powers of observation are world class."

He wiped more blood from his face as he blinked his one good eye. It appeared he was trying to make it to where he could actually see.

I knew he had important information…information that might cause someone to come back to kill him. I took a breath and thought about another approach.

"Okay, Ray, the cops don't have to know. Not now."

He didn't respond.

"But you need to tell me what's going on. My family members could be in danger."

"Eh, they don't know anything, so they're safe." He placed his arms on his desk and began to shift folders around as if he were searching for something.

"And me?"

He paused and looked up. In his one eye, I saw a web of red. "You need to pretend you didn't find me in this condition. And you need to let this all go."

"What are you saying?"

"We can't bring back your dad, Oz. I'm sorry." He lifted a folder from his desk and grabbed a small key; then he swiveled around to a filing cabinet.

"You know I can't just act like this never happened."

He didn't respond. I could only see him fiddling with the key in the filing cabinet.

"There's something you don't know, Ray."

A second of silence, and then he asked, "What's that?"

"They—maybe the same guys who beat you up—left a note on my car saying I should stop snooping into my dad's death. And then they apparently followed me to my buddy's place and tried to kill me last night. Fired seven or eight rounds. An innocent person was shot in the process."

"Damn." He finally yanked open the drawer, pulled out a backpack, and placed it on his desk. He pointed a finger at me. "This proves my point. There are some things that aren't worth your life or mine. We need to let this go and move on."

Sweat found my wounds and stung my face. With all of the towels being used by Ray, I dabbed my face against my shirt. "You ever heard of the Witness Protection Program?"

He tried to smirk, although his face didn't move much. "Government bureaucracy would take weeks to set that up. Even if I could survive that long—and that's not something I'm willing to risk—who wants to live their life under the thumb of the government? Not me."

He continued riffling through his bag. He pulled out an envelope and looked inside. I saw a wad of cash.

"What are you doing? What's in that bag?"

"Well, if you have to know—and by God, you can't tell a fucking soul—this is what I call my SHTF bag."

I could think of a few acronyms for some of the letters but nothing that made complete sense. "Okay, I won't tell anyone," I said, holding up a hand as if I had just sworn to tell the truth.

"Shit Hit The Fan. That's what this bag is for."

"When shit hits the fan…" I would have laughed had I not been looking at someone whose face had been used as a punching bag. "You've got a lot of cash. What's the plan?"

"To disappear, nimrod. Are you really that dense?"

"To where?"

"What's the old saying? For me to know and you to find out. Only, you won't find out. Hopefully no one will."

"This is crazy, Ray."

"Which part? Me getting pummeled or finally realizing that I can't sit around and hope it goes away?'

I thought about calling Brook. I knew she could help us figure something out. Plus, she might be able to convince Ray to start talking.

"So you're okay with the fact that Dad's killer is going to roam free, live an easy life?"

"Well, I'm hoping that karma catches up. But that's not my call. I got to protect *numero uno*."

"And me?"

"You got anywhere you can go?"

I shrugged. "I got shot at. I don't want to die, but I'm not going to let these fuckers make me fearful of every step I take." I jabbed a finger in his direction as I said this, a new round of perspiration bubbling at my hairline.

"You might regret that decision."

I blew out a disgusted breath.

"Look, Ozzie. If you want to continue going down this path, have at it." He grabbed a portfolio and placed it on the edge of the desk. "I jotted down some notes after some of my discussions with people your dad worked with and knew. It's all yours."

"Thanks," I said with little conviction. I picked it up and thumbed through the first few pages.

"Not much in there, honestly. You'll also see notes on my other current investigations." He twisted a few hairs on his mustache. "Arie told me your firm shut down."

"Yep. He's charged with selling it off. I get nothing, by the way."

"If you're not going to leave town—and don't get me wrong, that's my advice—what are you going to do? Join a new firm?"

"I suppose. Haven't thought about it much. But I have to do something. Nicole seems to have been possessed by the devil. She kicked me out of the house, took away most of my access to our money. I might have to start flipping burgers."

Ray picked up a soiled rag and blotted the cut near his mouth. "If you have any desire, you can take over this business."

"Quit joking, Ray. It's becoming painful."

"I'm not. I'm getting ready to walk out of here. I'll put in one call to my brother and give him a heads-up on what's going on. After that, I'm chucking the phone, finding an unregistered car, and hitting the road. If I'm lucky, by midnight I'll be across the border."

"You're going to Mexico?"

"I hear it's pretty cheap to live down there. You never know—maybe I'll start writing poetry or some shit like that. But then again, I may not go in that direction. It depends."

"On what?"

"On which way the wind is blowing."

I didn't really follow his logic, or his country logic, as the case may be. I looked at the piles of crap around his office and shook my head. "So, all of this, you'll give to me?"

"I know, it's a real gold mine. But if you stay alive long enough, you might be able to do something. You can tell my current clients that I had to leave to go take care of my sick Aunt Betty or something. After a while, they'll forget I ever existed."

"I'd need to get a PI license."

"I suppose. It helps in certain cases." He walked around his desk and held out his hand. I shook it gently.

"Ozzie, you're a brave man for sticking around. Crazy, but brave."

He walked out of the office.

"Hey, do you have keys to this garage?"

He pulled out his key chain, unhooked a key, and tossed it to me. "So you're going to give the PI business a run?"

"Just keeping my options open."

He nodded and took one step, but then he held up. "By the way, the first thing I'd do if I were you would be to put together your own SHTF bag."

"Thanks for the advice, Ray. Good luck."

He walked out of the garage, leaving me all alone, with bloody rags and a lot of questions.

Thirty-One

With his elbows anchored on the armrests of his high-back leather chair—imported from Italy, of course—the man at the top of the organizational food chain steepled his fingers and listened intently to his chief operating officer, a thirty-two-year veteran in the industry.

The silver-haired executive had this annoying tick, where his right eye would blink uncontrollably at the most unpredictable times. As he rattled off the highlights that would be communicated to the Wall Street analysts in the quarterly call the next day, the CEO couldn't help but be distracted by the eye that had a mind of its own.

"Which of my options do you think we should go with, Mr. Drake?" he asked, followed by two quick, involuntary winks.

Drake forced himself to look out the floor-to-ceiling windows to the darkening skies—anything to bite his tongue and not crack a joke about his right-hand man's condition. As he gazed across the Austin skyline that was bordered by Lady Bird Lake to the south and the state capitol on the north, he drew irony from his current meeting. In terms of architectural evolution and relevance in the business world, the development of high-rise apartment and office buildings in Austin had grown exponentially in the last ten years—the amount of time he'd been at Vista Labs. It had been like...the blink of an eye.

"You know, Tony, time is only pertinent when analyzing the cost benefit of the measurement being used." He spoke while counting the number of construction cranes in his current view. He preferred that to looking at his top lieutenant.

There was a silence. He smiled inwardly. He loved to baffle the members of his executive team. Sure, he knew they thought he was either too brilliant to relate to them or was starting to lose his marbles. Either way, he had an iron grip on the company, and there were only a couple things that could change that. The board, at times, was challenging. But what better way to exercise his broad skill set, one that had started years before on the inner-city streets of Dallas? It was possible for someone to connect enough dots to land a big pile of crap at his feet.

"Whatever you say, Mr. Drake."

Tony was placating him. He would have rather heard Tony attempt to understand the meaning behind his words. A verbal debate was good for the brain.

"You've been around a long time, Tony. What do you think we should tell the analysts tomorrow?"

"Well, sir..." Tony cleared his throat, then shuffled through a mound of papers spread across his lap. There was an elongated pause. He knew Tony was struggling with making the final decision. Making decisions—the tough ones—wasn't one of Tony's strengths, which is why Drake loved to watch him wiggle.

His mind wandered back to the day it was announced that he'd been selected as CEO and chairman of the board at Vista Labs. After many handshakes and even a toast of champagne with the board members, he had ushered his newly inherited executive team into a conference room and asked his new administrative assistant, Martha, to remove all the chairs.

196 John W. Mefford

"It's been a real honor working with many of you in the last few years. I've learned a lot, which has allowed me to shine. And for that, I thank you."

Everyone in the room had smiled, although he could see a hint of uncertainty since they were all standing up. He stuck his hand in his pocket, offering a casual pose. "I'm going to need two things from you as we get started on this journey together."

"We're ready to tackle the world," one of the younger executives said with a fist pump in the air.

"Nice," he said, although he thought the guy was a worthless piece of shit. "Anyway, I need for you, at all times, to call me 'sir' or 'Mr. Drake.'"

The team glanced at each other and then back to the front of the rectangular room. They all nodded, and a smattering of okays were heard from the crowd. He set his jaw. They didn't understand. He put his hand to his ear. "I didn't quite hear that correctly, did I?"

"Yes sir, Mr. Drake," the ass-kisser said with another fist pump. The kid was quick, if nothing else.

The rest of the team chimed in as well.

"Just so you know, I don't have any type of power trip going on here. My roots are humble. But I spent so much time being disrespected, called every name in the book, I figured that my new title should be accompanied by the proper amount of respect. I'm sure you can see my point of view on that, right?"

More nods. He froze for a second, waiting, and then they all showered him with praise. Satisfied, he looked at his watch. It was just after one in the afternoon. "So, your first task is rather simple. I need you to stay right here where you're standing until I get back to check on you."

Now the head nods came more slowly.

"Mr. Drake, sir, I'm late for a meeting right now, and I have meetings all afternoon," said the woman who headed up the Procurement Department. "So, if it's okay, I'll be heading off to my office when you're done."

He chuckled. "You have no meetings on your schedule."

"Actually," she said with a nervous giggle, "my phone is going off in my pocket. So, I really need to run, but I know you have something to say, so I won't be disrespectful...uh, sir."

He waved a hand across his face, as if he were casting a spell over them. "I said, no you don't. Are you going to dispute that?"

No one blinked.

"No, sir," she said as her face turned as red as a tomato.

"Well, then, I will see you tomorrow morning."

He turned and walked to the door as whispers filled the room. Before he left, someone finally asked, "Are you really serious? Tomorrow morning?"

He flipped on his heels. "You bet your ass." He pointed to the corner, where a small camera was positioned. "I'll be watching. If anyone moves from their spot, they're gone."

They all grumbled.

"Sir, Mr. Drake, you've got to be kidding," the woman said. "This isn't humane. We have work to get done. We have to eat, drink, and go to the bathroom. I have to take my daughter to soccer practice later. Now, if we were to plan some type of lock-in and make it a team-building exercise, I think that would do us a world of good."

He stared her down. "Do you enjoy your paycheck and all of your little perks?"

She nodded like a five-year-old.

"That's what I thought. So if you want that to continue, you'll do what I ask. And remember this: above anything else, I expect loyalty. I *demand* loyalty."

No one moved.

The one with the fist-pumps finally broke the silence. "We'll run through a wall for you, sir, but we have families and other commitments. It's just not possible. I'm not sure it's legal, for that matter."

Drake took one step forward. He could feel his veins throbbing at his temples. "This isn't a court of law, man. It's a company that *I* control." He raised a closed fist. "And I'll run it the way I see fit. Tomorrow morning—let's see who really wants it."

He left the room and came back nineteen hours later. The only person left was Tony. Still standing. His knees were knocking, his right eye fluttering nonstop, but he was there. When he asked Tony what had made him keep standing, even after everyone else had left, he had replied with a simple, "Because you asked us to."

And that was why Tony was his COO. Since then, he'd hired a lot of Tonys on his team.

Loyalty. If a leader had that, he could conquer the world, as that dipshit had said.

He pulled his eyes off the glow of the city lights and turned to face Tony. "I know you're nervous about the status of the vote with the FDA in two days. But trust me on this: it will go through."

Tony scratched his forehead. "If we tell the analysts that we have high confidence in this new Alzheimer's drug being approved, then, sir, uh…well, we have to come through. If not, then our eighty-five-dollar stock price will be shredded within twenty-four hours."

Drake's phone buzzed on his desk. He picked it up to read a text message, responded, and set it back down, steepling his fingers again. "Tony, I'm glad you're on my team."

"Thank you, sir." Tony's smile was strained, as if he were bracing for the next statement.

"You know how much I appreciate your loyalty."

"Yes sir."

"But have I told you which value I hold second highest?"

"No sir, I don't believe so."

"Respect of my intelligence."

"Right, sir. Well, I think you're very bright, sir."

Tony wasn't being honest, but he let it ride. "Just have confidence in my ability to navigate these drug-approval waters, okay?"

"I have great confidence in you, sir, but we did have that one mishap where—"

Drake chopped his hand downward. "It's been taken care of, right?"

"I guess so, although it was just kind of luck."

"Luck only happens to those who work the hardest and deserve it the most. Don't forget that."

Just then Martha opened the door to his office. "You have a call."

He looked to the landline sitting on his desk. No lights were blinking.

She added, "The one in your top-left drawer."

He dismissed Tony.

Thirty-Two

Mr. Drake waited until his office had emptied, then removed the spare phone from his drawer and punched up the call.

"What have you heard?" he asked without an introduction.

"No 'hello' or 'how's your golf game?' You're usually pretty good with the foreplay."

"Very funny. I just know that you like to get straight to it." He wasn't used to cowering to anyone, but in this particular relationship, it was a necessary evil if Vista Labs intended to remain a viable company, and if he hoped to see his net worth climb above a hundred million.

"I guess you do know me quite well. Hold on one second."

Mr. Drake swung his chair around to face north. In between the thirty- and forty-story buildings that were all in some form of construction, he could see the outline of the state capitol. The power brokers of the state seemed so close in many ways, but in reality, they were in their own protective bubble. To a degree, the same could be said for his world. But he knew if he didn't deliver what was promised to the analysts, the board would revolt against him as if he had a venereal disease.

Of course, that had nothing to do with Alzheimer's, the disease that had ruined so many lives across this great land. He could envision the adulation he'd receive once their drug was on the front page of every website, the greatest breakthrough in modern medicine in the last thirty years.

He could hear the man on the other line yelling at his staffers. Then, he came back on the line.

"Everything's okay, I hope," Mr. Drake said.

"Sure, just some ineptitude. You can't imagine what I have to deal with in my government position."

He rolled his eyes. "I'm sure it's unimaginable. So, I'm assuming that you called to tell me that you've spoken to your contact in DC?"

"I have. And she's not fond of the way you've gone about your business, Mr. Drake."

How the hell had she found out?

"And I have to admit, I'm not either. It's messy. And if you know anything about politics, we tend to steer clear of anything that is soiled."

Harking back to the first days when he'd joined Vista Labs as a salesman, Mr. Drake called upon his experience to close the deal. "Every operation of this magnitude has to deal with some unpleasant aspects. It's part of doing business. You yourself just mentioned the ineptitude of your own staff, and I would imagine you handpicked the best of the best. I haven't been dealing with the *crème de la crème* of society."

That drew a chuckle from the other end of the line. Drake smiled as his confidence surged. "Six months ago, after your initial investment, we were looking at the process taking three to four years. Now, we're on the verge of our dreams coming true."

"It has been an amazing project to watch from afar, Mr. Drake."

"So, can I be assured that you'll hold up your end of the deal?"

"Of course. We all win. Society wins, right?"

Not exactly, but he'd have his own island near Tahiti when it all came out. "Indeed."

They ended their call. He walked over to where his coat was hung and typed in a quick text to the other person who'd been vital to this project. The fact that she was the hottest piece of ass he'd ever touched was an extra benefit.

Just need to run a quick errand, and then I'll pick you up for the big event.

And out the door he went. He was a man who knew what he wanted, and no one could stop him.

Thirty-Three

The glow of the lone light affixed to the back of the building made it seem like Tomas had a halo just above his head. This made Alfonso think about a picture from Vacation Bible School as a child. A picture of Jesus. It kind of worked, since Tomas was standing at the top of the steps, acting like a preacher. He was spouting off about how they were going to rule their world with their new money and power.

"You hearing me, bro? We're going to the bank like nobody's bidness. I'm telling ya," Tomas said, smacking one hand into the other.

Alfonso glanced up and down the dark alley—the same alley where they'd knocked off that old man in the glasses. It was a little strange being back at the same place. Other than the fact that a Buick wasn't parked in the middle of the alley, the setting hadn't changed much. Garbage littered the space, it still smelled like rotten eggs, and there was a seam of light through the cracked door of the bakery and, of course, the thumping music.

Alfonso still had the man's briefcase back at his pad. The leather was nice and smooth. He'd found a bunch of papers in there with colorful charts. But what stood out was the repetitive use of certain words: "danger," "warning," "conspiracy." He'd tried to piece together what this guy was trying to communicate—some type of shit going down around the development of a new drug and how it affected the brain. It hadn't taken long for him to get lost in all the biological terminology. It had given him a headache. Still, it made him think about why they were given the job of ending that man's life. The guy was probably going to snitch to someone important.

Alfonso took a pull on his joint, closed his eyes briefly, and felt a tingle spread into his extremities.

"What you doing smoking dope at a time like this? It's time to celebrate, bro."

"I hear ya, Tomas. I'm excited, just like you. Honestly, it's the kind of break I've been hoping to get for a long time. My whole life, it seems."

Tomas hopped over the railing of the stairs with the nimbleness of a cat. Alfonso had heard stories of Tomas tearing up the competition on the soccer field before he got sucked up by the tornadic winds of MS-13. They all had been lured in by promises of gaining respect, getting even with the establishment for not giving them the same opportunities as others.

"Yo, dog, what you going to get when you get paid?"

Alfonso followed Tomas's gaze up to the sky, where a crescent moon illuminated thin clouds.

Before Alfonso could respond, Tomas started jittering his body like he was dancing while yammering away about buying three, four, five cars, all with custom wheels and chassis.

"Sorry, dude. I'm letting my dreams take center stage. What about you?" Tomas asked, his hyperactivity dialed back a bit.

"I don't know. I like to see the money before I get my hopes up. You know what I mean?"

"You got trust issues, Alfonso. This is happening, right here and now." Tomas pulled out his phone and checked the time. "Okay, I realize he's ten minutes late, but don't worry, man. He told me that this is just the beginning. He's got big plans for you and me. We've shown our loyalty, and now it's time to cash in."

Alfonso nodded in agreement, but he was having a difficult time controlling his nerves. In fact, it felt like one of those giant armadillos that had been digging up the foundation at his mom's place was clawing through his stomach. He tried to pinpoint the exact cause of his anxiety. He'd tried to forget the terrified look on that man's face just before he shot him. But being back in the alley brought those memories back again tenfold, and it didn't settle well. He sighed. *What's done is done. Can't undo the deed.* The guy had crossed the line with Boss Man, and he had to pay the price. End of discussion.

A thread of excitement was also front and center. He couldn't help but envision the look on Lupita's face when he showed her the wad of cash and shared with her how he'd be bringing in big bucks from that day forward. But he was most looking forward to picking up a couple of gold ropes to wear around his neck. People would see him coming from a block away. It would bring far more respect than any kind of cheap-ass tat.

A rattle off to the right. Alfonso shot a look toward the dumpster. Squinting, he reached behind his back at his waistband. Damn, he'd left his piece in the car around the block.

Tomas started laughing like he'd just seen one of those viral YouTube videos where someone would get their pants lit on fire. "Alfonso, man, you're all jumpy and shit. Look over there; it's just a damn rat."

Alfonso saw the long-tailed rodent slithering along the base of the brick building. He wasn't going to act like a wuss, but those things were beyond nasty.

Suddenly, a thought came to mind. Actually, it was more like a seed of doubt. "Hey, Tomas, you said tonight was going to be our big payoff. But you know, we weren't exactly successful on our last job."

"I know that. You think I'm stupid?"

He shook his head. "Just sayin' Boss Man may not think we should get a payday."

"Look, dog, he knows we did the best we could. He told me straight up that sometimes scaring the shit out of someone works even better than dropping them. It sends a message: *don't fuck with us.*"

"No doubt that dude is probably still curled up in a fetal position," he said, trying to muster a laugh.

Tomas popped him on the upper arm. "You worry too much, Alfonso. But, man oh man, I'll never forget you going Mike Tyson on his ass. How'd that ear taste?"

"Don't be harping on that shit. I was just in the moment, doing my thing."

"I'm down with you, man."

Hard-sole shoes clipped the concrete—four steps. Before he could turn his head, Alfonso felt the presence of a man just behind his shoulder. "Just like Tomas told you," the man said, "I'm down with you."

It sounded like he was mocking them. Alfonso looked up and saw the glow of the man's gleaming white teeth. They didn't look real. He decided to ignore the demeaning comment and focus on the long-term gain. He formally introduced himself, extending his hand. "Nice to meet you, Boss."

In the blink of an eye, the man pulled something out of his coat, swung his arm around Alfonso's neck, and pulled him against his chest. Alfonso felt the barrel of a pistol against the side of his head.

"He didn't mean it, Mr. D." With fear etched into his face, Tomas held up two hands. "Honest, I forgot to tell him."

Alfonso squirmed, but he could feel the bulge of the man's biceps against his neck. The arm felt like it was made of steel. He tried to speak, but all that came out was a mousy squeak.

"You're fucking hilarious. Are you trying to mimic these rats running around this shithole?"

Alfonso tried to respond, but his head was locked down, and he could hardly breathe, let alone speak. His eyes went to Tomas. Would he be able to talk some sense into this "Mr. D"?

"Mr. D, it's all a simple mistake. We meant no disrespect. We love working for you. We're your go-to guys for anything. Ain't that what you told me earlier? We'd be your A team?"

"For being a guy who supposedly has street smarts, you're pretty fucking stupid, Tomas."

The man loosened the grip around Alfonso's neck.

Alfonso sucked in air as if he'd been underwater for the last five minutes. But on the fifth breath, the gun fired. He literally peed his pants and then watched Tomas drop to his knees while pressing both hands to his chest.

Alfonso stopped breathing.

"You said we were your A team," Tomas said as blood gushed from his mouth.

The man moved closer and shot Tomas again in the chest. Tomas released a sound that resembled the pop of a tire; then his eyes flickered, and he dropped to the concrete.

Alfonso didn't move. He couldn't move. He was frozen in fear.

"It's kind of a shame," the man said, moving over next to Tomas's lifeless body. "There was some potential there."

"I…" Alfonso started to speak, but his brain couldn't find the words. He had no words. He had no way out. Tears filled his eyes as he felt the curtain of his life about to shut for good. With what little cognitive function he had left, he noticed the man was wearing gloves on both hands. The man set the pistol on the ground next to his foot. Was that the end of his retribution? Maybe he would spare Alfonso's life, ask him to work solo.

"Mr. ..." His brain was so fried he couldn't even remember the letter. He tasted the salt from one of his tears as the man lifted back up, removed another gun from his opposite pocket, and pointed it at Alfonso.

"It's 'Mr. D,' motherfucker."

Alfonso heard a crack and then felt his flesh rip from the bone. He looked down to see blood seeping from a hole. It had happened. He'd pushed it too far. He glanced up and saw only the man's teeth. Smiling. Enjoying it.

Another crack, and his body folded like a cheap lawn chair. His head bounced off the concrete. He tried to move, but his limbs didn't respond. Although somewhat blurred, his eyes remained open, as if he were destined to watch the final moments of his own life.

He saw the man place the gun he'd just fired in Tomas's hand. Then he grabbed the other pistol off the concrete and rested the gun in Alfonso's hand. Alfonso felt the extra weight. A signal was sent to coil his fingers around the grip and shoot that smug bitch in the face. To watch his pearly white teeth blow out the back of his head.

But he'd never get the satisfaction. As his vision caved inward and the odor of rotten eggs invaded his senses, he finally realized that his hunger for respect would never be fulfilled. His daughters would have no father. That was what now upset him the most.

And all he'd had to do was keep flipping burgers.

Thirty-Four

In some respects, the grand opening of "We, Three Kings" was a lot like any number of highbrow events in Austin. Lots of pretty people—some could even boast about not having to pay for their attractiveness—and a wide array of options at the free bar. Normally, I might go for a glass of wine. With Nicole, we'd typically name our top two options. She'd go for a chardonnay, and I might try a merlot.

I was a solo act now, so that plan was no longer feasible. Looking around the expansive art gallery on the trendy 2nd Street, it appeared that just about everyone else was paired up. Even Tito—one-third of the aforementioned three kings who had their work on display—was rocking a pretty woman on his arm when he wasn't explaining the inspiration behind one of his paintings to one of the high-rollers.

The ones with the real money, the folks who came to buy art, were at opposite ends of the social spectrum. Some wore belt buckles the size of a manhole cover, while some went with plain chinos and a solid-color shirt, usually a purple or beige. The female versions of each type were, for obvious reasons, more appealing to view. You had your typical bleached blonde who basically dared you to remove your eyes from her voluminous cleavage to stare at an array of diamonds that might be worth more than a house in South Austin. Then, you had what many called your tree hugger, the younger woman who was just as daring. As in, dressing so simply—baggy jeans, flats, a shirt that looked like it had just been picked up at Goodwill, and hair cropped at the neck—daring you to wonder if she was actually a female or someone who was going for the genderless appeal.

I sighed and grabbed a craft beer. As I brought the chilled glass to my lips, I could still smell the stench of blood on my hands. If the place hadn't been so crowded, I might have dunked my fingers in the suds.

With no one exactly bending my ear, I meandered around the gallery, stopping every few feet to take in the essence of each painting. The two other artists certainly had a different vibe than that of my old high-school buddy. I was looking at a painting that stood about five feet tall. It looked like some version of Jesus swan-diving off a cliff with Christmas lights along the banks of the shore. It was called *Lit.*

I tried not to lift an eyebrow and moved on. It wasn't long before I was thinking about Ray and his hammered face. Actually, it was his fear that had left a mark on me. He didn't seem to scare easily. He was born and raised in Austin, and I was sure that he'd been involved in his fair share of scrapes. He'd probably had his life threatened more times than a referee in a Texas high-school football game. All in all, he was laid back and seemed to let shit roll off his back.

But not this time. He had dusted off his Shit Hit The Fan backpack and left town, just like that. He didn't want to involve the cops; he didn't want to think about it. He was hell-bent on getting off the grid and starting life over again, far away from Austin. And he'd recommended that I do the same.

Then he'd offered his PI business for me to take over—*if I stay alive long enough*, I believe were his words.

That sonofabitch wouldn't tell me what had freaked him out so much, besides having his brains busted in. He had to know who Dad's mystery client was, or at least a good clue. He and I both had obviously spooked this client. Now, unless I just waited for another street battle with the bang-bang brothers, I really had no leads as to Dad's client and what had sent Ray on the run.

A nudge on my arm.

"You made it, Oz." It was Tito. I gave him a hearty handshake and was introduced to his lady friend. Her eyes seemed to be examining my face with its plethora of small abrasions and the nasty bruise on my forehead. "I cut myself shaving. And yes, I grow hair on my forehead."

She cackled like I'd just delivered the line of the century. Her response made us all laugh, especially when her laugh went falsetto. It was the strangest thing. Tito and I glanced at each other, eyebrows raised, and he shrugged as if to say, "You can't pick everything about your mate." Didn't I know it.

Tito was quickly ushered over to a potential buyer, and I restarted my lonely walk. Three steps later, I froze, nearly dropping my glass of beer. It was her. Nicole. Across the gallery, her arm hooked inside the arm of a man. He was shorter than I was by several inches and thicker through the chest. He had dark helmet hair and an obviously fake tan. He had to be "C."

I could feel the beer I'd swallowed defying gravity, making its way back up to my throat. As they moved through the gallery, I moved in the same direction. The man seemed to know everyone, at least in a surface-level way. A quick nod or passing handshake. He stopped, said a few words to another man, and introduced Nicole. She smiled. It seemed strained, as if she felt uncomfortable.

Other than that, she looked like a million bucks—a tight-fitting black dress that showed off her shapely legs. Her hair was up in a bun. I pushed away countless thoughts of her with her hair up, on top of me.

The glad-handing ended, and they were back on the move again. Neither seemed very interested in the art, which I found odd. Nicole—at least the Nicole I knew—would have been intrigued with the creative genius behind each picture. She would have sought insight from the artists, and then she might have tried to twist my arm into buying one of the less-pricey selections. Not that I had final say over anything really, but she had this cute way of leaning into my chest, and while convincing me it was what we should do, she'd goose me and pop her eyebrows. That would usually elicit a laugh and a wink—the kind that said we'd jump into bed as soon as we got home.

They walked behind one of the twelve-foot walls of paintings. I shuffled along, waiting for them on the other side, still keeping my distance. There were probably fifty people between us. More than a few seconds passed. I sipped my beer and tried to look casual. A young lady was on the verge of giving me a courteous nod; then her eyes looked closer at my face. She steered away from me like my nose had a foot-long wart growing on it. A second later, the man I believed to be *C* walked from behind the wall. I waited for Nicole to show her face. *C* was now a good ten feet past the wall, and there was no sign of Nicole. I'd lost her.

I flipped my head around and scanned the room. The crowd had doubled since I'd arrived. Great news for Tito and the other two kings, but not so much for me at the moment. I started retracing my steps.

I bumped into a person, tried to spin away, but somehow raised my hand and cupped a breast.

"Excuse me!" A woman who looked like my snooty mother had a scowl that could scare a scarecrow. I apologized as sincerely as possible and then offered to bring her a drink. She rolled her eyes and turned her back on me. It was for the best.

I whipped around, hoping to catch Nicole without the presence of "C." Would I have the guts to talk to her? I thought for a second, but that was all the time it took. The answer was a resounding no. I chided myself for even considering it, given she'd probably humiliate me in front of everyone.

So, Oz, why are you looking for her? She's old news. Put your focus on trying to find the person who killed your father, beat up Ray, shot at you. Move on already!

I tipped my head back and downed the last of my beer. Just as I set it on a tray, I felt my phone buzzing, and I plucked it from my pocket. It was...Nicole?

"Hello?" I sounded like a little kid.

"No time to get into anything now, but meet me at my house at one a.m."

The line went dead. My heart started pumping like it was bringing up oil from a thousand feet underground. I had more than three hours to wait.

Thirty-Five

Twenty minutes later, Nicole and *C* headed out the door. I watched from inside as *C* handed the valet his ticket. I couldn't hold off until one in the morning. Nicole had been direct, but it wasn't dismissive, like she'd been to me over the last several days. An alarm had gone off inside me. I had tried like hell over the last twenty minutes to objectively look at all the data points—her cold demeanor for the last two months, the way she'd unceremoniously ended our relationship, her flippant attitude to me since she dropped the divorce bomb, and how she'd cut me off from my money and our home. There was nothing, not one single speck of evidence, to suggest she still had feelings for me.

Yet she wanted me to meet her at one in the morning.

I couldn't debate it any longer; I had to follow them. I whipped around and spotted Tito. I rushed over and pulled him away from his conversation.

"Sorry, but can I borrow your car?"

"The Tube?"

"Yeah, the long green thing you drive around town."

"Uh, sure. You look like you're in a rush."

I looked toward the door. I could no longer see Nicole's bun above the throng of people. "I am," I said, holding out my hand. "I'll explain everything later. But it's important."

He riffled through his pocket, then stopped. "You're not going after those gangbangers, are you?"

"Not tonight. I need to figure out who shot Sam, killed my father, beat up Ray—"

"Ray? Someone else got caught up in this crap? What's going on, Oz?"

"Can't get into it now." I glanced at the door. "Has to wait until tomorrow."

He put the keys in my hand, and I rushed out the door. A moment later, I curled onto 2nd Street, which nearly flipped the Tube on its side, and drove by a two-door Jaguar at the curb. Nicole was in the passenger seat. The Jag pulled away from the curb. But I was in the wrong position. I was in front. Before I had time to figure out my next move, *C* turned the Jag left onto Colorado.

"Crap!" I banged the steering wheel. The entire dash rattled like I'd just kicked a doorstop.

There was too much traffic for me to do a U-turn. I quickly approached Lavaca, but it was a one-way street moving north, the opposite direction I needed to go. Next up was Guadalupe. The light turned red in the middle of my left-hand turn, and car horns blared at me.

Screw them.

One block down was Cesar Chavez Street, which bordered Lady Bird Lake. If *C* had headed east on Cesar Chavez, he would be long gone by now. I had to hope he'd gone west. I dodged around two slower cars and then hit the brakes at the stoplight. The Jag whizzed right by me.

I took a breath and executed a lazy turn onto Cesar Chavez. I quickly realized *C* was moving at a high rate of speed. I pressed the gas pedal to the floor, and the engine growled, but the Tube responded as if it were being fed water instead of gasoline. I kept my eyes peeled to the Jag's taillights, and slowly the Tube edged closer.

As both cars passed under MoPac, I had a good idea where they were going—my old home. The road turned into Lake Austin, and we zipped by a middle school and the Lions Municipal Golf Course. *C* hung a left on Redbud. He was taking the long way, but there was no doubt he was headed for my home. Ten minutes later, he pulled up to the curb; I killed the lights and coasted into the alley across the street, stopping in between two homes so I could see the Jag and the front of the house.

I wondered if they'd go inside...and then what? Had Nicole thrown out this bait, hoping I'd bite the hook? Did she want me to peer through the window and watch her and *C* doing it on our bed?

Don't go there.

I ran my fingers through my hair and waited. A second later, the passenger door opened. Nicole didn't get out for what must have been a full minute. Were they making out? Was she trying to convince him to come inside, or was she doing the opposite and convincing him she had a headache and she'd call him tomorrow? My head was swimming with a thousand theories. And I figured that nine hundred ninety-nine of them had a strong likelihood of making me look like an ass.

Just then, she hopped out of the car, leaned back in for a second, then shut the door and walked up the front sidewalk. She didn't turn around and wave. She walked through the front door of our home. The Jag took off.

Now was my time. Or was it? I glanced at the time on my phone. It wasn't even eleven yet. She had said one a.m. But was that to make sure that *C* would be long gone? Or did she have something else planned?

Another idea hit me. She'd become quite stingy with our money. Maybe *C* had convinced her to set me up. She could have invited me over, pretending she didn't know about it, and then she would kill me, or have someone do it, when I walked into the house as if I were a jealous ex out to get my revenge. She didn't have a gun, but given the bizarre world I'd entered recently, she could be a frickin' arms dealer, for all I knew.

The taillights of the Jag disappeared around the curve.

Stay or go? Dammit, I wanted to stay, to walk into our home, to feel her pressed against my chest.

Wake up, Ozzie. This isn't the make-believe city of Oz.

I fought off my primal urges and threw the gear into drive, following the Jag back into the city. C didn't speed or break any other laws. I figured he was headed to one of the high-priced, high-rise condos sprouting up every few months. At one red light, I was in the adjoining lane and caught a glimpse of his license plate: MRDRAKE. It was a vanity plate. Now I was almost certain he lived in one of those million-dollar glass condos.

He motored east on Cesar Chavez and neared the area where about twenty new high-rises either had been recently completed or were under development. The construction boom was insane. I waited for him to turn north onto Guadalupe or any of the other roads, but he never did. He continued his eastward trek until he crossed I-35.

Now he had my attention, and I inched up in my seat. You don't see many Jags on the east side of I-35, not unless someone was lost, and certainly not in the middle of the night. Sure, Tito lived east of I-35, but it was north of this area, in a pocket where a lot of artists lived. And even still, look at what happened to me. "C," or MRDRAKE, turned south on Pleasant Valley. We crossed the river, and the neighborhood quickly flipped for the worse. Rooftops and porches sagged as if the burden of everything connected to a poor area—drugs, gangs, violence—had weighed them down. Guys wearing do-rags were clustered every half-block or so. Every car I passed was unconventional. A few had purple lights outlining the undercarriage; others had tires that could have fit a 747.

A couple more turns, and we passed an old storage facility. A cracked streetlight illuminated red and black graffiti, and I had to remind myself to keep driving. I saw the number thirteen, or two numbers adding up to thirteen, sprawled everywhere. I spotted the words *Mara Salvatrucha*, and then *Maras*. That had to represent the "MS" in MS-13.

I felt a dry patch in the back of my throat.

The Jag veered to the right and stopped in front of a small home. I eased to a stop behind a parked pickup on the opposite side of the street, maybe fifty feet away, and killed my lights. Two guys walked out of the house and approached the Jag. Was this some type of drug buy? Maybe Nicole had caught wind of "C's" drug dependency and wanted to ask me for help.

I could only guess. I really had no clue.

A car drove by, and its headlights shone on one of the guys leaning through the open window. He took an envelope from the car and handed it to the guy behind him. He opened his mouth, and I caught a glint of metal. I could see his lips moving, but I was too far away to read them.

I decided to take a chance. Some might call it a death wish. I pulled out of my space and did my own version of a drive-by. It was slow, probably too slow, but for a good three seconds, I was able to stare down the guy leaning on the car, gabbing like nobody's business. I caught just a small snippet of what appeared to be a longer diatribe.

Bitch won't live.

I pressed the gas and turned left at the corner. I looked in my rearview. No one had followed me. Then I replayed what I was certain I'd seen the guy say. *Bitch won't live.*

I went to Peretti's to have a drink and mull over what that could mean.

Thirty-Six

I shook the ice in my tumbler and tipped my head back, sucking down the last remnants of my Knob Creek on the rocks—my second drink since arriving at Peretti's. It was achieving my goal: to soothe my nerves.

"You want another?" Poppy asked, flipping a fresh napkin on the bar.

I held up a hand. "Any more, and I'll be unable to resist her."

I'd filled Poppy in on the last few days, at least on the topic of Nicole.

She lifted an eyebrow—it had two piercings—and smirked. "Want to know what I think?"

"You're going to tell me anyway, so go ahead."

"She's playing you. She either wants something from you, or she's simply trying to lure you to her place."

"Our place." I eyed my empty drink for a second.

"Whatever. She knows she can yank your chain and you'll come running like a wounded puppy."

"But what could she possibly want? I mean, she has everything."

"I'm curious about this other guy in her life, the guy who wrote that love note. What did you call him? 'C'?"

A heavy nod.

"Yeah, well, sounds like a real douche bag. So, he could be steering her to do things."

"What did you have in mind? I told you, I haven't pushed back on anything."

Someone yelled for a beer, or at least I thought I heard that. She said, "That's either pathetic or real mature of you; I can't figure out which."

"If you don't mind, I'll go with option number two."

"Information," she said, pouring a beer into a glass for another customer. She set the glass on the counter and shoved it ten feet. The beer sloshed everywhere, but the guy who picked it up simply nodded and started drinking. The patrons at Peretti's were easy to please.

"What are you talking about…'information'?"

"You said she has all your money. She wants to find out something from you that she doesn't know. In the FBI, they call it intel."

"What do you know about the FBI?"

She put a finger to the side of her nose, which, like her brow, also sported two piercings. She was trying to be cheeky. "I know people." Then she barked out a brief, but obnoxious laugh. "Seriously, I read books, so I'm not ignorant. But don't get sidetracked here, Oz. No matter how good she looks, how much she sweet-talks you, keep your guard up. There has to be a motivation here, and there's about a ninety-nine percent likelihood it won't be about rekindling a lost love."

She was pulled away by another customer. *Information.* I scratched my head, accidentally digging a nail into one of my cuts. I gritted my teeth, thinking about what I knew that Nicole would give two shits about. I came to a quick conclusion—nothing.

My eyes shifted to the portfolio I'd brought in with me. Ray's notes from his initial interviews. I flipped a few pages. I saw more chicken scratch than real notes. And most of the notes were more of a profile of the person. I came to that conclusion by reading the notes he'd added for Arie and Stacy. There was nothing substantive there, unless he had hidden a coded message in one of his many tic-tac-toes. How did he expect me to use these notes to find Dad's killer? The whole notion seemed preposterous. And why the hell couldn't he have just told me the whole story anyway?

Hidden messages. Sheesh. I looked over at Poppy. She'd planted a new series of thoughts in my head, most of them negative. But she was probably being realistic. Then again, I was a man getting advice from his bartender. Could my life be any sadder?

I shut the portfolio and checked the time. I still had thirty minutes to kill.

I felt a tap on my shoulder.

I turned and saw the man I'd never seen smile.

"We need to talk," he said.

I followed him to a table.

Thirty-Seven

I stopped before sitting down and pointed a finger at Brook, who was already at the table. "Don't look so surprised," she said.

Bowser, the one who'd tapped my shoulder, kicked out a chair for me.

"You're quite the gentleman." I took a seat and eyeballed Brook.

"What?" Her palms turned to the ceiling.

I withheld any comment about her new friend. "How can I help you? Or, shouldn't it really be: how can you help me? I mean, you do technically work for the American people. I fall in that category last I checked."

"Sarcasm," Bowser said, drinking what appeared to be water. "I like it. Usually. But we don't have much time."

My eyes volleyed back and forth between the two law-enforcement officials. There was no way they knew about my one o'clock appointment with Nicole. "Do you have a deadline to hit?" I looked at Brook. "Maybe you're writing a sidebar story for Tracy?"

Bowser appeared confused.

"He's just an annoying reporter I know at the *Austin American-Statesman*."

Bowser nodded. "I'll get right to it. We want you to wear a wire when you go meet Nicole."

My heart pounded so hard I thought it might pop out on the table. "What are you talking about?" I asked while opening the portfolio and thumbing a few pages. I was thankful I had something to keep my hands occupied.

Bowser looked to Brook, who said, "Maybe we should have started this a little differently. Bowser decided to open up and share everything with me. I've done the same."

"Great to hear you have a new teammate." I looked down at the paperwork as my mind was flooded with theories on how they could know about my upcoming meeting with Nicole.

"Ozzie." Bowser set his hand on the edge of my portfolio.

I moved the portfolio closer to me, then locked eyes with Bowser. He said, "Time is running out. Will you work with us?"

I shut the portfolio. "How did you find out?"

"We have a tap on your wife's phone."

"You listened to our conversation a few hours ago?"

"It's the only way to get closer to her, uh…" Bowser again looked to Brook to bail him out.

"The man your wife has been seeing," Brook said. "We have good reason to believe that he was your dad's mystery client."

I pinched the corners of my eyes. This could not be happening. No.

Brook reached a hand across the table to make sure I was looking at her.

"What?"

"You remember that murder scene I showed you?"

"Dr. Harry Clem," I said.

Bowser jumped in. "He was the man who reported your dad."

I sat up in my chair. "What? For what? What?"

"Your dad, apparently, tried to convince him—intimidate him—to stop saying bad things about this new miracle drug being developed at a company called Vista Labs."

"My dad could talk a good game, but intimidation? Is this where all those charges came from?"

"Yes," Bowser said. "But I tried telling you that your dad wasn't our main target."

"So you did use him."

"I don't like that term. We thought it might cause the person who hired him to surface."

Heat rushed up the back of my neck, and I started lifting out of my chair. "You did it. You got my dad killed, you fucking prick."

Brook waved me down. "Ozzie, please. Just listen."

I saw Poppy looking in my direction. I turned back to the table and sat. "Who killed my dad? Are you saying it's this 'C' guy with Nicole? Does he work for Vista Labs?"

"We still don't know who killed your father. We haven't been able to piece that together."

"But it has to be this guy, right?"

"Maybe. Probably. I don't know for sure," Brook said. "But we have strong suspicions that he's behind the death of Dr. Clem."

It was all starting to make sense, at least one angle of it. "How do you know? Through this wiretap on Nicole's phone?"

"You have to swear to keep this to yourself," Brook said.

"I swear," I said, holding up three fingers.

She explained that Calvin Drake, the man in the Jag, was the CEO of Vista Labs. He was a former Dallas police officer who'd befriended members of MS-13.

Bowser jumped in. "I'm putting all of my cards on the table here, Ozzie."

I didn't say anything.

"You sure I can trust you?"

"You can trust him," Brook said with an annoyed look on her face.

I didn't say a word; I was listening, seething.

He leaned in closer. "We have a guy on the inside of MS-13. He found out Drake hired a couple of gangbangers to kill Clem. And then it made sense to us. He's the CEO of Vista Labs, and they're awaiting final approval on this new Alzheimer's drug from the FDA. Clem was being very public about the dangers of this new drug. Apparently, he was initially hired by Vista Labs to talk at medical conferences about the greatness of this new drug. But guilt set in, and he decided to tell the truth."

My mind was starting to catch up. "Then arrest this asshole Drake. Nicole is in danger, dammit."

"We don't have a clear-cut case."

"You just said—"

"It might not stand up in court. Our mole heard about it; he didn't witness it. Drake is loaded, and a strong lawyer could destroy our case."

I was trying to understand the task here. "So you want me to see if I can get Nicole to admit that she knows about her, uh…Drake killing this Dr. Clem?"

"Frankly, we don't know what she knows. We tried tapping into Drake's phone, but he talks business all the time. We think he might have a burner phone or something. Anyway, we have picked up a few things when she's talked to him."

"Care to share?" I asked.

"We don't have time to get into the details. But when she offered to see you tonight, we saw an opportunity to bring you in on everything."

"Can we count on you?" Brook said.

My mind was drowning with the weight of everything they'd dumped on me. I looked at the portfolio. I wanted to ask Brook and Bowser if Ray's name had come up in this investigation. But for now, I kept quiet. It certainly wasn't the priority.

"Ozzie, we need an answer," Brook reiterated.

I could hear Poppy warning me about allowing my protective nature to kick in regarding Nicole. And, of course, that was exactly what happened. I had to keep her safe.

"I'm in."

Thirty-Eight

Looking over my shoulder from the shallow front porch of my home, I realized I'd never seen our neighborhood from this viewpoint, not at this hour of the night. Outside of a few landscape lights throughout the hilly area, darkness ruled. The sky was a blanket of black, and a cold sprinkle had just started on my way up to the door.

I rang the doorbell, wondering which Nicole would answer the door, wondering how I'd respond to either persona. Then again, this wasn't exactly a private moment. A small mic was attached to the button on my blazer. Bowser, Brook, and a small FBI team were huddled in a van about two miles away.

A light came on above my head; then the door opened and Nicole stood there in her sweats, the ones that she always said made her look like a little boy. She was the most beautiful woman I'd ever seen.

"Hey," she said. Her eyes matched her tone of voice: kind.

"Hey."

"I know you must be wondering what this is all about."

I tried to chuckle, reset my feet. "Uh, yeah."

She licked her lips, then looked upward. "I'm—" She stopped short. Her eyes became glassy. Her hand jittered as she dabbed the corner of her eye. "I don't know what to say exactly."

Part of me wanted to take her in my arms, bury my face in the nape of her neck, and tell her she didn't have to say she was sorry. Whether it was Poppy's words, knowing the FBI was listening in, or my inner voice telling me to slow down, I caught myself before I said anything. I just waited.

"Ozzie, I don't know what happened to me the last few months. I just—" She stopped short again and looked at me with pleading eyes. My heart skipped a beat.

I clasped my hands together to make sure I wouldn't reach out.

She sucked in air like she was about to be dunked under water. Then, "There's a lot I need to tell you…that I want to tell you. But I'm scared. For me. And for you. Especially you." A single tear rolled down her cheek.

I could resist no longer. I reached my hand out, and she grabbed it. Her thin fingers squeezed my hand like never before. She pulled me to her. Her eyes began to close, her lips opened. I could feel her breasts pressing against my chest.

Something slammed into the back of my neck. I fell into Nicole, and we both toppled to the tile floor. I tried pushing up, to see what or who had hit me, but my neck felt like it had been stabbed with an ice pick. Loud baritone voices. Two sets of feet jumped across the tile. Under me, Nicole squirmed, her eyes wide. I swung my head to the right and saw a man holding a gun. But it was his gold teeth that made my heart leap into the back of my throat. *Bitch won't live.* It was him. I'd been so overwhelmed with information and so rushed, I'd forgotten to tell Brook and Bowser about what I'd seen when I passed Drake's car earlier.

"Yo, Hugo," Grill Man said to a guy half his size. "Tie them up; then we'll throw them in the back of the car. Hurry up, man!"

I was just about to throw my elbow in the direction of Grill Man's groin, when something leaped over my head. It had four legs.

"Baxter!" Nicole yelled; at the same time, I realized it was a dog. A dog who could have weighed as much as me.

Baxter, who appeared to be some type of Great Dane, clamped on Grill Man's gun hand before his paws touched the floor. The guy screamed bloody murder, and the gun dropped. Somewhere in the canine chaos, it was kicked ten feet away. I pushed up and started to lunge for it, but Hugo had beat me to it. He was midair. I swiped a hand upward and clipped his ankle. He dropped face first into our dining room table, but his body was still between me and the gun. Grill Man shook off Baxter and threw himself in the direction of the gun. I tried to thrust my body forward, but a hand grabbed my jacket and yanked me down. I looked up—Nicole was halfway out the door.

"Come on. Let's get out of here."

Grill Man was on his knees, reaching for the gun.

"Ozzie!" She'd stopped at the doorway. I got to my feet and ran toward her as she yelled at Baxter. He cut between us as I grabbed the doorknob and slammed the door shut behind us. A crackle, and the door splintered just over my shoulder. To say I flinched would be an understatement.

She yelled something at Baxter, and he bolted out of sight. I grabbed Nicole's hand. "I know where to go." She followed me into the thick of the night.

Thirty-Nine

Tearing around the corner of our home, Nicole slipped first, but I was able to hoist her back up and barely lose stride. Three steps later, my loafers went out from under me, and we both hit the ground. Hard. The wet grass was like running on sleet.

Up on my hands and knees, I was as still as a hunting dog that had just spotted its prey. "Do you hear anything?" I asked her, knowing I'd never be able to pick up slight sounds.

"Nothing yet."

I could make out her pale feet. We didn't have time to make sure her feet were warm. I tapped her on the shoulder, and we darted toward the back alley.

"This way," I said, heading west, which happened to be up a hill. As we ran, I touched the button on my coat, searching for the listening device planted there by Bowser's team. Then I put my hand on my front pocket. No phone either.

"Fuck!"

"What's wrong?" Nicole said, panting, as puffs of smoke curled above her head.

"The listening device. It's gone. So is my phone."

"You were wearing a wire?"

Now she sounded pissed.

"Nicole, don't go there. Some bad shit has gone down with your new boyfriend. I was dragged into this."

She didn't say anything as I spotted a house where I knew the owners would be home.

We slipped to the side of their eight-foot fence—everyone in Texas with any money at all just had to build their own fortress—and headed for the front door. Trying to shave a second or two, I cut across their lush landscaping beds.

It seemed like a hand reached up from the ground and grabbed my shoe. I flew through the air and landed face first into a rosebush.

I did everything I could to mute my groan, but something squeezed out.

"Holy…" Nicole dropped to her knees as I lifted my face. "Do you want me to pull out the thorns?"

"Screw it. No time."

She helped me up, and we jogged to their door. Not a light on anywhere, I rang the doorbell. My legs couldn't stop moving as I glanced left and right, wondering if the thugs would run up at any second.

"So, this wire…shouldn't they know we're in trouble?"

"I hope. I just don't know when it came off. Could have been when we fell on the side of the house."

"*Our* house," she said, as if she were redefining our relationship…again. I ignored it.

I rubbed the back of my neck. "Could have been when I was hit from behind, or any time during that fight. Hell, it could have been when you tried to kiss me."

"You mean when you tried to kiss me?" She cupped her hands and blew into them.

"What? You pulled me closer."

Whatever. I pushed the doorbell again, then plucked a thorn from my cheek.

She touched my arm. "You're right—I pulled you closer. I couldn't take being away from you any longer," she said, looking into my eyes.

She was hoping for a bonding moment, but instead I took a step off the porch and scanned the area.

"Jesus, Oz, your face. It's—"

"Made for Hollywood?"

"A sense of humor even right now. You haven't changed a bit."

I said nothing. "The Millers must be on one of their cruises."

"We could just climb their fence and wait in their backyard."

"I thought about that. First, we'd be sitting ducks. Second, I have no phone. We'd be waiting for hours. Come on. Let's try Mrs. Johnson."

Mrs. Johnson was related to THE Johnsons of Texas, as in the thirty-sixth president, Lyndon Baines, and his wife, Lady Bird. As least that was her story.

We raced across four yards. I thought about ringing a bell at each house, but I knew too many of these owners had guns. If they saw two people frantically running around, they might shoot first and ask questions later.

We managed to make it to Mrs. Johnson's doorstep without another fall and no sign of Grill Man or Hugo. I rang it twice.

"Maybe the two assholes got scared and ran off," Nicole said, rubbing a cold, bare foot against her sweats.

"Did you hear what they said? They were going to kidnap us. Not kill us, at least not initially."

She grabbed my arm and squeezed with the pressure of a medical cuff. "I'm so sorry, Oz. I should have never—I'm just so weak. I know you thought I was different. But I'm not like that. I'm weak, insecure, and flighty."

She was right. I had no idea. I'd read her all wrong, and she'd been damn good at portraying a very different person. "Thank you for saying that." I cupped my hand against a window and looked inside. No movement. I rang the bell again. "Come on, dammit!"

We waited another few seconds.

"What if we just broke in?"

"Two things: she might have a gun and an alarm." I started scanning the neighborhood, looking for any signs of the two thugs, as well as thinking about possible next stops.

"But if she doesn't have a gun," Nicole said, "the alarm would send the cops over."

"Grill Man and his sidekick would also hear the alarm. They'd beat the cops here, and then what?"

"You seem like you've been in this situation before," she said.

"No, I've just heard some crazy stories from my dad."

A pause. "Your dad."

I turned to look at her, as resentment coursed through my veins. "Do you know about how he died?"

She shook her head. "I swear I don't know. I just overheard Calvin in a phone call earlier. He said he couldn't leave any trail and that he'd decided to kill Nathaniel's son to ensure there was no trail."

"Do you know he killed Dad?"

She covered her mouth. "I feared that when I heard Calvin talking. I just...I can't believe it," she said as emotion crept into her voice.

I didn't reach out and console her and tell her everything was okay. It wasn't. And I wasn't sure it ever would be. "I thought his name was Mr. Drake?" That was a real classy line, but I couldn't think of anything else to say. So, I went low.

She sniffled. "I know, Ozzie. His ego is off the charts, but after I crossed the line, I wasn't sure what to do. I just kept up the charade. I knew it was wrong. I was wrong." She took in a shaky breath. "I had done so much to hurt you, it was impossible to face the truth. I couldn't bring myself to do it."

"What changed?"

"That phone call. He thought I couldn't hear him when I went into the bathroom to take a shower, but I could hear him through the wall."

The pang of jealousy hit me like a metal crowbar. "You two did it in our house?"

She opened her mouth, but no words came out. More tears streamed down her face. "Dammit, I hate myself." She gasped out a breath. "It just all happened so quick. He acted like he was being a good friend, listening to all of my complaints of the world. And then he started showering me with gifts. I was blind and selfish and couldn't face the truth, couldn't undo what I'd done to you...to us. I was weak, Ozzie. But now I just want to..." She sobbed, with her big eyes looking at me.

I pulled another thorn from my face. "That hurt," I said, knowing it actually felt good compared to hearing her unload this bagful of regret. My heart felt like it was being dragged through burning coals.

One more glance inside Mrs. Johnson's house.

"Now where?" she asked.

I ran my fingers through my hair, pushing all the emotional crap aside for now. Bowser and Brook had to know they'd lost communication with me. Wouldn't they at least drive by the house? I continued the thought. Then they'd see my car...well, Tito's VW bus. They could think that I was inside the house and that nothing had happened. They might even assume that the listening device had accidentally fallen off, especially if they knew the history of friskiness between Nicole and me. Or maybe not. I had little confidence in my ability to rationally think everything through.

The Tube. I felt in my pocket for the keys.

"We're going to circle around and try to make it to my car."

"You mean that old green thing? And we're going back to the house where the thugs are?"

"I'm open to other ideas."

She started running before I did. I caught up, and we made our way back to the house, but we took a different route. We stopped at every home, peered around each corner before moving forward. No sign of Grill Man or Hugo. We actually went farther than we needed, on purpose. We stopped two houses east of my former home. I knew this two-story had a large hedge of bushes. We got down on all fours, crawled into the middle, and stopped where there was a small hole. We could see the Tube and the surrounding street. No sign of any people or moving cars.

"It's eerie," Nicole whispered.

I nodded. "I'm worried they might be hiding somewhere, waiting for us to make a run for the car."

"You think?"

"Actually, I have no frickin' clue." A few seconds passed. "By the way, when did you get Baxter?"

She looked down for a second. "Right after you came into the house and looked through my things."

Wow. "So you knew that I knew about this 'C' man?" As soon as I said it, I realized what it might sound like—*semen.* "Damn, that sounds bad." We both smiled, although my stomach twisted tighter.

"Calvin put a few cameras in my house. Said he wanted to make sure I was safe."

I wanted to ask her why, but that would only lead to about ten other whys.

"I know I was naïve and immature," she said.

I ignored her and kept my eyes on the street and the surrounding yards.

"You haven't asked how he and I met or when it started."

"Does it matter?" I asked, my eyes on anything but her.

"It does if we're…" She didn't say it, and I'm glad she didn't. I couldn't go there. Not now.

"We met at a conference in Vegas about three months ago."

"I guess that's why they came up with their infamous phrase." I'd never been to Vegas, and now I never wanted to go.

She took my arm again, and I knew she was going to start talking about us. I waylaid that idea.

"You ready to run?"

She nodded. "I'm with you all the way."

Nice line. The old Oz wouldn't have been able to stop that arrow of love. He would have let it warm his heart. But right now, my wall was mostly intact. Only a small piece of the arrow had found its way inside. And I wasn't going to let her know that. "Let's go."

We crawled out of the bushes, then darted for the bus. Did I lock it? I wasn't sure, and that car was so old I'd have to get to the car and just yank on the door to see. I took aim on the passenger door. We crossed the sidewalk, and I did a quick three-sixty turn to make sure all was safe. Seemed so. I flipped around and yanked on the passenger door. It opened, and we jumped in.

Then we both froze.

"Has the happy couple renewed their wedding vows?"

It was Drake. My eyes went straight to his teeth. They looked fluorescent.

Bent over to fit in the bus, I shuffled a half-step toward him. He lifted a gun. It wasn't small. "I don't want to spray your brains all over your friend's car. Sit the fuck down."

We did as he said.

Forty

Through the rearview, I could see Drake put a phone to his ear.

"Get back to the bus now," he said into his cell phone. He placed it in his front pocket.

I tried to sneak a glance at Nicole to see how she was holding up. Her chin was trembling.

"Ah, is the little missus all upset?" Drake said as if he were speaking to a toddler. He laughed for a second. "Maybe I ought to pull you into the back here and let Oz watch a real man go to town on you."

I clenched my fists.

"Shut up, Calvin!" Nicole barked, then put both hands over her face. "You are a piece of filth. I don't know what I was thinking, being with you."

"Like I said, you finally wanted a real man. The whole thing was almost too easy."

His comment pierced through all of the anger and fear and found a way into the part of my brain that ran it through a series of tests. It didn't pass. "What was almost too easy?"

"Your wife, dickwad. She's easy, but not just in bed."

Nicole sobbed, and I fumed silently, although I could feel my eyes burning. It seemed almost certain that he and his two thugs would take us into a field and kill us, or maybe even throw us into one of the surrounding lakes. It almost didn't matter—we had no way out. But I had to know if he'd killed my father and why, although I was very curious about the role Nicole had played, apparently unwittingly.

"Easy in what way?"

"Stop, Ozzie. He's just trying to torture you." Tears covered her face and neck. I'd never seen her this upset.

"Easy in what way?" I repeated, still looking through the rearview.

"I guess it doesn't matter anymore," he said, as if he were talking more to himself. "She was the one who let my guys go through the outside back gate at the Belmont so they could plant the bomb that went off. She thought they were part of the crew. Like I said, 'easy.'"

We both gasped, and then Nicole screamed out. "You fucking monster. People died in that bombing!"

"I didn't mean to harm innocents, but sometimes sacrifices have to be made."

"What are you talking about?" I dug my fingernails into my arm to keep myself from lunging at the guy, which I knew would result in being shot.

"We learned that the good doctor would be in attendance. Turns out he knew one of the band members."

"Dr. Clem?"

Nicole asked, "Who's Dr. Clem?"

I saw Drake nodding, his eyes on mine through the reflection. "So you did piece it all together. That was my fear. That's why we're all here tonight."

"You killed my father."

"I paid Nathaniel a lot of money to be my mouthpiece. We tried to get the damn doctor to shut his trap without having to take irreversible measures. We tried everything, but Dr. Clem took this moral high ground, and I was left with no choice."

I could feel my rage boiling, and I was about to go off, knowing it might be the last thing I'd do on this earth. "You will fucking rot in hell."

"Might be so, but between now and then, I'll be a very rich man off this new drug. Of course, it might have some deadly side effects, but again, I say the evolution of this world is all about sacrifices."

Nicole whimpered, grabbed each side of her head. She was tormented by what she'd done, how she'd allowed herself to be used by this maniac. I could see it, feel it. I wanted to reach out and grab her hand, but I didn't.

"You had someone from MS-13 kill Dr. Clem, didn't you?"

"They owed me. I used to work for the force up in Dallas. I let them get away with so much shit. I finally called in my favors."

"And you paid them to shoot me."

"Those bozos fucked up. And it cost them their lives."

He'd killed the killers. This guy reset the bar for low-life trash. But I still had to know the fate of my father.

"How did you do it? How did you kill my dad?"

"Didn't do it. I guess that was a gift from the man upstairs. I was going to, especially with the Feds involved. I knew he'd eventually talk. And I thought he'd unload everything to you too. Which is why I was watching you."

The sliding door pulled open. Hugo hopped in, followed by Grill Man. With the interior light on for a moment, I could see blood seeping down Grill Man's arm. He caught my gaze. "Motherfucking dog." He lunged at me, slamming his gun against my head. I fell against the steering wheel. I literally saw stars for a moment, and my eyes went blurry. A cluster of noise sounded all around me, but through it all I could hear Nicole scream. I pushed myself up as Hugo pulled her out of the seat and into the back.

"Stop!" I made an attempt to reach for her, but it was pathetic. Within seconds, I was tossed into the passenger seat, my head still swimming. I tried to blink away my wooziness. Then I saw Drake climb into the driver's seat.

"I don't do anything unless I'm in the driver's seat," he said with a laugh. "You like my pun?"

I ignored him. I had to. I wasn't sure I could piece together two words.

Another scream from Nicole. I turned and saw Hugo pawing at her. I tried pushing out of my seat, but a second later, Grill Man shoved me back and pressed his gun into the back of my head. "Give me one damn reason to pull this trigger, motherfucker. Please. I'm begging you."

The engine started, and I caught the eye of Drake, who shrugged. "You swim with the sharks, you get bitten by the sharks. What can I say?" He knew they would rape Nicole, but he didn't care.

He put the VW bus in drive and pulled away. Nicole screamed again. I blinked twice and felt my brain starting to come back to life. I wondered if I could somehow move quickly enough to grab the steering wheel and yank on it. He'd swerve, maybe crash, but it would stop Hugo and give us a chance. That was all I could hope for at this point. A chance.

"What is—" Drake never finished his sentence. I heard a loud pop, and the Tube bucked upward. The back end fishtailed. All of us went airborne. My head hit the ceiling, and Drake face-planted into the steering column—old car, no airbags.

The crash seemed like it lasted a good minute, but probably took no more than a few seconds. The air was thick with burning rubber.

I took a breath, and everything was still. Somehow, the Tube had stayed upright.

Doors swung open. I glanced up and saw Brook with a gun aimed right at Drake. "Kill him, Brook. Shoot him dead."

She didn't do it. But she did throw him out of the car and onto the concrete. That would have to suffice for now.

Forty-One

Nothing to create a little neighborhood gossip like having a dozen law-enforcement cars with flashing lights in front of your house. I noticed a flurry of neighbors in robes and sweats, all outside a barrier set up by the APD.

Nicole and I stood next to the unmarked FBI van, each of us with a government-issued blanket over our shoulders. She'd been given a pair of cheap slippers. I watched them put Drake into a car with three other FBI agents and drive off. The two others, Grill Man and Hugo, were leaving in the back of ambulances. Hugo had apparently broken a bone in his arm, and Grill Man had accidentally shot himself in the foot.

I called that vindication.

We'd already been questioned by Brook and Bowser and were told to expect more before they were done with us.

"Did you think we'd ever be this popular in the neighborhood?" Nicole asked, looking at the people gathered outside of the yellow tape.

"We'll probably be fined by the Homeowners Association for creating a disturbance past midnight."

She turned to me and gave me a sly smile. "You're joking."

I shrugged and felt a smile tug at my lips.

"Is this guy your dog?" An officer had just walked up holding Baxter by the collar. Brook was just behind them.

"There's my hero." Nicole smiled in the way only she could and rubbed his ears. He immediately started licking her hands. She then introduced me to the newest guy in her life. Baxter sniffed my hand, then allowed me to scratch his back. Within a few seconds, he was leaning his body—I was guessing something north of eighty pounds—against my legs.

"That's his way of saying he trusts you," she said, curling a lock of hair around her ear.

We both froze, our eyes locked on each other. I glanced away first, my eyes darting around, looking for a safe place. Trust. It had been tossed away like a secondhand bike when it should have been cherished like a rare jewel.

Brook moved closer. I sighed, if only to clear my mind from the unsolvable push-pull I felt with Nicole.

"Are there others you need to arrest?" I asked Brook.

"The FBI is taking lead. Bowser said there could be further arrests. They believe Drake has a connection within the FDA for this drug that is up for approval, but they don't know who that connection is. Sometimes, he said, unless they find an email, audio, or video, then hearsay simply won't work on a government official."

"It's like catching a greased pig," I said.

"Never thought of it that way, but I suppose the analogy works. On many levels."

She said that, at some point in the future, Nicole and I might both be asked to testify in a trial, which might involve this unknown government official.

"Did you guys ever figure out what Clem used his lab for?"

A car drove up, and out popped Tracy Rowlett. Brook put two fingers in her mouth and whistled, then asked one of her officers to ensure that the reporters were kept away from the crime scene. Then she turned to me. "Apparently, he was trying to prove out the complications of the new Vista Labs drug. He was a very dedicated man."

As Bowser walked up, Brook said, "There is the matter of your father."

"Drake said he didn't do it. I'm not sure I believe him, though."

"We got back the toxicology report. And we have a piece of video from the hospital."

Brook lifted an eyebrow, while trading a glance with Bowser.

Within minutes, we all knew what had to happen.

Forty-Two

After the sun rose, I called Stacy and asked if we could move up our next lunch date at Franklin's barbeque. This time I was waiting in a booth when she walked in. She hugged me. Her face gave an impression that she felt my pain, both physical and otherwise.

"Your face is twice as bad this time," she said, her hands gripping my arms like I was fourteen again.

I explained how I fell into a rosebush. She asked more questions.

"Haven't you read the exclusive story by Tracy Rowlett?" I asked. Then I realized his story probably hadn't made the newspaper deadline and was available only in their online edition at this point.

Tracy had not only shown up at the scene within the hour it happened—he said he had sources within the APD—but he'd also sat down with Brook, Nicole, and me after most of the people cleared away, to get the full story. We asked him to keep the whole salacious affair out of the paper. He actually came through for us, which I found shocking.

"So, explain again how they stopped the car?" she asked.

"They used a spike strip. Apparently, my friends with the FBI and APD didn't have a clue where we were, so they put down spike strips going both directions on our street."

"You are so lucky to be alive, Ozzie. And Nicole too. I just don't understand her relationship with this Drake fellow."

In many respects, Stacy had been like a surrogate mother. She had taken care of so many things for me over the years, long before I joined the firm. She always seemed to be there for me, to lend a helping hand. But right now, I didn't feel like opening up and baring my soul. My face looked like it had gone through a paper shredder, but my heart had been shattered again yesterday, when Brook showed me the video they'd pulled from the hospital.

"I'd rather not get into it now, Stacy."

We both ate our barbeque. Actually, she ate and I picked at my food.

"Everything okay?"

She was watching me. She was a master people watcher. That was one thing we had in common. I had thought the other thing was our love for Dad. Apparently, I'd been wrong.

"Not really. Now that things have settled, I realize how much I miss Dad."

She reached across and patted my hand. "Over time you'll remember him fondly, and it won't hurt so much. And you still have me for our weekly lunches."

I didn't say anything. I only gave her a nod, but I could feel my cheeks go flush.

She put her fork down, clasped her hands, and anchored them under her chin. She looked at me with a blank stare. That wasn't Stacy. She usually showed something in her expression, even if it was annoyance at one of the lawyers or paralegals for leaving a mess in the breakroom.

The stare-down lasted a good minute. I wasn't going to give, no matter how long it lasted.

Finally, she said, "Your father and I had an affair that lasted over two years."

I felt a jab to the gut, but after everything I'd endured, the impact was more like that of a mosquito bite. I remained expressionless. My eyes didn't blink.

"He hurt me, Ozzie. He promised me that he'd leave his witch of a wife. Sorry, but you know it's true about your adoptive mother."

She'd never used that term around me before…"adoptive mother." I could feel my jaw clench, but I was like a statue. She continued caving.

She pulled a tissue from her purse and dabbed the corner of her eye. "I was devastated. I loved that man like no other woman could. And he tossed me aside. I'd become too old for him. He moved on to Bianca," she said, exaggerating her name with an accompanying eye roll. "That woman was nothing more than a sex machine. She was after his money. And…" She tried to laugh, but she was stuck with a stiff smile. "I guess it all worked out for her."

I finally broke my silence. "It did for you too, since Arie is selling off the firm. But you knew that if Dad died, Arie would be forced to sell it off and give it to the older employees."

Her smile stuck around, but a shadow crossed her face. "I did, yes. I knew just about everything that went on in that office. Well, except all this crazy stuff with Drake and the killing of the doctor."

"But when he was arrested and had the heart attack, you saw your chance, didn't you?"

She quickly reached across to grab my hand. I pulled it back and gave her a venomous look.

She began to cry, but the burden she'd been carrying apparently pulled the words out of her. "My mother, it's just been so painful. And costly. I needed help."

"And so…?"

"I can't hide the truth any longer, Ozzie. Your dad's heart was weak. You don't know this, but he'd had fainting spells many times in the last year. He was on the verge of dying; I know it."

I couldn't lead her to say it—it would be inadmissible in court—so I just had to wait and somehow hold back from lashing out, or from breaking down.

"I promise you, when he died, it was peaceful. He basically died in his sleep."

"What are you saying?" I bit into my lip until I tasted blood.

Tears cascaded down her face like a river that had just poured over muddy banks. Makeup was everywhere. "As a trained nurse, I knew that an extra dose of potassium chloride given right into his bloodstream would stop his heartbeat. I then unplugged his machine. There was a shift change going on. No one noticed a thing." She paused and tried to plug the open dam of tears, but it was no use. "I wasn't certain that I wouldn't get caught, but I suppose it was meant to be."

"And I thought you cared, Stacy."

"You and I both know that he would never change his habits. He would have kept eating, drinking, working. He was a creature of habit. He loved that firm more than any woman. He wouldn't have lived another month. I guarantee you."

"And I guarantee *you* that you're going to spend the rest of your life in prison."

A moment later, Brook, Bowser, and six other officers appeared at our table. Stacy didn't seem too surprised.

"He treated me like a throwaway tissue, Ozzie," she said as an officer cuffed her.

I started walking away, but she yelled across the restaurant. "A person can only take that for so long. You know that, right?"

I walked outside and threw up.

Later, Brook told me that Stacy admitted to writing the death threat and leaving it on my car. She had used her left hand to write the note, believing I'd never connect it to her. She also admitted to slashing my tire. She said she never intended to follow through and hurt me. She just didn't want to get caught. She said she knew, ultimately, that Nathaniel would just want her to be happy.

I threw up again.

Forty-Three

I watched Arie's fingers work the ten-key like a concert pianist. It was three days later, and I'd somehow awoken from my catatonic state. "You called me here, so what do you need?"

The office had boxes stacked to the ceiling. There was one desk and two chairs left at Novak and Novak. My body and my senses were numb, but I still felt a sense of loss, a cavern of emptiness that made me question so many things in my life and the people who had touched it.

"Sorry for the wait. I was just running some numbers about the FFE," he said, scooting up his chair.

I didn't give him a quizzical look, but he must have thought I did.

"Furniture, fixtures, and equipment. It's a term used in the sale of companies." He paused, but I said nothing. "So, first things first. Stacy's demise does not mean that you get her share. Unfortunately."

"I never thought it would. This world, Novak and Novak, is all behind me now, Arie."

He rested his elbows on the table. "What that woman did to your father…I'll never forgive her. If I wasn't such a religious man, I'd hope she would rot in hell."

I'd never before heard Arie throw out the religious card. I was sure he needed some way to express his anger and hurt. We all did.

"Sometimes we think we know people, but I guess we don't." The words just came out. I wasn't just thinking of Stacy. I'd included my dad and Nicole in that thought. I'd lost my ability to filter very much in the days since everything had finally come to an end.

Arie nodded. "Sorry for everything you've been through, Ozzie. I know it's been rough. Maybe this will help."

He handed me an envelope. It was sealed but had my dad's handwriting on it.

"What is this?"

"A letter to you. From your father."

I thought I had no emotion left in me, but I was wrong. Tears welled in my eyes, a convergence of about a hundred emotions.

"Your father loved you very much, Ozzie. He never once considered you less of a son because you were adopted."

I flipped the letter over a few times.

"Read it later, when you have a quiet moment."

I shook his hand, and he said he'd keep in touch. I walked out of the office and got on the elevator. I was alone, so I tore open the envelope and read the letter:

Dear Ozzie,

If you're reading this letter, the world must have been turned upside down. And you're probably wondering if I ever really loved you.

The answer is yes, unequivocally. Your mother and I took you in when you were just two weeks old. You had some rough spots around age two, but other than that, you stole our hearts. And as you grew up and listened to this old man's stories about his work life, I began to feel a bond with you that lasted forever.

You probably have a lot of questions. I'll do my best to answer them.

Early on, I didn't want to give you partnership in the firm because I thought you needed to earn it. Eventually, I wanted it all to be yours, or maybe you and your future son's firm. But to get there, I didn't want your colleagues to resent you for thinking you had the world handed to you on a silver platter.

And then my life changed when I decided to work with Calvin Drake. Early in our arrangement, he paid me huge sums of money to complete menial tasks. I didn't want to admit it, but I knew eventually he would ask me to cross the line. And when he did ask, I tried like hell to not do it. But the man proved to be a formidable negotiator: he said he'd pay me more money than I could ever earn with ten other clients, and he threatened me. He said he'd hurt my family if I didn't comply.

It tore me in two. I was stressed beyond belief, but knowing I couldn't take the risk of seeing one of you hurt—and yes, that includes your mother—I complied.

Again, if you're reading this note, then a lot of stuff has happened. All I can say is, I'm sorry we couldn't have been partners. You will always have a special place in my heart, even if I'm looking down on you from the Pearly Gates. I just hope they let me in.

Love,

Dad

As the elevator door dinged open, I shoved the letter in my blazer and thought about the comment Drake had made about swimming with the sharks. Dad was definitely swimming with sharks, but what struck me was that he never realized the pain he'd caused the women in his life. It was rather apparent he never understood that treating people with so little respect would have such a lasting impact. On their lives. On his life. And now on mine.

I made my way out to the street and spotted the space where Sam was normally set up. It was empty. I knew he was at his sister's place, healing, but I wondered if he'd find a new way to make money.

I had no car. I'd walked all the way from Tito's place. I'd told Tito that Nicole and I would pay to get his car fixed. He was just relieved that we were still breathing. I felt like I could walk another hundred miles. I flipped around and nearly ran into my brother.

"Tobin?"

"Hey, Oz. Mom said you were dropping by the office to talk to Arie."

She'd called earlier in the morning to express her concern, in her own unique way.

We exchanged small talk for a few seconds. "Look, I'm not really in the mood to get into everything."

"You don't have your Cadillac back yet?"

I shook my head and watched two college kids stop and give a homeless guy some money. I had to blink to make sure I wasn't dreaming. Maybe humanity wasn't on the decline.

"You were saying?" I turned back to Tobin.

"Come on, I'll drive you wherever you need to go," he said, waving me toward the garage.

"I'm good. Seriously. Thanks, though."

He stuck a letter against my chest. "What's this?"

"It was in my pile at Mom and Dad's place. You know how we sometimes receive mail there and she has two stacks for us?"

Another letter. I nodded, and found the letter had already been opened.

"You read my mail?"

"Sorry, dude. I thought it was mine." He shuffled his feet. "You might want to be sitting down when you read it."

"You read the whole thing?"

"It was hard to stop. Just let me know if you want to talk to me about it."

I gave him an annoyed look, then emptied my lungs. I couldn't be mad at Tobin for long. Annoying as he was, I knew he meant well. I popped him on the shoulder and started walking.

A few seconds passed, and I opened the letter. I read the first sentence and stopped in my tracks. Just then, my phone rang. I looked at the screen. It was Nicole. She'd called me about ten times since Brook and Bowser had saved us from sure death. I'd actually picked up twice. I'd told her I needed more time. I could tell she was looking for an anchor. But I just couldn't be that for her. Not now. And I wasn't sure when. Or if.

Back to the letter. I looked at the return address and the name above it. It took me a few seconds, but then it slammed into the front of my mind. End of high school, senior year. Prom night.

I read the first sentence again and kept going from there.

I'm sorry I never told you, Ozzie, but you have a daughter. She's in danger. And I need your help. I didn't know how to reach you, so I'm sending this to your parents' house. I remembered their address from when we dated in high school. This isn't a joke. I'm telling you the truth. I'm just sorry you had to find out this way. I wasn't sure who else to turn to, or who else would care. Please call me or send me an email and let me know if you can come.

Truly,

Denise

Denise, a friend from my past. We'd dated, had some fun, and then moved on with our lives. I looked up and felt the cold wind bite into my face. Family had meant so much to me growing up. I'd always pushed the thought of my blood family to the back of my mind. I had no need to conjure up any emotion about that topic. But a daughter? I'd never gone there. Usually, you're aware of that before you get a letter ten years after you last saw the person.

My phone buzzed again. This time it was a text from Nicole. She'd sent a picture of the two of us from back in our college days, taking a selfie with the Golden Gate Bridge in the background. Damn, we looked happy and carefree.

I didn't bother responding to Nicole. I couldn't invest any more of myself in her, in our relationship. Instead, I sent an email to Denise. I headed to Tito's to pack and then went to the airport to catch a plane to go meet my daughter.

My daughter. Saying it out loud didn't make it any more familiar. Yet, something pulled me to her.

I couldn't turn my back on the one true relative I had. Not like my birth parents had done to me. Blood relatives had to mean something.

Excerpt from Game ON (Book 2)

One

$\mathbf{A}$ battle between my senses of sight and smell raged mightily in my brain. Off to the side of a small apartment building sat a rusted, dilapidated swing set. It was on the verge of being devoured by weeds and vines. In fact, the vines had wrenched the metal into a pretzel-like configuration.

An intake of breath brought with it an aroma that, on its own, would normally move you to a place of harmony and peace. The sweet scent of bougainvillea, plumeria, and orchid was both organically intoxicating and—because of this odd sense of dread that had clawed at me since I'd landed at the airport—toxic.

I lifted part of the lei that hung around my neck—full of vibrant pinks, reds, whites—and asked myself why I hadn't left it in the minivan. The sweet smell was over the top. Or maybe the odor had crossed into the pungent zone because of my body composition. My stomach churned like that of a little kid who'd overdosed on Halloween candy.

Indeed, the sensory overkill had done a number on me. As a person with a hearing impairment, that wasn't too surprising. I relied upon my four other senses as if I were clinging to a float in the middle of the ocean. An ocean as big as the Pacific, which, according to street signs, sat about fifty miles to the east of Fern Forest, a small, forgettable community set inland on the Big Island of Hawaii. Or as the countless travel guides had called it on the plane ride over from Austin—the Orchid Isle.

I put my hand on a rickety wood railing to cross a muddy moat, and my fingertip felt the prick of a nail. I wiped the hint of blood on my jeans.

"Smart one, Ozzie. Add 'Get a tetanus shot' to your list of fun-filled activities on your first trip to Hawaii," I muttered to myself.

Just then, a woman slammed a door on one of the downstairs apartments. She trekked through weeds with an open purse tucked under her arm. I held out a hand, prepared to ask if she knew Denise Emerson, but it was obvious she wanted no part of me. Her sunken eyes stayed on her direct path. She wore a hairnet and a brown dress uniform that said she worked at a diner. She brushed against my shoulder without a word, then slipped behind the wheel of an ancient sedan and drove off.

Why anyone would choose to live in this place was a mystery. Then again, as I walked across the small bridge and contemplated the upheaval I'd experienced in the last week or so, perhaps they were just unlucky in life, going through a period of time when one bad thing built on top of the next.

A breath clicked in the back of my throat as a sobering fact took hold of my thoughts.

Your daughter—a person you didn't know existed until about twenty-four hours ago—may very well live in this wondrous dwelling.

I stopped at the edge of the U-shaped complex, looking for an indication of which apartment might be "Unit E." From where I stood, I saw nothing on the doors. I raked my fingers through my hair, which normally had a bit of a wave to it. In the salty, humid air, the ends had begun to roll into curls. Poppy, a bartender friend of mine back home, would, at about this time, smack the counter and ask me, "Love your hair, Oz. You want me to make you a Shirley Temple?" She loved to razz me. I would then quickly point out that she looked like a member of a reggae band from Mars— she of the red dreadlocks pinned behind her head.

Enough screwing around. I pulled the folded letter from my pocket and verified the address. "Unit E" was written in the upper left-hand corner of the envelope. I popped the letter against my opposite hand, contemplating the letter's authenticity. From what I could recall, ten years earlier, Denise seemed like a straight-up person. We'd dated briefly toward the end of our senior year in high school. She was fun, happy, the life of the party. I never got the sense she would be the kind to screw with someone's life just for the hell of it.

But again, that was ten years ago. Under normal circumstances, most people go through at least two metamorphic stages between eighteen and twenty-eight. And as of right now, nothing about this felt normal.

My thoughts flipped to the key part of Denise's letter. *I'm sorry I never told you, Ozzie, but you have a daughter. And she's in danger.*

That had ignited an action on my part that some might say was a desperate attempt to flee all of the drama back in Austin. Some of those same people might also point out that such an action was counter to my training as a lawyer—to first logically walk through the theoretical permutations on why Denise would send me this letter now, ten years after the fact.

Danger.

The word had prompted my nearly instantaneous response to travel to Hawaii; it was one of those trigger words for me. But there was an additional draw that had pulled me to the Big Island. The very real possibility that I might actually have a living relative.

My adoptive family had raised me since I was an infant. While it was a dysfunctional family—and still was in many ways—I'd never really put much thought into finding parents who'd tossed me into the expendable bucket. Their loss, my gain, I figured.

You don't even know her name, Oz.

Oh, yeah—there's that part. For whatever reason, Denise, or possibly someone posing as her, had forgotten to mention my daughter's name. That had limited my ability to verify that this daughter of mine existed at all. Was that because of the urgency or emotion of the moment when Denise, or perhaps her proxy, had penned this letter? Or could it have been by design?

That's right, I was actually going there. A nefarious plot to lure me out of the moderate chill—not meant as a euphemism of my current relationship status with my wife, Nicole—of Austin, Texas, so that I could be screwed over by some bizarre scam in one of the most popular travel destinations on Earth.

But here I was. Two thousand miles later. And while this section of Fern Forest could have been a rundown corner on the east side of I-35 in Austin, I recognized the contradictory irony of crisscrossing words like *nefarious* and *scam* with the paradise of Hawaii.

Ah, the games that your mind will play when sitting on a charter airplane for eight-plus hours with wall-to-wall college kids who clearly couldn't go for long without taking a shot of something over eighty proof.

I circled the rim of the inside of the first-floor apartments. No sign of "Unit E." Hell, no sign of human life. I toddled up to the second floor, where the sidewalk dipped toward the railing. I paused and eyed each window from the top of the steps, trying to get a bead on whether there were any inhabitants in this place. All I could see were plastic blinds and doors with tic-tac-toe games etched on them.

I wiped a drop of sweat off my forehead; then I glanced to the courtyard below. Was there any way that one of my old lawyer buddies, maybe someone from the old firm, could have played a trick on me? Wouldn't that be the ultimate prank? Tell a guy with no blood family that he has a long-lost daughter in some exotic paradise, one who was in grave danger, nonetheless.

Okay, I added the "grave" part. Still, though, it worked with the plot.

But, if for some bizarre reason, someone had pulled off one of the greatest pranks in modern history, provoking me to impulsively jump on the next flight to Hawaii, then the real fool would be them. I'd check out the apartments just to make sure there was no sign of Denise or a daughter who looked anything like me. Then I'd jump back into my minivan and head for the nearest all-inclusive resort and start the rejuvenation process.

I could already taste the Knob Creek on the rocks.

With a little extra energy in my step—I stayed as far from the railing as possible—I ambled down the walkway, stopping every few feet to cup a hand against a window. No sign of life anywhere. I wondered momentarily if the woman I'd seen earlier had the whole place to herself.

I completed one leg of the U; then I turned left. At the first door, I noticed something different. The letter "G" was carved into the door. I leaned backward while glancing left and counted down two more doors.

The adrenaline rush was so fast and unexpected, I felt like the base of my skull had been zapped.

The door was open, just a crack. My other sense, that sixth one, had been pinged.

Two

Given my lack of quality hearing, I instinctively put my head on a swivel and started to shuffle close to the partially open door. The last thing I wanted was not to hear someone coming up behind me. Despite the absence of life in this place, I wasn't about to take any chances.

I made it to the door, and sure enough, I found an "E" carved on it, although it was waist high. I dipped my head and peeked through the crack. It was dark, but I could just make out a kitchen table with books and papers on top.

Another glance behind me. All clear.

I knocked twice. "Anyone home?"

I waited a few seconds, but no one responded. I tried the same routine again and waited even longer this time.

All was quiet. Too quiet.

I nudged open the door and took a single step into the apartment. My eyes went straight to the green, wooden kitchen table in front of me. Coloring books covered it, some of them open to reveal the colored images. These weren't little-kid coloring books, for sure. The person had used colored pencils to embellish the detailed designs. One was a beautiful depiction of a waterfall cascading off a breathtaking cliff.

"Hello?" I was at a disadvantage. If someone were calling out in a soft voice from another room, I probably wouldn't hear them. I walked through a living room with furniture that didn't match and found a single bedroom. An unmade queen bed, the smell of perfume in the air, but no people. The hall bathroom had makeup, a hair dryer, and hair-care products. No people, and no real sign that a kid lived here.

Except for the coloring books, and even that was a stretch. An adult with aspirations of learning the art of drawing could have created those pictures. I spun on my sandals and headed back to the kitchen.

A chair was toppled over. Not sure how I missed that a minute ago. My eyes picked up red marks on the drab linoleum. I lowered to my knees and ran my fingers across the floor. Under the table, I spotted some colored pencils that had been smashed into tiny pieces, as if a heavy shoe had crushed them.

I tried to swallow, but my throat had gone dry.

On the other side of the table near the wall, I found an envelope on the floor. I crawled over and picked it up.

It was addressed to Denise Emerson. *So she does live here.* Unless this was a different Denise Emerson than the one who was my prom date.

My pulse ticked faster.

I eyed the front door. People don't leave their doors open like that—not unless they were in a huge rush.

She's in danger, the letter had said. Had Denise actually been referencing herself, thinking that if she mentioned a daughter, I was more likely to come than if it were just her? Given the dreadful condition of the complex, her life had taken a wrong turn somewhere.

Again, *if* it was her.

Pictures. She had to have photographs around here somewhere. I probably missed them in the one bedroom.

I quickly pushed up to head back to the bedroom.

Footfalls peppered the walkway. With no weapons on me, I plucked a dirty skillet off the stovetop and held it above my head. The door popped open.

"Ozzie!"

It was Denise. Makeup snaked down her face, but I could never mistake her eyes, the same icy blue. She looked worn, and her hair was a different color, but it was her.

"What's going on, Denise? Did you write me this letter?" I whipped it from my pocket and waved it at her.

Tears sprung from her eyes, and before I could take another breath, she barreled into me with open arms.

"They have her, Ozzie. They took our daughter." She fought through the sobs, then looked me in the eye. "They have our Mackenzie."

Three

My heart sank. I set down the skillet, slowly inhaled and exhaled, and then gently took Denise by the arms.

"Tell me what's going on, please."

She gasped a few times, as if she were having a difficult time getting words out. I found a cup on the kitchen counter and poured her some water. As she chugged the water, I ripped a paper towel from a roll and gave it to her. She wiped her face and got her breathing under control.

I gave her a minute. "You feeling better?"

"Thank you." Her voice was raspy, as if she'd been yelling.

"Start from the top. Where is...Mackenzie?" The name sounded strange coming off my lips.

"It's the *yakuza*. They took her from me."

I was a master at reading lips. That had always helped me piece together words I didn't quite hear. I wondered if I'd heard her correctly. "*Yakuza*—the Japanese crime syndicate?"

She nodded repeatedly. "Yes, it's them. You've got to help me get her back. Please. She's all I've got, Ozzie. Will you help me?" She was firing off words so fast it was hard to keep up, each phrase more animated than the last.

"Of course I'll help. I'm here, aren't I?"

A breath, and then she dialed back the intensity a couple of notches. "You are." Her eyes scanned me from head to toe. "You got my letter."

"You must have mailed the letter a week ago or so?"

"I'm worried about her, Oz. Mackenzie is…" She raised a jittery hand and wiped a tear from her face. I noticed her fingernails were down to the nubs. She'd ignored my question, or she'd been too rocked by the situation to listen clearly.

"I'm just trying to take this all in. I'm a lawyer—"

"Of course you are. Wow. Just like your dad."

I offered a tight-lipped smile. We could talk about Dad and everything else that had transpired over the last decade once we got Mackenzie back. "I need to understand the timetable, okay?"

"Okay. Right. Makes sense. What did you ask me?"

"You sent a letter. You must have been worried for a while. When did you send it?"

"About a week ago."

"Okay, when was she taken?"

"After she got home from school."

"Today?"

"Yes, today. Do you see why I'm so worried?"

She should be worried regardless, but I saw this as a small positive. "Better today than a week ago. So, have they communicated with you at all? Asked about a ransom, or said what it would take to get her back safely?"

"No, nothing."

I looked off and found a framed picture above the couch. It was a painting of a black-sand beach with steep cliffs in the background. Seagulls flew overhead at dusk as waves crashed into rock formations. It had to be a knock-off of a print.

I turned back to Denise, her glassy blue eyes as clear as the ocean water. "The door was open when I got here. Why?"

"I ran out of here when I came home early and found that she'd been kidnapped. The door is a piece of crap and doesn't shut well unless you really play with the lock. I didn't have time to screw with it."

"Where did you go?"

"Back to the school, about four blocks down. Sometimes she goes back there and plays with friends."

"You don't think she's at a friend's house?"

She held up her cell phone. "I called the parents of her four best friends. No one has seen her after they walked home together."

I felt a trickle of sweat bubble off my sideburn. I used my shoulder to wipe it off. "This *yakuza* angle. I have my doubts, but it—"

She pounded her shoe into the floor. I then realized she had on heels and was wearing a navy-blue pantsuit with a blue-and-white polka-dot silk shirt. Outside of her smeared makeup and frizzed-out hair that was a combination of red, brown, and blond, she looked almost professional. She didn't match anything else about this place.

"You don't fucking believe me," she said, taking a step back.

"No, Denise, that's not it. Look, I used the wrong word. I don't doubt you. I'm just wondering why the *yakuza* would bother to kidnap your...our daughter."

She put a hand to her face, but it didn't stop the new surge of tears. "I fucked up, Ozzie. And I think it might cost Mackenzie's life."

Four

There was something about Denise that seemed off, other than the obvious. I couldn't pinpoint it exactly. Perhaps I was being influenced by this ghetto-like apartment.

"Look," I said. "Nothing you could have done justifies kidnapping a child. Nothing. So get that out of your head."

I wasn't sure she believed me, but she gave me a single nod.

"Okay, let's just call the police and get their resources on this."

"Are you kidding me?" She pushed me in the chest, although she was the one who went backward a step. She probably weighed less than half of my two hundred ten pounds.

"What? What did I say that was wrong?"

"You haven't listened to me," she said, poking herself in the chest. It was so violent I felt certain she was bruising herself. I tried not to stare at her chest, which in the past might have been an issue. Now, not so much.

"Denise, I'm here for you…for Mackenzie. Which is why we need to call the cops." I pulled out my phone. Before my thumb could punch the nine, she slapped the phone out of my hand.

"What the hell are you doing?" I bent down and picked up my device. Scowling, I looked it over. The screen wasn't cracked, but there was no telling if any internal damage had been done.

"You can't call the cops." She smacked one hand into the other three times. "They'll kill her, Oz." A gasp, as she put a hand to her face and fought back more emotion. "Do you hear me? They will kill my precious little Mackenzie."

Her voice seemed to echo—I wasn't sure if that was my hearing aid or an actual reverberation. Her sobs ceased, and there was a moment of silence. We just stood there and looked at each other. For the first time since she'd walked through the door, her face, while blotchy, gave no indication of what she was thinking. Me? I had no clue which way to take this or how to fix it, how to bring back a girl I didn't know, a girl who had my blood in her veins.

At least a minute passed, and as I stared into her eyes, my mind couldn't help but shoot back to prom night, when I'd borrowed my father's Cadillac, walked up to the door of her home, and rang the doorbell. Her mom had answered, and, before I could ask if Denise was ready, she swung back, and there her daughter stood. The lighting hit her just perfectly. She looked angelic. My heart had kicked into another gear, and I'd just gawked at her like boys at that age are prone to do. I remember not being able even to speak. She wasn't just beautiful, though. She had this graceful confidence about her, as if I were about to take the arm of a princess. It had sounded cheesy running through my head even as I was thinking it, but that didn't negate the butterflies fluttering in my stomach. Was it love? It was difficult to pinpoint, actually. Lust, certainly. But, for one night, we'd connected on a level I'd never experienced before that moment, as if we had this perfectly aligned energy. We ended the night in a hotel room, making love. That must have been when Mackenzie was conceived. The next morning, with birds tweeting and the sun peeking through the trees, I had kissed her goodbye. A week later, we graduated and, like most high school couples, knew it was time to move on, to experience college without trying to juggle a long-distance relationship. I think she was headed out of state, but I really couldn't recall.

She sniffled, and I let out a sigh.

"Why didn't you tell me?" I asked.

"I…" Her eyes momentarily found the floor; then she looked at me, her lips pressed together. "I was just confused. I didn't know what to think. I found out when I was here, in Hawaii."

I tilted my head.

"I visited my aunt and uncle here on the Big Island. It was all part of a big graduation present. I planned on staying here a month. But that's when I found out I was pregnant. I struggled with what to do, whether to call you, or whether to even have the baby. I couldn't make the decision, and then the next thing I know, my aunt is taking me to the doctor, and I'm hearing the heartbeat. I connected with her at that moment."

"Wow. Sounds powerful."

"You don't have kids?"

I followed her gaze to my left hand. I was still wearing my wedding band. I twisted it on my hand, feeling a bit awkward. "No kids for me."

Her mouth opened, but no words were spoken.

Then I replayed what I'd said. "I'm sorry. I just meant that I have no kids with my… Well, I guess she's still my wife."

Something crossed her face, just for a split second. It was the smallest hint of the girl I'd taken to prom. Maybe she thought there was something there for us to rekindle. My stomach felt like it was trying to push its way into the back of my throat. I had so many emotions and thoughts waging an internal battle.

"You know I can't just sit here and not do anything to find Mackenzie."

"That's why I reached out to you, Ozzie. You always seemed like you had a good head on your shoulders, like no moment was too big for you."

I wasn't sure whether to thank her or be pissed at her for not telling me about my daughter. Again, the competing emotions. The knot in my stomach only grew larger.

"But that was when I was just scared. Now, they've taken her. I don't know what to do. But the *yakuza* has people everywhere, including the police department. That's a known fact on this island."

An idea, one that might not go anywhere, came to mind.

"I need to make a call."

She reached out and touched my arm.

"It's okay. I'm not calling the cops."

Not on the island, anyway.

John W. Mefford Bibliography

The Ozzie Novak Thrillers
ON EDGE (Book 1)
GAME ON (Book 2)
ON THE ROCKS (Book 3)
SHAME ON YOU (Book 4)
ON FIRE (Book 5)
ON THE RUN (Book 6)

The Alex Troutt Thrillers
AT BAY (Book 1)
AT LARGE (Book 2)
AT ONCE (Book 3)
AT DAWN (Book 4)
AT DUSK (Book 5)
AT LAST (Book 6)
AT STAKE (Book 7)
AT ANY COST (Book 8
BACK AT YOU (Book 9)
AT EVERY TURN (Book 10)
AT DEATH'S DOOR (Book 11)
AT FULL TILT (Book 12)

The Ivy Nash Thrillers
IN DEFIANCE (Book 1)
IN PURSUIT (Book 2)
IN DOUBT (Book 3)

BREAK IN (Book 4)
IN CONTROL (Book 5)
IN THE END (Book 6)

The Ball & Chain Thrillers
MERCY (Book 1)
FEAR (Book 2)
BURY (Book 3)
LURE (Book 4)
PREY (Book 5)
VANISH (Book 6)
ESCAPE (Book 7)

The Booker Series
BOOKER – Streets of Mayhem (Volume 1)
BOOKER – Tap That (Volume 2)
BOOKER – Hate City (Volume 3)
BOOKER – Blood Ring (Volume 4)
BOOKER – No Más (Volume 5)
BOOKER – Dead Heat (Volume 6)

The Greed Series
FATAL GREED (Greed Series #1)
LETHAL GREED (Greed Series #2)
WICKED GREED (Greed Series #3)
GREED MANIFESTO (Greed Series #4)

To stay updated on John's latest releases, visit:
JohnWMefford.com

Made in the USA
Monee, IL
21 April 2020